The Nature of Denial

by Madelyn March

Madelyn March

This is a work of fiction. The events, characters, and dialogue in this work are inventions of the author's imagination.

Copyright © 2015 Madelyn March
Printed in the United States.
All rights reserved. This publication may not be reproduced without permission of the author.
ISBN-13:
978-1508844433

ISBN-10:
1508844437

Cover design by Ana Grigoriu at Books-design.com

DEDICATION

This book is dedicated to my husband, Bryan. He has supported me in all my endeavors, even the outlandish dream to write a novel or two.

ACKNOWLEDGMENTS

I want to acknowledge those who volunteered their time to read and critique the earlier versions of this book: Judy Bobrow, Linda Grischy, Deby Henneman, Sharon Quiroz, Paula Roth, and Kathy Wheeler.

I also want to thank my husband and two incredible sons who called me a writer before I dared to utter such words. I am in debt to you all. Thank you.

Part One

The Sacrifice

The screeching sound of bending, twisting metal stopped abruptly and created a bubble of silence within the car. The pounding of her heart and the hissing radiator broke through the quiet. Anna pushed the airbag away from her face and looked around the car. Things were strewn around the seats as result of hasty packing and the impact. Anna gruffly gathered what she needed--a few pieces of clothing from her bag, a large envelope of money, her purse, a water bottle, some snacks--and shoved them into David's hiking backpack. It took her a few moments to find the flashlight, which she then crammed into her pocket. She found the gun resting on the passenger side floor and secured it in her waistband. Then she covered herself with every piece of winter gear she could find and exited the car. The heft of the weight on her back calmed her. The layers of gear protected her from the cold outside, but they couldn't touch the chill within.

The desolation on Interstate 75 in northern Michigan was a stark contrast to the highway's southern counterpart, with which she was more familiar. The monotonous miles of darkness, held back only by the Lincoln's headlights, had lulled her to sleep. The result was mangled metal and steam. She was lucky to be alive, but didn't appreciate it. She ran her hand through her hair, momentarily shocked as her fingers reached the end of the strands prematurely, before she remembered that she had cut off her long, black locks of hair.

Ready for a long journey. Time to walk. She walked on the side of the highway, flashlight in hand, loose gravel scattering under her feet. The stench of the radiator dissipated with distance. The darkness offered ample warning of approaching cars, so she could hide in the thick brush. After trudging over what felt like many miles, but what was likely less than one, she turned back and shone the flashlight toward the Lincoln, to no avail. What did she expect? A flashlight didn't have the power to illuminate such distance. The car had vanished, swallowed by time and darkness. An old life--disappeared.

I'm awake now. A sarcastic, dark smile swept across her face, then faded. *Andrew is safe now. Just keep walking.* Looking back anymore would break her, so she walked and willed herself to focus forward and keep her mind clear. The sound of her steps and the weight of her pack created a rhythm of movement that calmed her, allowing her to live in the present moment. *Is this what David means about losing himself?*

A far-away rumbling sound grew gradually closer. Slow to process the sound, she finally recognized it as an approaching vehicle and flashed her light upon the side of the expressway which looked like an impenetrable fortress of underbrush and snow. She pulled off the backpack and shoved it in front of her like a shield against the underbrush. On her knees, she pushed forward in small increments sheltering herself behind the pack. Back on the road, the headlights came closer. She pressed onward. Sticks and branches snapped in discontent as Anna tried to penetrate the brush. She wanted to slink down as low as possible, but was unwilling to put her face or body directly in the snowy cage so she compromised and laid on the pack.

The sound of a nearby animal startled her. She carefully pulled the gun out of her waistband. *Just wait, it will pass soon.* The vehicle slowed down and stopped behind her abandoned Lincoln, illuminating it in the darkness. *It is probably just someone doing a good deed, making sure no one is hurt.* It felt like an eternity before the engine started up again. A hunting spotlight on the vehicle probed and canvassed the roadside. Now frantic, she pushed further into the scratching bushes and mocking weeds. The lights drew near and she froze.

Oh shit. I need a story. The light moved forward like a seeking serpent, persistent and unyielding. *They will find me. Maybe I can get a ride. I need a new name.* The vehicle's loud muffler, guided by the bright light, was now only feet away. A man's twangy voice called out, "Anybody there?" and then, "Need help?" The light passed, reversed, and landed on her, briefly blinding her. *I can't breathe.*

"Hey, little lady," the man called out to her, "don't be afraid." He left his truck running as he walked toward her, his gait unsteady. He smiled, his brown teeth exposed under tendrils of greasy facial hair. "Are you okay?" he slurred.

Anna's heart beat fast, and she feared that she might faint.

Frozen with indecision, she couldn't move or talk.

"Why don't ya come out of there before ya freeze to death?"

Anna realized that she must speak or else he was going to come and get her out of her make-do shelter.

"I'm fine," she called. "Just resting. Someone's coming to get me. They'll be here any minute." *Please leave, please leave.*

"Ain't nobody coming, girl. Get yourself outta there and we'll get you taken cur of." The man's lips contorted to form what looked like a cross between a smile and a grimace.

"Really, I'll wait. It won't be long."

"I'm telling ya. Get out here!" His voice changed, became more demanding, and he yelled, "Now!"

His eyes squinted and his lips turned down. He reached down to his waist and pulled something from his belt. Anna continued to hold her gun at her side, hidden beneath her thigh, hoping this man would leave. He slowly exposed a large hunting knife, partially pulling it from its sheath.

"We gonna have ourselves some fun. Get outta there now!" he growled at her.

"No," Anna said flatly.

He pulled the knife out completely. "Okay by me. I don't mind if we do it the hard way. That's more fun." He started to push through the underbrush. Anna realized that the man intended to rape her or kill her, maybe both, it was written in his black, flash-lit eyes. She forced herself to stand up and revealed the gun, pointing it at the man's stomach. He stopped moving, as if running into some invisible barrier. "Whoa, lady, I'm just playing. It's alright. Put that down before you shoot your foot."

"Drop the knife, asshole! Hands over your head or I'm gonna shoot *your* foot off!" Her voice hinted at the shaking inside her.

"Okay, okay." He threw the knife aside in the underbrush, and it clanged against the ice coating the ground, making a sickening sound. *That could have been me.*

Confusion over what to do stalled her. Leaving the man here was not an option. He would be able to point the finger at her because she planned on taking his truck. She knew that if she got rid of her car and drove him some distance it would be more difficult, if not impossible, for him to identify her.

She walked him over to the truck and made him lie face

down on the ground so she could frisk him for other weapons. Satisfied, she tied his hands together with a tank top she found in the backpack and looked over his vehicle. She found a shotgun, rope, tape, whiskey, a cell phone, and a nasty smell. *Who knows what this man is capable of? I've got to keep him quiet for a few hours.* Inspiration struck.

After she tied up the man's hands more securely with some of the rope from his truck, she led him to the passenger seat and asked him if he wanted a drink or two. She offered him some pills from her backpack. "They won't hurt you, it's just Motrin. I feel bad about your face." She had made sure that he took a tumble when he got up with his hands tied, and his face was covered with small scratches.

"I'll take the drink, but I'm not taking no pills. I ain't stupid, bitch. When I get my hands untied, I'm gonna smash your face, right after I fuck your ass."

A tough act was required since she couldn't drive him unless he was passed out. He would kill her if he had a chance, she was certain of that.

Anna slid out of the truck and walked over to the passenger side where he sat. She opened the door and pointed the gun at his head. "I'm trying to do you a favor … uh … I didn't catch your name." He stared blankly at her in response.

She'd never hit anyone in her life, but it had to be done. Using the butt of the gun, she hit him on the head like she'd seen in those ridiculous movies David watched. "I'm sorry; I didn't catch your name," she repeated.

"Fry," he responded, glaring.

"Fry?" she repeated. He nodded slightly. "Okay, Fry. I don't want to become a murderer, but I'm willing to make an exception for you. Catch my drift?" He nodded again.

"Do you get me? Fry?"

"Uh huh."

"So, you're going to enjoy some pills and whiskey. Then you are going to be okay and I'm not going to be responsible for murder."

He sighed and his body slumped with resignation. Anna got back into the truck and lifted the whiskey to his mouth so that he could sip. Acid and repulsion rose in her throat as she fed him four Motrin PM and gave him drink after drink of whisky. She tied his feet together and secured his tied hands to the door handle to be sure he was completely immobilized.

It's time to make a phone call. Climbing out of the truck, she dialed Kate, her best friend for nearly two decades. When Kate answered, Anna relayed only the most important details.

"Kate, I need your help, but please don't ask a lot of questions."

"What's going on?"

"I got in a small accident, and I need you to take care of my car. I need it out of here before the police or anyone else sees it and--"

"--Are you okay?"

"I'm fine. It's banged up and leaning against a tree, but I think it's towable." She gave precise directions to her smashed car, which was nearly three hours away from her house, and demanded that Kate tell no one, not even David.

Anna explained that she was leaving for a while and didn't want to be contacted. She told Kate she'd be at her mom's cabin in Alpena. It was a weak lie—she had been there only once as an adult—yet it was the only lie that came to mind.

"This is crazy, Anna. You can't. What the hell is going on?"

"Kate!" Anna screamed into the phone, "Just trust me and do what I've asked. I need your help, not your advice. Please? Just do it. Take care of the car."

Admonished and beaten, Kate complied. "Okay. Call later and let me know you're okay?"

"Of course," Anna lied again. "I've got to go now. Please, get it out of here quick. Bye." There was no time for emotion. No time for tears. It was time to drive.

At least he's not dead. Car theft is a much lighter load than murder, she thought as she drove off in the rusty Ford pickup. A pamphlet showcasing the beauty of Michigan's Upper Peninsula pushed against her hip from within her pocket. It was a destination she would never have chosen, unless she didn't want to be found. It was a perfect place to hide for a while, or maybe even permanently. Time would tell. Thankful that the Ford's engine sounded solid, although the body surely was not, she drove on, passenger in tow.

***

Anna wore gloves in the truck for warmth as well as discretion. During the hour she drove, she mentally explored her options. She could drive to an airport and fly somewhere but they would likely find her. If she drove to a large city, the truck would stick out like a sore thumb. She decided to stick with her plan to hide in the far reaches of the Upper Peninsula, at least for a while. She looked over and saw that although Fry was trying to resist it, sleep had begun to claim him.

She drove south despite the fact that her destination lay to the north. There was no way she was going to take this grimy, evil man any closer to where she planned to hide. Now the fear of losing her sanity was compounded by the fear that this man could find her. She knew she couldn't drive the truck all the way to the Upper Peninsula, as it would lead him right to her. She needed an untraceable ride. Thoughts of stealing a car, renting one, and hitchhiking all rotated through her mind, each one shot down by its shortcomings.

Her mind wandered back to her teenage years. Once when she and Kate were on the extreme far reaches of town, in the middle of the sticks, at an outdoor party, they were left by their ride and stranded. It was the night Kate got in a fight with Melissa Prince. The bonfire roared and the drunken teenagers were loud and boisterous. Their ride, Kate's date, was upset because Kate wouldn't put out in the backseat of his Chevelle. He decided to show her and left them both stranded at the party which was miles from town and even further from their homes. The other teens were either too drunk to drive with or unwilling to leave. A friend of theirs, Matt Drunn, offered to walk with them, having no car himself. Anna suspected he had a crush on her, but maybe he worried about them walking so far alone.

They walked for miles down the dirt road and then onto a main road that would eventually lead them to town. Away from the road, down a long driveway, they saw a man inside a large barn leaning over the engine of a semitruck, perched precariously on a makeshift scaffold. Intoxicated, with sore feet, and exhausted from their long walk, Anna suggested they ask him for a ride.

"Are you crazy? I don't want to be found in parts somewhere. It's the middle of the night. What's that guy doing out there anyway?" questioned Matt.

"Fixing his truck, obviously," said Kate. "My feet are blistered, not to mention frozen. Do you know how many miles we are from town?"

They walked up the long driveway, and the large-bellied man turned to look at them. Anna stated their case: "I know this sounds crazy, but we were wondering if you might be able to give us a ride to town. We've got a couple bucks."

He didn't even hesitate. "Sure. Let me finish this and we'll take her for a spin," he said, apparently referring to his rig. They waited quietly for the man to finish his work. He stepped down from his makeshift scaffold and introduced himself as Joe. "Climb up, kids," he said with a smile.

They were amazed by the truck's size. The seats seemed enormous and behind them was a large bed. The bed made the girls hesitate, but they were young and stupid and got in anyway. Matt provided the girls with a false sense of security.

They were lucky that the man wasn't a creep—a little unbalanced, maybe, but not violent. When they drove past his ex-wife's house, he started in on a rant.

"That's where my ex lives. Crazy bitch. I should kill her. Sorry, I know I shouldn't talk that way, but I hate that bitch. She cheated on me and took all that I had."

The girls exchanged a look of alarm and kept their thoughts to themselves. Matt sat stiff with fear. They were not used to adults being so open about their personal lives. When the truck approached town, they were thankful.

"This is good," Kate said.

"You sure?" asked Joe.

"Yep, we live right around here. It would be too hard to explain if a semi pulled up in front of my house."

He stopped the rig and let them out. They thanked him and offered him money, which he declined. The girls walked to Anna's house, and Matt walked home. Anna was thankful because even in her intoxicated state, she realized that they had gotten off easy. Never again, she vowed, would she take a ride with a stranger.

Reflecting on her impulsive teenage self inspired her next move. She needed to find a truck stop. Maybe she could find a ride north that way. At least she had protection this time. She pulled over to the side of the road, searched on her phone, and learned that there was a truck stop twenty miles ahead.

Fry leaned so hard and lifeless against the door that she worried that she might have killed him, but then he began to snore. When she arrived at the enormous truck stop, she parked far away from the building, so no one would see Fry if he woke and no cameras could track her if he failed to wake. Asleep, he looked innocent enough, and she had him covered with a blanket to hide the rope binding him. The building housed a restaurant, a convenience store, and a gas station. There were semitrucks everywhere, even though it was late.

Before she could think of anything else, Anna had to relieve herself. Her bladder had reached full capacity and her gorged breasts felt like they were filled with rocks. She found a Styrofoam cup by the coffee counter and bolted for the bathrooms. She sat on the edge of the toilet seat and pulled her tender breast out of her bra. It radiated heat in her hand. It felt heavy and hard. She carefully squeezed to expel some milk into the cup. The fluorescent lights observed her shame, yet she tried to will it out of her mind. *I hope I dry up soon.* When she finished, she poured the collected milk down the toilet, unused and unwanted. *I'm sorry, Andrew. I'm sorry I couldn't do better, but you'll be safe now.*

***

Outside, a tall woman stood gassing up her rig. She wore a short sleeved shirt, oblivious to the cold outside. Anna decided maybe she would be a good source of information, especially since no one else was around who seemed approachable. The woman looked cheerful, and Anna hoped she would be helpful.

"Hi," Anna said. The woman looked up. "I was wondering if you could help me."

"What's the problem?"

"Well ... I'm looking for a ride north. I'd be willing to pay. I was wondering if you might be able to give me a ride."

"You sure you want to hitch a ride? Don't you have a car?"

"No. It's a long story. I'm writing a book about trucking. I got a ride this far from Kentucky, and now I'm trying to get to the U.P., where I have family."

"We're not supposed to take any hitchers. I'm headed south myself or I'd help ya. I would be careful, being a woman and all. These men don't see their wives much. I can tell you're full of it, but maybe someone will buy your story. I'll help ya anyway. We girls gotta stick together. Right?"

They walked around the parking lot. The woman pointed to two empty logging trucks. "Those are your best bets. Those trucks are empty and probably headed north to load up. There's lots of logging up there."

Anna approached one of the two truck drivers.

"Hello, sir," she said to the man, who was adjusting a large strap at the back of his empty truck. Even in the dim light, she could make out the oil-stained fingers on his massive hands. He stopped and looked at her, one eyebrow lifted, waiting.

"I ... um ... I need a ride north. Are you heading north? You see, I'm writing a book about trucking and I—"

"You need a ride?" he asked her in a deep voice.

"Yes, I—"

"I can give ya a ride. But I don't want to hear no story. I like it quiet. You understand? Those is my terms. Take 'em or leave 'em."

"Okay, I'll take them, thanks."

He showed Anna where to step to get up into the cab of the semi.

Thirty minutes later, they were on the road. Anna took one last look at Fry's truck as they left the truck stop, but she couldn't see inside it.

They drove north retracing the drive Anna had already completed before she had backtracked in Fry's truck. She remained silent as they passed by the tire tracks where her car went off the road and into the tree. Although it had been only a few hours since she phoned Kate, it seemed more like days.

Thank goodness Kate took care of the car. At least now I'm heading in the right direction.

She sat quietly as her phone vibrated yet again, reminding her of the life she was reluctant, but determined, to leave.

Now Anna had nothing but time to think while the trucker drove. How ironic David would find it if he knew her destination. He'd tried for years to convince her to travel north and enjoy the outdoors, but Anna's opinion was that if you'd seen one tree, you'd pretty much seen them all.

Her decision to go to the Upper Peninsula hadn't entailed deep thought. The week before she left she noticed a trail book that David had left on the side table. The back of the book showed a map of the Upper Peninsula, which reminded her of a fish, above the easily recognizable Michigan mitt. She looked at the map and realized he would never think that she would hide there. He knew her preference for the city. On the map, she saw that Marquette was a good-sized city if she needed anything. She wanted to reside in a smaller town, so she randomly picked Mikamaw, a little town west of Marquette, off the map.

Anna liked to be prepared, so she did some research about Mikamaw on a computer at a coffee shop so it wouldn't be traced. She learned that Mikamaw grew during the heavy copper mining and logging years. The stores that supplied goods and entertainment to the working men had long since been renovated for the tourist industry. The town lost residents each year to other states with more job opportunities, but the tourists were relatively consistent. The Ottawa National Forest was less than an hour away, and people visited in different seasons for outdoor adventure there or in one of the other areas nearby.

She read that Lake Superior, which bordered Mikamaw's northern end, deeply influenced the moods and weather of the town. People who lived there were hardy — they had to be because the weather could change in an instant, not much grew there, and snowstorms of epic proportions were regular fare. The day she read it, she wondered how the hell could a lake change people's moods? She pondered it again now.

After miles of quiet and hours of napping, Anna awoke when the truck's brakes squeaked as the driver slowed down.

"I need to stretch a minute," he said before he got out of the truck. Anna went back to sleep until she heard the door open again.

"Where ya headin' to, anyway?"

"I'm going to Mikamaw, but if you need to drop me somewhere else, as long as there's a hotel, I'll figure out how to get the rest of the way."

"I'm headed right through there, if ya like."

"Thanks, that would be great."

"Yep."

"And uh … sir … if you don't mind, don't tell anyone you drove me here. I -"

"I don't talk much to anyone, so your secret's safe."

"It's not a secret. Just—"

"I don't care what from where."

"Okay. Well, thanks."

Mikamaw City

Through the grime on the window Anna could make out a smudged "help wanted" sign with the word "office" scrolled across the top. The door squeaked as she opened it, and Anna was enveloped by a strong smell of oil, sweat, and gas. The smell of gas always made Anna nauseas. A short grungy man approached. He walked with an odd gait, like he had been broken in half and incorrectly reconstructed. His eyes swept up and down her, not in a sexual way, but laden with judgment. He sighed. His voice was a mixture of dry smoker's throat and deep southern twang, even though they were far from the South.

"What you want?" he asked.

"I want to apply for the job. Can you tell me about it?"

"You don't want that job."

Anna was taken aback. Did he mean she *couldn't* have the job?

"I really need a job, and I can do office work. I'm new to town and I need some—"

"Ok. Let me get to the chase. My boys are gonna be staring at ya like a piece of meat to a starvin' bear. Catch my drift? I don't think it gonna work. Sorry."

Irritation started to boil over within her as Anna realized this man was not going to give her a chance. She tried to contain it.

"You don't belong here. No offense," he said and turned to leave.

Anna held him back with her words. "You have no idea where I belong," she said and paused, not knowing what to call him, "mister. I have been through hell and back to get to this shit hole, and I need a job. I get that you're not going to give it to me, but don't you *dare* tell me where I belong and don't belong, because you don't know a thing about me."

He gave her a big, surprisingly white smile under all that smudged grease and said, "I'll give you a chance, but don't come biting my head off if it don't work. Deal?" He looked down, smirking.

It was hard to reconcile her heart-pounding anger with the

relief she suddenly felt. The only answer was laughter. Anna burst with it. Tears streamed from her eyes as weeks of pent-up tension released. The man stared at her, eyebrows lifted. He'd missed the joke.

"When can ya start?"

"Right now."

"How about tomorra?"

"While we're working out details, I know this isn't very appropriate, but I need to be paid ... uh ... in cash. I need to be under the radar for a bit, if you know what I mean."

"Ya kill someone?"

"No! Why would--"

"Ya rob a bank?"

"No."

"Why you want cash? That's risky. I need more than that."

"I have an asshole husband looking for me. I don't want to be found," the lie rushed out.

"I think we can come up with something. Come back at nine."

"Thanks. I didn't quite get your name."

"Name's George. Yours is?"

She decided to keep it simple and use her real first name and a false last name.

"Anna Jones."

"See ya tomorrow, Anna."

***

Like bears anxiously waiting for the ripening spring berries, people pay close attention to changes in small towns. Not many secrets escape scrutiny, and newcomers are a studied curiosity. Nelly Pattis was always studying. When an unrecognized car drove by on Lincoln Street, she would look out her window to judge the situation. She noticed right away that someone was staying at Walt's hotel. She watched with binoculars as a woman she didn't recognize walked toward town. Clearly, the woman with dark hair wasn't from around here and didn't belong. Nelly figured she was likely a traveler passing through, probably one of the artist types who occasionally did. Nelly was wrong.

Alice Russel called Nelly with the news.

"Someone new is working at George's shop," Alice announced. "I had to get new brakes on my car and I saw her myself."

"Where'd she come from?" Nelly wondered aloud.

"I don't know. She must have somehow bullied George into a job. Maybe with her good looks, because it's obvious she doesn't know anything about cars."

"It's got to be the woman staying at Walt's. Did she have shoulder-length dark hair?"

"She sure did. I caught her name. It's Anna," said Alice.

"Well, we'll have to keep an eye on this Anna. Find out her story," Nelly said.

"There's bound to be some kind of story. She's got to be crazy. Working at George's. No woman in her right mind would choose something like that."

"You're right," agreed Nelly. "Keep your ears open and I'll do the same. Let me know what else you learn about her."

They had an unspoken agreement to find something not to like about this newcomer.

***

Leena rolled her eyes when she saw the women from the ladies bowling club come in Bart's Bar. They were chirping like chatty chickadees. She wondered what had them all worked up today.

Alice looked over at George across the bar as they took their seats, and then back to the women. "Did you hear that there is a new girl in town?" She said with a conspirator's tone as she moved close to discuss the situation.

Nelly chimed in, "She's staying at Walt's. God help her. And you'll never guess where she's working—"

"—George's shop," Alice interrupted.

"That poor thing," said Rhonda Dawlson.

"Trust me. You don't have to feel sorry for her," said Alice.

At that moment, Leena interrupted to take drink orders. "Leena, have you seen the woman working at George's yet?"

"What woman would want to work there, eh?" Leena laughed, genuinely perplexed at who would torture themselves with George as a boss.

"Exactly. You get it," said Nelly.

"Get what?"

"That there must be something horribly wrong with a woman who would work there," Nelly whispered.

Right then Leena got it. Alice and Nelly were on the trail, ready to pounce on any woman they found intimidating or any interesting gossip they could vicariously live through for a while.

"I don't know about that," Leena told them. "Lots of us have to work. I'll have to check it out. I need some work done on my baby anyway. Don't be too hard on her. We don't know a lick about her."

Rhonda nodded in agreement. Alice rolled her eyes but said nothing.

When the clutch of women left, Leena asked George about it. "I hear you've got someone new working at the shop, eh?"

"You ladies are always talkin'."

"Well, I'm more the listener, but anyway ... what's the story?"

"I don't like talkin' about people, but for you, I will. Her name's Anna. She walked in with the help wanted sign and basically said she's takin' the job. She seems okay. But she don't belong there. She's o.k. 'n all, just not fit for the job."

"I see. Well, I need some work done on my truck. It's stallin' all the time. I'll come by and say hello to her too."

"Bring it in."

"Okay. Wednesday work?"

"That'll work. Maybe you can get this employee off my hands while yur there."

"I don't know about that," laughed Leena, feeling bad for any woman who would work for George. He wasn't known for treating women, or anyone, for that matter, very well, but Leena didn't have any problems with him.

***

Anna hated it at the shop, but thought maybe it was justice to have a job she detested. She deserved misery after the pain she had inflicted on Andrew and David. *I hope David can forgive me for leaving. I should have explained it better, but it's too hard. I miss them both so much.*

The fumes at the shop made her nauseous and the men drove her crazy. George was much wiser than Anna had realized. He was spot-on that some of his men would leer at her, although a few were nice. Ignoring the ornery ones was almost impossible, and she found their attentions irritating. Two mechanics in particular, George Jr. and Adam, bothered her so much that she wondered how any cars got fixed.

Adam walked up to the front desk, his body odor preceding his large body. How did he maneuver around the cars to fix them? Anna wondered.

"How you doing today, pretty lady?"

Ugh, thought Anna. "That Cavalier needs a new muffler. It's next in line. It's got your name all over it," Anna said, hoping this would move him along in his work.

"I'll get to it when I get to it. I want to talk to the pretty lady first." He smiled and Anna's skin crawled. His eyes shifted from her eyes to her chest. Papers in hand, Anna shifted them around, trying to look busy, hoping Adam would get the hint and leave. He stared at her, making no movement to leave while his eyes groped her.

She could feel herself begin to simmer. What right did this guy have to stand there and leer at her? Turning toward him, she asked, "You got a problem, Adam?"

"Not since you started working here."

"Lay off it, will ya?"

"Don't get your panties in a bunch, eh?"

Anna leaned in closer to Adam, gave him a sexy smile, and said, "Back off, Adam. I've got a gun and I know how to use it. You're getting on my last nerve, and I don't think anyone would miss you." His jaw slacked and he stood in front of her, speechless.

"Do you understand what I'm telling you or do you need me to say it again?" she asked.

"I get it. Calm yourself down. I'm going to work now," he said as he walked away.

Annoyed and relieved, Anna started organizing work orders for the day. Thank goodness I threw the gun in the field, because I swear I could use it on that disgusting man.

Anna wasn't desperate for money. Her hidden bank accounts were well stocked, but not enough for a lifetime, and she wanted to save it. She needed work, if not for the money, then to keep her mind occupied and away from missing her family.

Two weeks into Anna's employment at the shop, an old, loud, bright yellow Suburban pulled in, coughing exhaust and piteously puffing along. When the car door opened, out stepped a woman clearly stuck in the eighties. She had heavy, waved bangs and frosty blonde hair. "It's on the shitter again, George, please bring 'er back to life," she said to a smiling George.

She looked toward Anna and walked right up to her. "You're a new sight here," she said as she gave Anna a warm smile. Anna couldn't help but like the woman.

"Yeah. I'm Anna."

"Well, Anna, I'm Leena. Nice to meet ya. Are you *really* working here?" She paused, looked around, then added, "No offense."

"George was kind enough to give me a job. I'm new in town."

"I thought so. Hey, when you're done with work, why don't you come over to Bart's Bar? I'll be workin' and I can fill ya in on the two streets and five places available in this wondrous town. And feed ya. Looks like you could use it. What do you say?"

Anna wanted to say no. She didn't want to make friends right now. She wanted to be alone and try to forget all that had happened. Lacking a good lie off the top of her head, however, she was surprised to hear herself say, "Sure, I'll see you there."

"Great. Bring good news about my baby," she said while pointing her long, pink fake-nailed finger at the equally bright vehicle.

Baby?

***

When Anna pushed open the heavy wooden doors to Bart's Bar, the welcoming smell of fried food greeted her. A polished bar made of beautifully stained oak stood before her. The full array of liquor bottles caught the light from the small lights that twinkled in front of the long mirror, and in front of the mirror were rows of shined glasses. The lights were dim, but in a comforting way. It wasn't at all what she had expected in a bar. Something about Bart's felt almost homey.

Leena invited Anna to sit at a booth, and they ordered drinks and fries.

"So, what brings you to our little town?" Leena asked.

"I don't know. I've always wanted to travel up here. I had some time, so here I am."

"I see," said Leena. "Where ya from?"

"I've traveled so much these past years, I wouldn't say I'm from anywhere," Anna replied.

"Fries are up," a man yelled from behind the kitchen window. Leena got up and brought a basket of French fries over to their table. Leena dipped her fry in ketchup and continued their conversation. "You don't belong at the shop. We need some help here, if you're interested."

"I've never waited tables in my life. I'd be a disaster."

"If you ever cooked food for friends, or waited on an ornery man, you'll do just fine. Have you done any of that?"

"Sure." Somehow it seemed that Leena was asking more of Anna than just a job and she wasn't sure that she wanted what was being offered.

"Give it a go. I can see you need some kind of help. Don't worry, I'm not asking no details. There's also a room upstairs Ron needs a tenant for. He's the owner now that Bart's gone. That was his dad. Anyway, you might not get to bed early on weekends. But, who wants to sleep life away, eh? You don't want to sleep at Walt's motel anyway. Do ya?"

"I'm going to have to think about it. Thanks for the offer. I'm just not sure I want to commit to a lease or anything like that. I don't know what I'm doing right now. I'm kind of in limbo."

"Alright, I'm sure Ron would be willing to have a short lease," she smiled. "Keep in mind, there are pretty gals coming to town daily who might steal this job opportunity," Leena said, smirking.

***

Anna looked around her room at Walt's Motel. It would be nice to leave, but Leena seemed a bit intense and like a person who might ask too many questions.

Walt's Motel was the first place Anna had seen when coming to town. It frightened her, but less so than the other motel down the street. It was dimly lit and frequented by questionable characters with no bedding standards. The flowered bedspread seemed oddly out of place and pocked with more than a few burn marks. Smells lingered that could not be accurately identified, and grime grew in tiny mountains in the corners of the floor, indicating that thorough cleaning was not a priority.

The first week, Anna could barely sleep. The room disgusted her as she analyzed it while she handled her still-aching breasts. Yet, the sleepless nights caught up to her, and when they finally did, she slept through all of the dark sounds of the night and had the first uninterrupted nights of sleep she had experienced in months.

The night after she met with Leena, she woke up, urged by her bladder. Anna sat on the cold toilet seat and screamed when she saw cockroaches on the floor. She didn't handle bugs well, even in well-lit and expected environments, like outdoors. Years ago, when she and David had brought a kitten home only to find out it had fleas, she moved frantically to fumigate the house and threw things away that couldn't be properly cleaned. She couldn't rest until she had returned their apartment to a flea-free zone.

Anna tried to settle herself down by pacing the small room. Light came through the darkened curtains from ancient outdoor lights that lit the snowy parking lot. Peeking out around the edge of the curtain, she noticed a large silhouette at the corner of the long line of motel rooms across the way. *It couldn't be.* A moment passed and the shadow didn't move. Then a small light, a lighter, dimly lit the face—Adam. She knew he didn't live here; he had to be watching her.

Anna packed her bags, looking intensely through each piece of clothing and each pocket of the backpack to make sure no creatures took the journey with her. That night she didn't get any more sleep. After she calmed down some, she watched *Seinfeld* reruns, kept a keen watch over her things, and occasionally peeked out the window. Adam left after she turned on the lights to pack, and as far as she could tell, he hadn't returned. As soon as there was a light on in the front office, she checked out and walked to work with everything she owned in the backpack on her back.

"Sorry about the short notice, George, but I quit."

"Thank goodness."

Anna looked at him curiously.

"No offense, but we're not getting as much work done since you got here. Where you going to go now?"

"Leena offered me a job at Bart's. I'm gonna give it a go there."

"You know, it's hard to get around these parts without wheels."

"I've managed so far, but you're probably right."

"I have an old beater, I'd be happy to loan it to you."

"Loan?"

"Yeah. You can't put anything in your name if you don't want that husband to find you. I'll keep the insurance in my name and you can make payments."

Anna stared at him, dumbfounded. She hadn't expected generosity from George.

"I don't know what to say."

"Thanks would be a place to start."

"Thanks! I'll pay you monthly."

"Damn straight."

"Thanks," Anna said again and wrapped her arms around his stiff body. He didn't lift his arms in return. She pulled away.

"Thanks is enough," George said.

"Thank you!"

"I believe you already said that."

He wished her good luck and she was on her way.

***

Ron Tulsky thought his father would be proud of what his restaurant, his dream, had become. Bart, Ron's father, had poured himself into building Bart's Bar and keeping it going. Maybe it was his spirit that made it more than just a bar. People came for food, but they also seemed to come for comfort and community. Ron had seen his share of bars, and the ambiance of Bart's was something unique. His dad would be proud. He was certain of it, because before he died, Bart told his son about all he went through to build his bar and he held nothing back.

His father grew up in the town of Mikamaw. He would have stayed there, but employment was scarce, and he wanted to earn some money to realize his dream to open up a bar in his hometown. He moved downstate and found a job at GM. When his mind had time to wander, he imagined how his bar would look and what kind of food he would serve.

He put this dream on hold, rarely thinking of it, while he married the love of his life and raised his two boys. It didn't take long, however, for him to realize he had married a fair-weather wife. (This part was hard for Ron to listen to.) She began to ignore Bart and the children, and did so more often as the years went by. Bart knew in his heart that she was like a caged bird, but he couldn't talk to her about it. He wouldn't have known where to start. He hoped it would get better on its own. One night, though, she up and left them. Bart knew she wasn't coming back. He was devastated, but moved on the best he could, for his boys. When he was offered an early retirement from GM he took it, his savings, and his sons and moved back to the U.P.

Ron and his brother Chris were not keen on moving to the middle of the sticks from metro Detroit. They missed the people and the action and knew they would be in for a hard time entering their teen years at a new school. The first day of school, Ron beat up Martin Carey in the boy's bathroom. Martin started taunting him, and Ron knew that he must make it clear, in no uncertain terms, that he and his brother weren't targets. It was a dangerous plan, but successful. He and his brother were left alone and made some friends in Mikamaw High School. They also tried some things they hadn't done below the big bridge: skiing, snowmobiling, four-wheeling, and more.

Over time, they found their place among the local teens and came to enjoy what the small town had to offer. When they weren't with friends, they helped their dad build his dream. After workers framed Bart's Bar, his dad decided to do much of the finishing himself, to save money. He poured his soul into the place. That's why the locals accepted it, Ron thought. They didn't like people who came from downstate and tried to open a business, but Bart was a Mikamaw native and his work ethic was strong. Not to mention that there weren't a lot of bar choices in town and people were excited for a new place to frequent.

It went through rough patches, but Bart's Bar was a part of Mikamaw, as much as the Lake Superior shore. It ingratiated itself into the landscape, natural as the sand. Bart had spent so much time over the last twenty years of his life working at Bart's and talking to the regulars that it seemed as if a part of him still resided there. In the occasional drunken haze, Ron sometimes imagined he saw his dad's shadow pass by or heard the echoes of his familiar phrases.

Ron couldn't decide if he was thankful or bitter that his father had asked him to take over the bar. He liked the people here, and they accepted him as he was and didn't give him looks for his tattoos or biker wear. Downstate, people assumed things about a man covered with body art and leather, but here, they knew he was an academic, a writer who liked motorcycles and tattoos, and they didn't give him trouble for any of it. A few times at Ohio State University, he had gotten some strange looks when he walked to the front of the class to start the lecture on the first day of classes. He didn't want to be pegged into anyone's idea of what he should look or be like.

He could have used his looks to his advantage at the university. He'd been approached by more than a few college girls but that wasn't his style. People often assumed he was a ladies' man, but he wasn't. He had only two loves in his life, his ex-wife, Shelly, and Leena. He rarely thought of his ex-wife anymore, but

Leena tortured his heart and libido daily.

Years ago when he had left Mikamaw to start college downstate at Central Michigan, he'd known that he would always love Leena, but it was hopeless. She only had eyes for Frank, and they would soon be married. Ron wouldn't interfere with Leena's happiness. He realized that he might not be marriage material anyway since he hadn't figured out his own life at that point.

He did his best to let her go. Yet her image would cross his mind at the most unexpected moments over the years. Even in the midst of the few happy years of his marriage with Shelly, he sometimes awoke from vivid dreams about Leena. It seemed that no matter what, he couldn't erase her from his subconscious. Ron drove the 10 hours north once or twice a year to visit his father, Bart. On those rare occasions, he'd done his best to avoid Leena and the torment it brought him to see her. His efforts were in vain. Leena worked too often at Bart's for Ron to hide from her.

He had come back to Mikamaw for good when his father became sick. The cancer slowly claimed his father's body, but Bart couldn't find peace until he knew his beloved bar would go on. Ron knew that he would have to take over his father's pride, at least for a while. He decided to write. It had always been a dream of his, and he figured this was probably the only chance he would have to put some time into it.

***

Anna sat for hours in front of Bart's with her few belongings, waiting for anyone to show up, hoping for someone soon because it was cold and snowing—a constant state, she noticed. Lloyd, the cook, arrived first. His eyes drooped atop his six-foot lanky frame and he reeked of cigarette smoke and marijuana.

"Leena said you might be comin' by." Lloyd held the door open for Anna and ushered her in with overly polite humor. "Here ye go me lady," he said, smiling.

Inside Bart's kitchen, they chopped vegetables wordlessly while listening to Led Zeppelin. The smell of baking pasties, a northern Michigan stew-filled pie pocket, reminded her of her days at Savory Scents, where she had worked for so many years. She missed starting her morning with her friends amidst balls of dough, the scent of coffee, and baking bread.

    A few hours later, Ron showed up. He had a tough but handsome look. He wore leather, intricately inked skin peeked out around his collar, and he had more piercings than Anna had seen in these parts. Despite his appearance, he was quite a gentleman. He gave Anna the keys to her upstairs apartment and insisted he carry her bags. Her temporary abode was nicer than she expected, although small, and apparently bug free. *At least it isn't Walt's,* she thought as she unpacked.

Water

"For a small town, this place gets busy," said Anna. She and Leena had just finished with the dinner shift at Bart's and sat eating their own dinner before they parted ways.

"Ya haven't seen nothing yet. You've only worked Wednesday and Thursday. Tomorrow you'll see what a Friday is like. You're doing good though," said Leena.

"Yeah, except when I gave Harold a medium-rare burger instead of medium-well. Did you see the look he gave me?" She didn't mention the fact that Harold was the truck driver who drove her to Mikamaw in the first place, and she hoped he wouldn't mention it either. She hadn't realized at the time that he was *from* Mikamaw.

"Oh, that?! That was nothing. Harold is always griping about something. He let you off easy. He's yelled, and I mean *yelled*, at me for less. Like the time he swore at me because his beer wasn't cold enough. Had a fit, I tell you!"

They ate their greasy food. Ron walked over to their table. "How's the food, ladies?" he asked, then sent a shining smile Leena's way.

"Good," they chimed in unison.

"How are ya learning the ropes?" he asked, looking at Anna. "Do you have everything you need? Have any questions?"

"I'm good," Anna said, covering her mouth full of food.

"Good," he nodded. "You're in good hands here," he nodded toward Leena. "She's the best," he said, then winked and walked away, a chain on his belt jingling as he walked.

When he was out of earshot, Anna asked, "What's up with you two? Are you a thing or what?"

"Or what. We've known each other for years. That's all."

"Oh," Anna nodded like she understood, but it seemed like Leena had given her only part of the story. "Well, thanks for showing me around. I think I've finally got the computer system figured out. Mine was similar, but it didn't have so many choices."

"Yours?"

Anna felt the blood drain from her face. How had that

slipped? "I mean, the one at the place I worked before. Their system was kind of like yours." She stretched. "This job wears me out. I'm gonna get some rest so I'm ready for the onslaught tomorrow."

"Alright. See ya tomorra," Leena called out to Anna's retreating form.

***

Friday and Saturday passed in a whirlwind of slinging beers, fizzy soda, countless burger-fry combos, and numerous customers (many of their faces growing familiar at their reappearance). The work kept Anna's body busy and her mind occupied. Sunday felt like screeching brakes, as everything became still and quiet. With the day off work, Anna didn't know how to fill the time. Quiet was not her friend.

Was Michigan weather always so depressing? Now that she thought about it, people usually seemed grumpy this time of year. The end of winter often dragged on, the dreary weather refusing to leave and settling itself for the long haul, and the winter's clouds were reflected in people's eyes. Their voices became tenser as the clouds rested unyielding in front of the sun. Then eventually it changed. David always said, "If you don't like the weather here, wait five minutes and it will change." Now, as she contemplated this, she waited for an hour. No change. She couldn't remember when she'd last seen the sun. She didn't mind the accumulating snow banks, now taller than the houses, which littered the landscape, but where was the sun?

Movement eluded her. Invisible tendrils rooted her to the couch. Even though she was hungry, the thought of getting off the couch to find food sounded like an exhausting endeavor. She sighed. She sat. Her arm stretched for the remote to the small TV. Flipping through the channels brought no relief, so she clicked the television off and dropped the useless remote to the floor.

Her cellphone sat on the small table near her, mocking her for being too afraid to turn it on. It sat silent, immobile and useless since she had hopped in the big rig with Harold. *God, I miss them.*

Would it hurt to look once? I'm sure they couldn't track me with one quick look. Just one?

Anna looked out the window. Thick, wet snow fell outside, a curtain of white hiding all in its path. She was stuck indoors. A run might do her good, but her legs were like wood and refused to move at all. She reached over and tenderly grasped the phone. She held it reverently for many moments. *Should I?*

Although she didn't remember the moment of her decision, she looked down and the phone was on. On her background picture, David cradled Andrew in his arms. She remembered taking that picture. It was a beautiful moment. Now all those moments were tainted with her mistakes. She was a failure. She'd failed them both. At least she had known enough to free them from her — crazy, evil.

Tears streamed down her face as she scrolled through picture after picture of the life she had left behind. Her husband, her baby. *What a mistake. I should throw this away and make a clean break, for his safety.* She gently stroked the phone with her thumb.

Then it vibrated. The word "home" surfaced below another picture of David holding Andrew in the glow of Christmas lights. She silenced the call. *I'm so sorry, David. You didn't deserve this.*

Curiosity pulled at her, sixty-two messages waited for her. David had been unyielding in his attempts to contact her. She started listening to them. "Anna, where are you? I love you," was typical of the first handful of voicemails. Then they became desperate. David cried, "Let us know you are okay. I don't care what happened; I just need to know you are alive. I don't even need to know why you left … for all we've been through … let me know you are alive!" Then they became more resigned and a little report-like: "Andrew is sitting up now. His eyes have changed …"

There were messages from her friends at Savory Scents. Bev's voice sounded uncertain of what to say, very unlike her. Of course, Kate left her share of messages, chastising Anna in one message and pleading with her in the next. Anna thought that listening to her friends might distract her from her thoughts of David and Andrew, but it only made her ache for them worse.

Against her better judgment, she decided to listen to the last message David had left. "Andrew is incredible. He looks at me like he knows the secrets of the universe, like he knows me. He laughs with a chuckle that for some reason makes me think of Trent. Come back soon so you can see. I love you."

The mention of her father overwhelmed her. She sank into her pillow and cried until her face hurt and the pillow was soggy. *What would Dad think? I've let them all down. Become worse than my mother.* She started a text to David, and then stopped. No words would be acceptable, she thought.

Anna cried until she was empty of tears and then sleep mercifully took her away. Briefly. She woke feeling empty and dead inside. *I can't live like this.* She hated herself for what she'd done. Hate fueled her body, and her legs were unbound, finally moving. She bundled up for an icy walk, holding her head low to hide her red-rimmed eyes. She was on a mission to numb herself.

Anna walked to Ned's Grill which was hopelessly devoid of customers. *No hope of blending in with the crowd tonight. Maybe I should move to a bigger city. But they would find me.*

"Beer and a shot of whiskey," she told the bartender. He gave her a single nod and wordlessly filled her order. She stared blankly at the TV, pretending interest in the football game.

"So, how are things going at Bart's?"

"No offense, but I can't handle small talk right now."

He looked startled, but then a polite half-smile crossed his face and he stepped away. "I get it. Let me know if I can get you anything," he said as he pushed through the doors to the kitchen. The ambiance of Ned's, dark and empty, fit her mood.

He poured her four more beers and two more shots before she left. Numbed, she stumbled out and walked, uncovered, wet snow sticking to her sweatshirt. She pulled on her coat and then walked into the liquor store, where she bought a six-pack. The cold walk back to her apartment sobered her enough to make it to the toilet to vomit.

As she stumbled around the apartment, trying to calm herself, she mumbled incoherently. Three beers later, she stumbled out of her apartment door, stepped shakily down the stairs, walked past Bart's, and headed toward the Lake Superior shore. The temperature had dropped. The wet snow under her feet turned to ice.

She could hear the waves long before she saw them. A fierce wind pushed the waves forward like angry buildings battling to the Lake Superior shore. The bluish-green waves were illuminated by hazy afternoon light. The churning water promised to take and destroy anything in its path. It almost made Anna happy. *This will be easy work.* She remembered that Leena had told her that the long pier at Springport Beach lingered from an old lighthouse that was no longer used. It was a remnant from the busy logging and mining days. Useless information, she thought.

Anna leaned deeply into the wind as she walked along the pier. Her intention was to end her life; the only question was where she would do it. She sat down, frozen inside and out, thinking about the best place to jump. Images of David and Andrew passed before her eyes. *Is it too early for my life to flash before me?*

Something tickled her thigh. It took a moment for her to realize that her phone was vibrating in her pocket; she thought she'd left it at the apartment. The message, difficult to hear, over the howling wind, was to the point: "I'm so sorry to tell you this way, Anna ... but your mom had an accident." David sighed, and his voice sounded groggy. Was he crying? "She didn't make it. I'm so sorry. Anna, you need to call. I need to know you are ok. I have to hear your voice. I'm so sorry. I love you."

One last selfless act before I go, she thought. She texted, "I am ok. Tell Joanne sorry. Please find happiness and peace. I'm not coming back. I love you and Andrew forever." Then she placed the phone on the pier. Taking it would be like drowning David and Andrew with her, and she couldn't bear that.

The irony was not lost on her, even in her inebriated state. *It is fitting, that we go close together. I hope you found peace, Mom, and I hope to find it too. I guess I'm more like you than I ever realized.*

She decided the best approach was to run. She ran toward the end of the pier. *I hope it ends quickly.* Her legs slipped from under her and she heard a grotesque thud. *Did that come from me?* She looked at the darkening sky above. *Where are the stars?* Before she had time to contemplate the answer, blackness enveloped her.

She imagined her body slinking into the water, loose like a rubber band. Was she dreaming? Was it real? *It doesn't matter, because the view is amazing. No, it does matter. I want it to be real, to be over in this peaceful way. I haven't had peace in months.*

Thousands of bubbles rushed at her ears simultaneously as

her body sank like unwanted metal. Thought was impossible over the noise. The rushing sound slowed to a calming trickle, like a small brook. Her feet landed softly on the lake floor. As she looked around, the visual clarity underwater surprised her. In the distance, a shipwreck rested peacefully with fish swimming around it, oblivious of the raging waters above, a serene, watery grave. Lake Superior's floor alternated between rocky and sandy. Something dark emerged from the murky distance. Anna did not fear the dark shape that slowly approached. It started to resemble a person. Then the vague form coalesced into her mother.

"What are you doing here?" her mother asked, waving her hands at their surroundings, seemingly oblivious to their astounding location. "You should be somewhere like here ..." and suddenly Anna found herself in her old room.

"No, I don't want to be here," Anna screamed, and then she covered her mouth, ashamed that she had yelled at her dead mother. "How are we ..." she began, but her mom waved her hands again and suddenly there was a blinding light. They stood on a warm beach, one Anna remembered as the scene of the last good memory she had with her family intact, at a Lake Michigan beach. Her eyes slowly adjusted to the brightness, and her skin soaked in the warm sun until agony and realization filled her. "I'm dead, aren't I? I'm sorry, Mom. I didn't do any better than you did. I'm sorry I haven't been a good daughter. I was wrong."

"Baby girl, you have nothing to apologize for. I am at peace, and you can be too. I have accepted my life. What it was ... and wasn't. I was recently taught that acceptance is the way to peace. Don't keep my sickness and your reaction as an anchor. I forgive you."

Anna started to cry, and her tears floated outward, instead of down her cheeks, remaining whole and surrounding her, floating heavily in the air around her face. Each tear revealed more of the Lake Superior floor, like a tiny television set, until she was back where she started, standing in view of the shipwreck. Her tears didn't mix with the Superior water. Instead they began to multiply and grow, creating a person-sized bubble of tears around her. Then suddenly they mixed with the cold Lake Superior water, and a rushing sound bellowed past her ears. She reached out to hug her mom before her image faded in the whirling water. "I'm sorry, Mom. I love you!" Anna yelled.

"I love you too," her mom said and reached out to her, but she was no longer solid. Anna's lungs began to burn. *This is it. They are filling with water."* She fought to take a deep breath; nothing filled her but regret over what she had done.

Part Two

The Break

Anna's family started to change when she was ten. To her, it seemed that her parents were happy, and then, suddenly, they weren't. Their happiness faded, and smiles were replaced with scowls or indifference. What followed was months of nervous silence, disrupted by occasional hushed arguments that Anna tried unsuccessfully to hear.

Her older sister, Joanne, much wiser in Anna's eyes because of her five years' advantage, caught Anna with her ear against the hallway wall, trying to make sense of the muted, unhappy words of her parents.

"You're not going to hear anything from there," Joanne admonished. "You have to go in here." She led Anna into her small closet and cleared a spot for them to sit.

They sat quietly, ears to the wall, and listened for clues, but found none. The words weren't loud enough to be heard.

Anna's heart raced. "Can you hear *anything*?" she whispered.

"I hear lots. I just can't understand it."

"What do you think they're fighting—"

"Shh—" Joanne insisted. The words were getting louder on the other side of the wall. The volley of words sounded angrier.

"I know you fucked that whore! Stop denying it and maybe we can move on!" their mother, Clare, accused.

"I'm tired of this bullshit. I didn't do anything. What makes you keep saying this shit?" their father asked.

"Women *know*. Women know when their men are on the prowl. I'm not stupid."

"Maybe not, but you're acting like a lunatic."

"Fuck you."

"I just don't know what to do to make you believe me." Anna's father continued to talk, but his voice disappeared below the audible threshold of understanding.

Joanne and Anna looked at each other. Tears streamed down Anna's face. Joanne reached for Anna's hand and motioned with her finger for Anna to be quiet.

They heard more arguing, which they couldn't decipher.

Then their mother's voice rose: "You love your job more than me, your whore more than me. Why don't you just leave?"

"I don't know where you are getting this from. I do everything you ask. I'm here with you and the girls. I do what you ask around the house. Yet you nag, nag, nag. I think we're at a standstill. We need help."

"You may need some, but I'm just fine!" The girls heard the door to their parents' bedroom open, followed by footsteps and then even louder footsteps. Garbled, angry words moved further and further away from them, and then the door to the garage opened and shut and silence returned.

Joanne and Anna walked out of their closet hideout and stood by the door leading to the garage. Anna knew the garage was the place of preference when her parents could no longer rein in their voices.

"What should we do?" Anna asked after a few tense moments. "Are they okay?"

Joanne was uncharacteristically speechless. She looked at Anna blankly, then said, "I don't know."

"I'm going to look. Real fast," Anna said. She quickly opened the door a crack to look into the garage. Joanne and Anna squeezed close to one another to peek through the crack in the door. In the garage, their parents embraced and shook with intense sobs. Trent saw Anna and waved them back inside. Anna had never been more scared than in the moment she saw tears falling down her strong father's face.

"What do you think it means?" Anna asked Joanne after she shut the door.

"It looks like they've made up," Joanne answered, but Anna heard an edge of doubt in her voice.

Trent and Clare stayed in the garage another hour after that.

The next day the family went to their favorite pizza parlor for dinner. The air felt calm and peaceful, as if the anger had dissipated between her parents. Joanne was right, Anna thought.

With dessert, Anna finally relaxed, trusting her intuition that all would be well.

"Your father and I are getting a divorce," her mom said between bites of her chocolate sundae.

Anna choked, "What?"

Joanne sat statue still. Anna looked to her for help, but she was clearly stunned. She would be no help.

"Clare! I thought we were going to ease into it," Trent said.

"Cat's out of the bag. I'm sorry girls," said Clare.

"How could you do this?" Anna asked.

"It's complicated," Dad calmly responded.

"That's what adults say when they don't want to explain! Tell us!" Anna yelled. Other patrons turned to stare.

"We should continue this at home," Mom insisted, leading her daughters out the door.

The ride home was silent. Anna kept looking to Joanne to respond, but she didn't. *What's wrong with her? She looks like a mannequin. I need her help!*

At home, Anna sat and listened to her parents' empty words, which she supposed were intended to convey something, but they did not. Their words were like puffs of smoke, with nothing concrete to grab onto. They didn't explain *why* her family was breaking apart, only that it was.

It seemed to Anna that as soon as the divorce was decided, her parents seemed less angry and more civil toward each other. Maybe if they had acted like this before, they wouldn't be divorcing, thought Anna. Trent stayed for weeks after the announcement while he made arrangements for a permanent departure. Clare walked with extra bounce in her step, seeming almost giddy. Anna noticed, and it burned a pit in her stomach. Adults were just like big kids, she thought. They pretended to have it all figured out when they got it backward just as often as anybody else.

***

Even months after the divorce, Anna couldn't make sense of it. She felt undone. She imagined pieces of her everywhere, like puzzle bits strewn across a room—a piece with her mother, another with her father, a few at school. This disjointed Anna couldn't make sense of what had happened to her family. How did things go so wrong?

She had a vision of what her family *should* be—a memory she often turned to in order to replenish her lost stores of hope. A sunny summer day at the Lake Michigan shoreline on Ludington Beach epitomized the family she wanted. It was the last time she remembered her parents happy together. The weather was hot with a refreshing breeze, the water surprisingly cool. Her mom and dad held hands and walked down the beach in search of Petoskey stones and other rock treasures. Anna watched as they made their way farther down the beach, the waves lapping up their footprints. They stopped to investigate something in the sand. In another moment, Dad splashed Mom with water and chased her back toward Anna. He caught her and they embraced, laughing, their eyes bright with love.

Later that same day, Joanne and Anna ran out into the waves under their parents' watchful eyes, greeting the water like an old friend. They bounced in the waves together. Each blue wave gave them the brief gift of weightlessness as they jumped in it and squealed with delight.

When the sisters were exhausted from swimming, their fingers wrinkled and cold, they dried off on the shore. The Cromley family sat on an old, blue blanket. They ate a gratifying lunch, many of their favorite foods lovingly prepared and packed by Clare, sandwiches with cut crusts for her daughters and cold chicken for Trent. Anna ate until she thought she might burst. Then she leaned back on the blanket and rested her body after its work in the waves.

The sun warmed Anna's body and she felt warmth from within as well. Joanne lay beside her, and they were at peace with one another. Trent and Clare talked quietly while they looked out at the water.

Anna held this memory, like treasure, and locked it in a special place in her mind. On occasions when she was empty and hopeless, she brought it out for comfort, but over time its powers seemed to be dwindling.

***

When Anna was eleven, almost a year after the divorce, she woke up in the middle of the night to the sound of squeaking and bumping. She imagined an enormous eight-foot-tall spider suspending itself from the ceiling with its legs scrambling over the walls. Anna ran down the short hallway, yelling wildly, to her mom's bedroom door, where the sound originated, and hurriedly opened the door, yelling, "Mom!"

Her mother held tight to the pole of the paint roller and frantically pulled and pushed it up and down the wall. Sweat dripped from her face. Bright pink strips of paint marked her progress on the wall. The paint roller squeaked hideously with each push and pull. Her arms continued their movement, oblivious to Anna's presence.

"Mom?" Anna questioned, her voice shaking.

Her mother turned her head with her arms held high, holding the paint pole against the wall. With a calm voice, she said, "Hi, sweetie, I'm painting. Do you want to help?"

Anna squeaked out a small, "No." *I must be dreaming. Is this the mom in my dreams? She seems so real. The smell of paint is burning my nose.* She pinched her arm. *Ouch.* "Mom, why are you painting in the middle of the night?"

Her mom rested the paint roller on the paint tray. She stretched her arms and smiled at Anna. "Lots of reasons, peanut. Paint dries faster at night. I will have more time during the day to do other things. I can paint dreams on the walls. And, of course, pink is perfect." She smiled grandly, "You want my room to be perfect, right?" The words came at Anna so fast from her mother's lips, it took Anna a moment to comprehend them.

"Oh . . . okay. Goodnight, Mom." She plastered the fake smile she used for school pictures across her lips and nodded like she understood, but she didn't. *At least it's not a monster on the other side of the wall, but why is Mom doing this in the middle of the night?*

Anna walked quietly down the hall to her sister's room. Leaning over her sleeping body, she gently touched Joanne's arm. She worried because at sixteen, Joanne treasured her sleep, and she could be mean when she woke, but this was an emergency. "Joanne," Anna whispered until the form under the sheets stirred. Finally, two dark eyes, lit by one of the many nightlights adorning the room, looked at Anna sternly.

"What are you doing?" she growled.

Anna quickly blurted out, "Don't get mad. Something's going on. Mom is painting her room Pepto-Bismol pink and it's two in the morning. Isn't that weird?"

"The only thing weird, twerp, is that you are waking me up in the middle of the night and there's school tomorrow. What's your problem?" she grumped as she grabbed Anna's arm, hard.

"Never mind. It *is* weird, but I wouldn't expect you to know the difference."

Anna whipped her arm out of Joanne's grip, left her room, and walked back to her own. She could still hear squeaking. She slid her toy box in front of the door, as she did whenever she felt scared. Lying in bed, she just couldn't make any sense of it. It *was* weird. Wasn't it? People don't paint rooms in the middle of the night when they're supposed to be sleeping. What would her dad say? Should she even tell him? Thoughts floated in her mind like wisps of smoke that couldn't be grasped, until finally she drifted off into a fitful, disturbed sleep.

***

The house transformed over the following weeks. Her mother's energy seemed endless. Furniture arrangements shifted while Anna was at school. She couldn't imagine her tiny mom moving the large couch and chairs alone—she didn't want to. Every room in the house donned a new color of paint in the wee hours of the night. On those nights, Anna braved the basement, which she feared, to find refuge in the downstairs guest room from what she dreaded even more—her mother's late-night painting. Swatches of color came alive and others diminished under her mother's control. Clare's actions were evident in the colorful displays, but the reasons behind them were mysterious to Anna.

After she had painted all the rooms and moved all the furniture, her mother turned her attention outdoors. She feverishly dug up bushes and perennials and moved their rooted balls to plant them in odd arrangements of tightly joined plants. It didn't make any sense to Anna. It looked all wrong. She watched her mother through an open window on a Saturday morning in the midst of her work. Words escaped Clare's lips, which Anna overheard, "The plants will make it better. I must make them right. The right landscape for the right life."

What on earth does that mean? Goosebumps ran across Anna's skin and nausea bubbled within her.

Anna decided to approach her sister again, this time awake, about their mom. Later that day, she plopped down next to Joanne on the green-cushioned chair on the porch, looking at the disarray created by their mother in the yard.

"How do you like how Mom has changed the yard?" Anna asked, hopeful that the innocent remark would urge her sister to discuss the strange behavior.

Joanne turned her head slowly, her eyes squinted, emanating cold, "The thing is, twerp, you can't tell how these things will turn out until they regrow. That is, unless you can imagine how the plants will grow. Which, obviously, Mom can."

"Oh," Anna said, her determination to talk about her mother briefly thwarted. Desperate, Anna decided to seize the moment and ask what was on her mind.

"Aren't you worried? I mean, doesn't any of this seem ... weird to you?"

Joanne jumped up and put her face a nose away from Anna's. "The only thing I see weird around here is you," she sneered in her face. Anna thought Joanne might hit her, but Joanne just shifted back, still eye to eye with Anna. "You need to stop causing trouble. Mom's getting through ... a rough time."

Anna stood up out of the chair and took a few steps back. "I am not causing trouble. Something's wrong!"

"Don't you ever say that!" Joanne gave Anna's shoulder a push.

"Maybe we should talk to Dad and—"

"If you do, you're dead." Joanne grabbed Anna's shoulder hard between her fingers.

"Stop, Joanne, I'm worried about her."

"You'd better start worrying about yourself, because if you don't stop this crap, I'm going to beat you up." The anger of her words burned hot like boiling water. "I don't ever want to hear you talk about Mom again like this, understand?"

Anna stood, silenced with disbelief.

Joanne shook her shoulders. "Do you get it?" she yelled.

"Yeah, got it," Anna said and ran into the house. She closed her bedroom door behind her and squatted behind it, crying and alone.

***

The paint fumes still permeated the air the night Anna's mom brought home a man. Clare stumbled into the house, drunk again. This drunken bender resulted in a man at the door. The only man Anna had seen wrap hands around her mother's waist was her father. Joanne rolled her eyes and huffed, apparently speechless. Clare and the man danced an unsightly jig, laughing and stumbling about the living room. He didn't glance at the girls, staring at this intrusion. Clare stopped the dance and glared at her daughters.

"You gals need to be in bed. You've got school tomorrow!" She stood taller, adjusted her shirt, and continued on dancing down the hall, leading the man into her bedroom.

Anna looked at Joanne to gauge her reaction. Joanne glared in return. "What are you fucking looking at?" she seethed. The shock of hearing her sister cuss rendered Anna speechless.

Her focus shifted to the banging and yelling down the hall.

"What are you doing in my house? Get out!" Clare screamed. She chased the drunken man down the hall with a tirade of insults and screams. She held one fist in the air and used the other hand to hit him with her pink shoe. The man looked bewildered as he fled.

Mom looked at Anna, sweaty and bewildered, "How did he get in here? Lock the doors, for goodness sake," she ordered as she careened unsteadily back down the hall to her bedroom.

***

Days passed after the strange man incident. Something felt different to Anna inside the Cromley house. The air itself tingled with electricity, and Anna imagined that her hair might start standing straight up or that lightning would strike her dead. The source of the energy must be her mother, she decided, but somehow the quality of it had changed since her frantic transformation of the house.

When Anna stayed with her dad, she could almost relax. A weight lifted off her shoulders as she packed her things in the car and sat behind her sister on the ride over to Dad's house. She breathed in deeply, smelling the odors of her father's less-than-clean car. Her mother stared at them from the doorway, waving, looking lost. Anna sat a little straighter, her body stiff. She reminded herself she must not let her guard down completely and let normalcy creep through the cracks of her skin, because it would make the return to her mother that much harder. *I wish I could stay with Dad all the time instead of two or three days a week.* Her stomach filled with something sour at the thought. *What would Mother do without us?*

"How has your week been, girls?" their father asked as he drove away from Clare's house.

Anna quickly responded, "It's been busy. I finished my report on the rain forest and I rode my bike lots this week." Stories of physical activity always pleased her dad.

"Excellent, Anna."

"What are we doing this weekend, Dad?"

"I don't know about today, but tomorrow there's a Tigers game."

"Yes! I can't wait."

Joanne emitted a drawn-out sigh.

"So, how about you, Joanne? What's new in your life?"

Joanne sat in the front seat, arms crossed, lips unmoving. Anna sighed at her sister's seething anger. She seemed to hate Dad lately. *What's her problem? She's so angry lately, at Dad, at me. She won't even talk about what is going on with Mom. I don't get it.*

"How's school going?" he urged. He waited in silence for a response.

"Tell me *one* thing," he kindly pressed.

"I hate going to your house. One thing!" Joanne said, her

voice shaking with anger.

"Watch your tongue, young lady," he scolded. A few moments passed and he sighed deeply, stewing in his thoughts. "Listen, honey, I know it must be hard. You miss your mom, I get it. Make the best of it, ok? Let's have a good weekend together. What do you say?"

Joanne sat tree-like. She didn't move or bend. Anna breathed deeper to try to rid herself of the tension filling the car.

Trent turned the music up and spoke no more. Anna looked at him through the rearview mirror. His face showed no sign of what he thought or felt.

Later that afternoon they were stuck indoors because of rain so Trent took them to the movies, followed by ice cream. Anna wished he didn't feel the need to placate them with treats as if they were fragile or only special visitors. She had never dreamed a girl could become so sick of ice cream. Joanne spoke little the whole afternoon, and her face never cracked from its fierce scowl. Anna tried to fill the space for them both, telling her father most of the details about her week, but never speaking a word about her mother.

Sometimes at night, Trent would invite a friend over to keep him company after the girls were in bed. This night a woman named Veronica sat in the living room with him, drinking beer. Anna liked to eavesdrop from the top of the stairs when he had friends over. She discovered that the secrets of the adult world could be uncovered in this way.

"I'm sorry to keep going on about it," he said.

"No, it's good to talk," Veronica said in a syrupy voice that annoyed Anna.

"I try to be patient, but she's just so angry. I thought she would be happier by now. It's been over a year since the divorce. I know it has to be hard, but why does she hate me?"

"I'm sure she doesn't. Kids just take things out on parents. That's all. It will get better."

"And why don't they talk about her? I've never said a foul word about Clare. They act as if she doesn't exist when they're here. It's weird."

"Maybe they're trying to be loyal to her by doing that. I don't know," she said. "Keep in mind, too, that your oldest is a teenager. It's hard being a girl at that age. Hormones raging, one minute you want to cry, next minute you want to rip someone's eyes out. It's not easy."

"Yeah, I guess so."

"I know so," Veronica said. "Just give it time."

The room grew quiet after that, so Anna left her perch and snuggled back in bed.

At least tomorrow, she had baseball. It was part of the world she shared with her dad. He had to work the next day, and he promised to take them along. He announced the Detroit Tigers' games for a small station in Detroit and wrote reports about sports, specializing in baseball, for a local paper. His dream was to be like Ernie Harwell, his idol of sports casting and a Detroit icon. Trent's excitement for baseball, very boy-like, was contagious (occasionally enough so to get Joanne excited about the games, though she'd never openly admit it), the peanuts were phenomenal, and they always had great seats. Yet, a sadness existed behind the enthusiasm because they were one family member short.

***

Later that week when Anna came home from school, she noticed a change. The noisy, frantic movement inside the house had been replaced by a complete stop of life and intense quiet. Her mother barely moved from the couch and didn't want to talk. Anna envisioned her mom as a science experiment, her motion suspended in formaldehyde. Anna wondered if her mother moved to use the bathroom while they were gone.

Days passed like this, and the only thing that changed was that Clare lay unmoving in her bed instead of on the couch. Anna worried that her mom wasn't eating. No dishes were in the sink besides her own and Joanne's. *She is going to starve to death. I need to call Dad. But if I do, Joanne will kill me. I've got to get Mom to eat.*

Anna searched the kitchen for food to make. In the fridge were cucumbers, milk, apples, and an unpleasant odor. In the bare pantry, a lonely jar of spaghetti sauce stood next to elbow noodles.

Anna slowly read the directions and boiled the pasta. She carefully cut the cucumbers while the sauce splattered like angry blood on the wall behind the stove.

Joanne jeered at her attempts. "She's not going to eat that junk. What makes you think you can cook?" she asked, laying her arms across the counter.

"I don't think she's eaten in days. We've got to get her to eat."

"You are such a drama queen. Of course she's eaten. Don't be ridiculous."

Anna wanted to punch her sister, but instead focused on her task. "Leave me alone or I'm telling Dad about Mom."

"You wouldn't. I will smash you to bits."

Anna stopped cutting and met Joanne's eyes. "Try me," she said.

"Hey, I'm only kidding. Don't be so uptight," Joanne said before she walked off.

Anna persevered, determined not to let her mother die. She propped her mother up in bed and brought her food on a makeshift tray made of a Monopoly board folded in half. Her hard work was rewarded as her mother ate. No words were shared, no thank you, just flat-faced eating. Anna was ecstatic. In that moment she had saved her mother. She imagined her mother saying words of gratitude and amazement at all her daughter had done.

Life progressed for months with Clare's erratic behavior of energy and decline. Anna grappled daily with whether she should tell her father. She hoped he would see on his own that things were odd, but instead, he filled their time with special trips and more ice cream. Despite the dairy overload, Anna grew thinner, and anxiety filled her belly instead of food. She yearned for the boredom of normalcy, but didn't receive it. Their secret was kept, until one day Clare went too far.

***

Clare believed her children were extraordinarily special in a way that exceeded normal parental pride. She knew her daughters were meant to do something great in the world, although she wasn't sure what. Somehow, they would monumentally change the world, or at least improve it vastly, maybe even be famous. To her, they glowed with bright, unique potential. She saw light emit from their skin, felt the warmth from their glow.

In the living room, a camcorder stood atop a sloppy stack of books sitting on a table. The lens pointed toward the window, the on button lit green, facing the Nabs house across the street. Clare turned it off and then rewound to review her video footage. Anna walked in while she frantically searched through the video, trying to learn more. Damn that tiny viewfinder!

"What are you doing, Mom?"

"Oh …" Clare searched her mind for a plausible lie. "… bird viewing, of course. I'm recording birds!" she declared.

"I didn't know you liked birds so much."

"It's a new thing of mine."

"Oh, okay," Anna said before leaving as quickly as she came.

Clare noticed in the footage that the Nabs were moving a lot of boxes into their garage, but there was no "for sale" sign in their yard. What could this mean? She thought on it for days. Something was wrong. What were they doing, moving so many boxes? Surely they were up to something unsavory, she thought. She had never trusted those Nabs.

Cynthia Nab came over days later and told Clare that they were getting ready for a temporary move because Joel Nab was going on sabbatical to Europe. Clare could see from Cynthia's eyes that she was lying. All of Mrs. Nab's "hellos" and neighborly conversations with her daughters were a ruse. How had she not seen it before? Clearly, they wanted to steal her daughters. The thought made her pulse race. It made perfect sense. They didn't have any children of their own, so they wanted hers. They would live off Anna and Joanne's fame or use their special light for evil. Once she made this discovery, Clare stopped sleeping.

Two days later, a moving truck arrived at the Nabs' house. It sat there, tormenting Clare, with its gaping tailgate ready to accept boxes and special children. She knew, without a doubt, what the Nabs wanted. She understood that they must be planning to do it that night. Why else would the truck be sitting there, waiting? Surely they would have help and weapons to accomplish their thievery.

Clare would not let her lights—her girls—go out with the Nabs, down the road in their moving truck to an unknown town where she would never see them again. While the girls were at school, she ripped through drawers, frantically packing clothes and food into their minivan. She picked Anna and Joanne up from school early that day, her minivan left running while she walked them outside. Her actions were so frantic and jumpy, she felt as if she'd overdosed on caffeine or uppers, which she hadn't.

Once in the car, Joanne asked, "Where are we going, Mom?"

Clare didn't answer until they were down the road. "We're leaving town."

"What do you mean?"

"It's a long story, and I don't want to scare you, but the Nabs were going to abduct you. I'm taking you away. Keeping you safe."

She saw the girls exchange frightened glances. They would understand eventually. "What about Dad?" Anna asked.

"I'm sorry, but Dad can't know, because he can't keep a secret. He'll let the Nabs know where you are, and they will come to get you."

"What are you talking about, Mom? The Nabs are nice people. We can't leave Dad! We—"

"Sweetie, you have to trust me. I know!"

Finally the girls were quiet. They must have finally understood, Clare decided.

Clare was a good mom. She knew how to protect her children, and no one could say that she couldn't.

Anna and Joanne stayed silent. She was sad to see tears run down their faces, but she knew she was doing the right thing. After hours of driving, they finally fell asleep.

They woke to the sound of their mother's agitated voice. "They found us, they're behind us!"

Clare stared out the rearview mirror. They were chasing her and trying to trick her with those lights. She pushed down harder on the accelerator and drove onto the off-ramp.

Joanne screamed, "Mom, it's a real cop. Stop!"

"It's a trick. Can't you see? They put lights on their car, but I'm not falling for it."

"They will put you in jail if you don't! Stop, Mom! Stop!" Joanne's voice cracked as she screamed.

Anna sat mute.

Clare slowed down enough to turn and ignored her daughter's screaming pleas. She knew what was best. In hopes of losing the pursuer, she turned down a wide dirt road, surrounded by peaceful farmland on rolling hills. *I'll lose him on this curve,* she thought as she slowed down for a curve. She didn't slow the van enough. The minivan fishtailed around the corner and they were off the road, stones flying, weeds and branches scratching against the van. The broken minivan stopped short of a thick forest abutting the farmland. Clare's head bled from impact with the side window. Despite the pain of her body's position, she couldn't quite move, though she could hear the screams of her daughters.

***

The girls moved to their father's house after the accident. Anna would turn twelve in a week, and this was her gift. The sisters' bags sat in the living room, unpacked, when they sat down and talked with their father.

"Your mom is sick," Trent said.

Like we don't know that, thought Anna.

"What's wrong with her? Is she going to be okay?" Joanne asked.

I've been trying to tell you something was wrong. Now you get it? It takes all that?

"Yes, she is going to be okay." Trent rested his head in his large hands, then started rubbing his hair. Anna knew that motion; he was stressed.

"She has what's called manic depression. That's what they're helping her with at Sandy Creek. She needs medicine, and it takes time to find the right kind. She is going to be fine."

"We're going back to her house when she gets home then, right?" Joanne pleaded.

"I don't think so, honey." When he looked at Joanne, his eyes were filled with tears. He looked down and wiped at his eyes.

"You will see her all the time, but you'll live here. That way there will be less stress on her. Not much will change, you'll see, you'll just spend a little more time here."

Joanne's face turned red, and her lip trembled. "How can you do that to her? Leave her all alone. You just said she's sick. You don't do that to people." Her red-faced words came so fast and loud that spit came along with them.

"We are not leaving your mother alone," he said loudly. He took a deep breath and continued in a softer tone, "Don't think for a second that I don't care about your mom. I will always love her and care for her. I will make sure she gets the best care. We are part of that. We will help care for her."

Subdued, Joanne leaned back into the sofa, arms crossed and mouth quiet.

Anna didn't know what to think. She ached for her mom but also feared her. She hoped that her Mom wasn't scared right now at the hospital. It had been terrifying to watch the strong arms of the EMT's pull her out of the car that night, and Anna prayed silently the whole time for her mother to survive. *How could this happen? Why?*

***

Weeks later, they were allowed to visit Clare. Trent led the way down the long corridor, his daughters at his side and flowers in his hand. He had warned them in advance that no matter what their mother said or looked like, they were to be positive and loving.

Like we needed to be told that? thought Anna. She didn't know what to expect. Would her mom be wrapped up in a crazy vest like she'd seen in the movies? Which mom would she see—the one zipping around or the one vegetative on the couch?

They walked into a room that looked like the living room of a house, but larger, with upholstered furniture that had seen better times. Her mother sat on a chair looking out a window. She looked deflated to Anna, obviously not the zooming mom, but not the depressed one either. When she noticed her daughters, she ran toward them and put her arms around them. She cried. Joanne looked up at her, eyebrows furrowed in alarm.

"It's okay," Clare said. "I'm just so happy to see you and that you're okay."

They stood for a moment, embracing, until it felt uncomfortable to Anna. She pulled out of Mom's grasp. Clare turned her attention to Trent. They embraced. "Thank you so much for watching over my girls."

"They're *our* girls," he kindly chided. "And you don't have to thank me." He stepped back, "So, how are they treating you here? How's the food?"

Clare smiled and motioned for them to sit. They sat and talked about the food at Sandy Creek Health Center, the weather, school. They talked about everything that had nothing to do with the reason that Clare was there, and an hour later they left.

Anna wanted to know how her mom was doing. She wanted to ask if she was better now or not. She needed answers. Adults always avoid, she decided as they walked back down the long hallway.

***

Anna sat in her eavesdropping spot, crouching in the hallway, out of view, but not earshot, of the kitchen. Why couldn't her parents get along like this when they were married? It infuriated her sometimes, but it comforted her that her dad seemed to have things under control. She felt sorry for her mom, but she definitely didn't trust her.

"I feel like something has been off for a while, but nothing like the last year. I can't even remember everything that happened. It's scary," Clare confided to Trent, who sat across from her in her kitchen.

"Well I'm glad you're okay. You're getting the help you need. If you need anything, tell me," he said.

"You've been so good to me. I mean, we're divorced; you don't have to do anything. I—"

"We're *friends*. We'll stay friends. We'll be the happiest

divorced couple around." They both laughed at that.

"For a while, I thought it was the divorce that was making me feel ... like that. I didn't mind the ups. I could get so much done. The downs, though, they were unbearable."

"You've been through a lot. I'm sorry."

"Don't be. I'm just grateful that my cocktail of meds is making me feel normal. It feels good to be off the ride."

"You've really got an amazing outlook on it all."

"For the moment. Other moments, I'm mad as hell."

They laughed again, but Anna didn't see what was funny.

Tired of eavesdropping, she slunk back down the hall to visit her room. This was now her weekend room. She'd grown up here, and now she felt more like a visitor. When she thought hard about it, it made her happy. Moving in with her father marked a new beginning. Her spirit was no longer heavy with worries. A weight was lifted. For good or bad, she tried to erase her mother from her memory when she wasn't with her. Occasionally guilty thoughts would snake through her consciousness, insisting on being noticed, but Anna did her best to keep guilt at bay.

While Anna was elated to move in with her father, Joanne seemed to harbor different feelings. Maybe it was because she had to drive farther to get to her old high school. Their dad lived close to Clare, but far enough away to be in a different school district. Anna didn't mind. She didn't have many friends and welcomed the change. Joanne refused to switch and so she drove. In one of their rare conversations, Joanne confided that she stopped over at her mom's after school at least a few days a week. This news shocked Anna. Why would Joanne choose to leave the comfort of their dad's? Anna loved her mother, but didn't think she'd visit more than necessary. It was too hard to confront all that had happened.

Each day brought more tension between the sisters. Joanne's words often whipped at Anna, condescending and angry. Then came silence. Anna wasn't sure which was worse, but she began to avoid Joanne altogether.

Anna felt that her true self emerged when she lived with her father. Her chrysalis opened and she became humorous, quick witted, and determined to find joy. She was a butterfly set loose — free from the cowering child she imagined herself when living with her mother, free from straining anxiety, free.

Cooking and baking became an essential part of her life when she moved in with her dad. As skilled as he was writing and talking about baseball, he was equally unskilled in the kitchen. When she lived with her mother, Anna had learned how to finish meals her mother had started and forgot, or to make meals when Clare was too exhausted to move. This skill that the other Cromleys had lacked brought Anna strength.

Friendship

Kate was always full of ideas, and Anna ready to follow, keen for adventure. Together they found the strength to do things they wouldn't do alone.

Like the night they taught Tom Beauford a lesson he sorely needed. He considered himself a gift to all and ridiculed nearly everyone in his path. He used his good looks and expert manners to fool adults, but when teachers weren't listening, his taunts were ruthless. One day at school, he asked Anna if she was starting to grow boobs yet or if she had a penis hidden in her pants. The way he glared at her with contempt and hatred stirred the fear that wafted through her soul frequently, but to have someone nurture it besides herself was unbearable. He knew better than to say much to Kate. She had once smacked him in the face for singing, "Kate, Kate gained some weight," which didn't even make sense because she was a thin girl.

The girls waited an hour after Kate's parents went to sleep before they left the house. They slowly opened the sliding door window and sneaked out. Luckily Oscar, Kate's dog, was so old and mellow that even a burglar standing outside his cage wouldn't rattle him. He looked vicious with his thick Rottweiler body and menacing face, but at heart he was like a friendly, sleepy, old man.

Dressed in black, Kate and Anna walked swiftly and silently through the neighborhood. Darkness shrouded the sleeping neighborhood except where streetlights revealed the sidewalks and the occasional street-parked car. Kate and Anna whispered and ran outside the light, down the street. Their weapons were a pillowcase filled with rolls of toilet paper and a carton of eggs. The target: Tom Beauford.

Kate lived in a sprawling neighborhood. It passed through two main roads, and neighborhood roads zigzagged between them. Tom lived at the far end of her neighborhood. Retribution drew near. Anna nearly burst with joy—an emotion she'd nearly forgotten.

"We should've brought a bag of Oscar poop," Kate laughed.

"Yeah, can't you put it in a bag and light that shit on fire and it does something?" They both laughed quietly but deeply.

As they closed in on their target, they made jokes about how Tom would react when he saw that he'd been chosen. Usually it was only the bullied kids who were selected for the TP ritual, not those who doled it out. Kate and Anna had never done it, but intended on doing it right. The cherry on top was the forecasted rain, a near certainty, which would make it difficult to clean up the toilet paper. That would make it more humiliating — little toilet paper remnants waving like flags in the trees to remind everyone of Tom's humiliation.

As they approached the house, they donned their ski masks. Tom's bi-level house was brown and white, the inside dark with sleep. A large maple tree stood sentinel, marking the middle of the front yard. They decided efficiency was the best approach. They each took two rolls and pulled the end of the toilet paper to get it started. Then they threw them, silent streamers, which left a paper trail across the limbs of the maple tree. The paper covered more area than they thought it would, even with two rolls lost, caught somewhere in the branches. The quiet sounds of ruffled leaves accentuated the sound of muffled laughter.

Anna soon realized that the second bottle of pop was a mistake. Her bladder stretched to fullness. Earlier, they had decided to fuel themselves with caffeine to keep them from drifting to dreamland while waiting for Kate's parents to slumber. She pushed the thought out of her mind.

There were small bushes in the yard that punctuated the property lines and the front of the ironically brown house. Six rolls were empty by the time they decorated the bushes by the porch with the paper. Then it was time for the eggs and the announcement. They had their hiding spot already picked out. Hearts pounding and blood racing, they threw the eggs and rang the doorbell. Then they ran like whipped animals to a house three doors down and across the street. The thick evergreen bushes hid them and they sat back to watch the show. Lights turned on and Tom's mom opened the egg-drenched door. She looked around in alarm. Tom followed her.

In a whining yell like a five-year-old he said, "Who would do this, Mom?" Her words weren't audible as she shushed her son and ushered him back indoors. It took all their willpower for the girls to be silent in such circumstance.

When the downstairs lights went off, they bolted down the road. The laughter they tried to mute built and built until it could be contained no longer. It rolled out of them from a deep place, pressure released. They had to stop running to breathe. Something warm dripped down Anna's legs. She couldn't believe it—she wet her pants in her fit of laughter.

"I just peed myself!"

"Oh, my gosh, I felt like that too."

"No, I *really* peed myself! What am I going to do?" Her joy suddenly changed to alarm, fear, and embarrassment.

"You're going to rinse out your pants at my house, beanie!"

Beanie was Kate's nickname for Anna because of her lankiness.

They ran, wet pants and all, and made it to the safety of Kate's house. Anna washed her pants in the basement sink, thankful that Kate was the kind of friend who wouldn't poke fun at her mishap.

Dressed in pajamas and dry, they laid in their sleeping bags.

"That was hilarious!" Kate whispered.

"I know. He got what he deserved."

"You think we should tell him it was us?"

"No, I don't," Anna answered.

"Why not?"

"This way, we get the satisfaction of knowing we made the world a better place," Anna said importantly. "Maybe it will make him think twice about being such a jerk if he doesn't know who did it. Anyway, if we tell, we'll have to worry about him getting us back."

"Yeah, I guess you're right. We won't have to look over our shoulders if we're quiet, right?"

"I didn't know boys that age could whine like that! Boy, what a baby!" They laughed until slowly silence and sleep took over.

Although at the time Anna wouldn't have been able to articulate the thought, she realized that day that Kate was the kind of friend you keep for life, a true treasure.

***

Anna and Kate's friendship remained strong through the years. They weathered the tumultuous experience of high school together and remained best friends. Naturally, they had their ups and downs, but nothing came close to pulling them apart. It took more effort to maintain their friendship, however, when Anna was at Michigan State University and Kate at the University of Michigan.

Anna made a point of calling every few days to catch up with her best friend. She closed the door to her small room, sat on her bed, and dialed the numbers.

"Kate, you've got to come out here this weekend. My roommates and I are having a party, and you've got to meet Ben."

"I don't know. I've got a huge test on Monday."

"You've always got a big test. Come on. You haven't met him yet. I'm in love and you haven't even met the guy."

"Three months and it's love?"

"It's not about time. It's about feeling."

"Oh, *please*, don't tell me anymore about *feelings*." They both laughed at the reference. Anna had spent much of their time lately talking about her sex life with Ben.

"I can't help it if the sex is incredible. Don't be jealous," Anna chided.

"How do you know? You don't have anything to compare it with," Kate teased.

Anna dated little in high school and her first year of college. Boys frightened her with their constant urgings of more, more, more. With Ben, she couldn't resist. He caught her wandering attention with his bright blue eyes, blonde hair and incredible build. She loved how his smile could be devious and sexy. She discovered sex with Ben and learned its merits.

"I could respond to that in a mean way, but I won't."

"What? Just because I've had lovers. Sex is not love, that's all I'm saying. Sorry if I know the difference."

Anna worked to loosen her irritation at Kate's insinuation that her feelings were somehow flawed.

"So are you going to come or not?" Anna asked.

"I'll get studying now and see how much I get done. I'll give you a call tomorrow and let you know."

***

Anna greeted Kate at the driveway. As they stepped up onto the porch of Anna's house, she said, "Don't embarrass me by going right after Ben, okay?"

Kate had a bad habit of interrogating the few guys that Anna had dated. It didn't usually go well. Her strong personality could intimidate others. Anna knew that Ben would pass with flying colors. He was hot, smart, and nice. What more could Kate want for her?

"What do you mean?" Kate raised her voice to be heard over the thumping music emanating from inside.

"You know, just don't ask him a bunch of questions right when you meet him."

"I don't know what you mean. But I'll be cool."

"Okay, let's get you a drink."

They filled their cups from the keg outside and walked in. Kate said hello to Anna's roommates, and they found Ben in the living room standing with a group of guys.

He turned his attention to Kate and smiled warmly. "So, this is the girl I've heard so much about. Nice to finally meet you." He gave Kate a big hug.

They made small talk and a few rounds of shots passed by the group. Relief flooded Anna that Ben and Kate were getting along so well. Kate's opinion mattered.

"So, what do you study at the school which should not be named," Ben asked, alluding to the intense rivalry between their schools.

"Very funny. I'm in engineering."

"Ooohh. Very nice. What kind of engineering?" Anna zoned out as they talked about Kate's dream to become a chemical engineer. Anna had heard it a million times. She drifted over to another group. They heatedly discussed the Monica Lewinsky scandal, and Anna joined in.

The Nature of Denial

Time passed and somehow Kate and Ben were on the other side of the living room. Anna watched them. Ben leaned close to Kate's ear. Kate's cheeks looked red. They look too close, she thought. She reprimanded herself for being jealous and walked over to them.

"Your friend here is a funny one," Ben smiled. "Excuse me, ladies, I'm going to see how my buddy Todd is doing over there." He walked off through the sea of people.

"Well, what do you think of him?" Anna asked.

"He seems ... nice. He really does. And he's hot, if you don't mind my saying so."

I do mind, thought Anna. "Well, I'm glad you like him."

They made the rounds, talking to other friends and keeping their cups full. Ben resurfaced from the sea of faces, and the three started talking again. Anna left the two to empty her bladder. There was a lineup at all the bathrooms. It seemed ridiculous to wait so long to use the bathroom in your own house, she thought. She made small talk with the other waiting girls and finally got her turn.

When she walked back toward Kate and Ben, she knew something was off. Kate's face was contorted with anger. Her lips moved quickly with strings of words. Ben's body stood tense while his finger pointed at Kate's face. Anna hadn't seen his face look so angry before.

Anna turned away and walked outside. She didn't want to know what had turned things so vicious. It disgusted her. What right did Kate have to ruin things for her? She couldn't just visit and not make a fuss over something. She was always getting worked up over something.

Kate slammed out of the house, red-faced, "Did you know Ben is a racist?" she hissed.

Anna drunkenly stumbled, stepping away from the beer keg that had supplied her current disorientation, away from the porch and the ears of others. Kate followed.

"You're drunk. Ben is not like that! Don't accuse people like that when you don't know! He has never said anything like that. I would know!" Her sweet, sexy Ben never said anything bad about anyone. He got along with everyone.

Kate and Anna shared many views. High on the list was their

strong belief that the world was filled with assholes, but you couldn't tell if someone was one until you had an actual conversation with him or her. They found any kind of prejudgment of others intolerable.

"It's true! We were talking about affirmative action and he said that if blacks were as smart as whites, they wouldn't need it. Does that leave room for questions?"

Anna sighed, wishing the night had been different, that her moments with Ben could remain untainted. The sleepy soft moments of the morning when she woke up with him, still wearing the smell of sex, were now violated. Yet she wasn't ready to accept this new reality. "You must have misunderstood. He's a nice guy. I've been with him for months. He's not like that."

"He *is* like that. That's what I'm telling you."

"Well, you're lying. Are you jealous or something?"

"What do you mean by that?" Kate asked, rage flickering across her face.

Anna walked back inside, snatched her purse, and walked away. Kate tried to follow, but Anna set her straight: "Just because you haven't gotten laid in a while doesn't mean you have to ruin things for me. Why don't you fuckin' leave?"

Kate didn't have to be told twice. She stared at Anna for a long moment, her lips clamped tight, then walked inside.

Anna wondered if Kate had exaggerated the situation. Maybe she was jealous that Anna had found happiness that didn't involve her. Confused and very drunk, Anna's stumbling legs took her downtown. She ended up in front of one of the many bus stops and took the 89 bus to a friend's house. It wasn't someone she knew well enough to impose upon, but she couldn't face Ben or her roommates at the moment. A balloon of possibility had burst.

***

The next morning she woke feeling mortified that she had stayed at Lisa's, whom she knew so slightly. It made her wince to think how pitiful her drunken self must have seemed to Lisa. To avoid further humiliation, she slipped out early in the morning, reeking of beer and still tipsy, the taste in her mouth an odorous reminder of the night's events. She walked downtown and waited stretching minutes for a bus.

When she got home, she noticed Ben sleeping suspiciously close to a girl on the floor amid a handful of people. Anna realized that his good looks and sensual ways had reduced her abilities to think rationally. What did she really know about him? Nothing. That would never happen again, she vowed.

It took two days for Anna to call Kate, tail between her legs, with an apology.

"Ben's history. What an asshole."

"I'm sorry. I know you liked him."

"I thought I loved him. But how could I? I didn't even know him."

"Don't be so hard on yourself."

"I give up. Men are schemers. I'm on a permanent hiatus from them," Anna said.

"Don't let one bad apple scare you from the fruit. Just don't give up *your* apple until you know more about them. Then you can think with your brain instead of..." she paused and they laughed, the healing balm between them.

Even though Kate could drive her crazy, she could trust her to tell the truth, even when Anna didn't want to hear it.

***

A semester passed and Anna was over Ben. She rarely thought about him during of her busy schedule of work, school, and partying. It filled all her time. It seemed that things were going pretty well, most of the time. Except in those quiet moments, when thoughts of Ben or her family would drift into her mind and then she would have to work to erase them.

It had been a week since she'd spoken with Kate. They were both busy that they often played phone tag. Anna was surprised to receive a letter from Kate one day. She read it several times, trying to make sense of the words.

Dear Anna,

I'm worried about you. We haven't talked much lately and when we do, you seem to talk a lot about getting drunk or you are drunk. I'm all about having a good time, but there is such a thing as too much. Are you doing okay? I found this quote and it made me think of you (don't be offended). Let's talk soon! – Kate

Everyone has their demons – the issues of their past which are difficult and must be dealt with in order to find happiness. Personal demons left unchecked tend to grow, like festering sores, bound to leave scars. People are often desperate to escape their demons – to hide truths from themselves with denial. The problem is you can't outrun yourself, no matter what the pace. When you get to the finish line, your self is always there to greet you. Sometimes people try to lose themselves in the fog of mind-altering substances, a haze of smoke, vein-pumping toxins, overloaded liver. In the end, when sobriety arrives, you are faced with yourself. The only way to slay a demon is to face it, head on, preferably with the help of friends.

What the hell does this mean? Who is Kate to judge me? thought Anna, picking up the phone and dialing.

"What is this crap you sent me?" Anna asked.

"Well, hello to you too!" Kate teased.

"I'm not laughing here. I'm pissed."

"Hey, whoa, I'm sorry. I'm not trying to upset you. I'm genuinely concerned about you. You seem to be partying a lot."

"Everyone parties, Kate. It's MSU, not U of stuffy M. Anyway, I'm doing fine. I work my butt off between work and school. No alcoholic could do that."

"I never said you were an alcoholic, Anna. You're really getting worked up here."

"What is this quote about? What demons? What are you getting at?"

Anna heard Kate sigh deeply. "You know what? Never mind."

"No, spill it. If you've got something to say, say it."

"I don't want you getting mad at me. Let's just drop it."

"Too late for that." Anna waited.

"I just wonder if maybe it would help if you try to talk to your mom, even your sister."

"You've got to be kidding me. You're going *there*? I do talk to my mom. My sister, well, I'm going to ignore you said that because that's ridiculous and you know it."

"You talk to your mom when you're dad makes you at holidays and stuff."

"Kate, I'm going to forget we had this conversation. You need to take a walk because your studies are getting to you and you're becoming delirious. There's no drama going on here. All is fine. But I do have to let you go because I've got some homework to do. I'll talk to you later." Before Kate answered, Anna hung up.

Kate had a lot of nerve psychoanalyzing her. Who did she think she was? Didn't she know how hard Anna worked? Freedom didn't come for free — she worked for it. Three mornings a week she trudged off to the bakery before the birds chirped at the sun. In her free time, she attended classes and studied, just enough.

The empty pockets of time were the problem because thoughts about her mother tried to sneak into them. It made Anna feel unsteady when this happened, like a chemical reaction with an unpredictable outcome. Kate was right. She did try to avoid her mother. Her father did his best to mitigate this by inviting Mom to every family event and holiday. Despite his efforts, Anna put a wall between herself and her mother. She wasn't rude, just apathetic, which could be equally painful. It wasn't right and she knew it, but she didn't know how else to be. Gnawing guilt caught her by surprise at times, but keeping busy kept it at bay.

When other people spoke of their mothers, it made Anna wonder if she had been too harsh. Joanne seemed to think so, but Clare accepted whatever Anna offered. Her mother didn't push too much. Anna sometimes wished things were different, but felt powerless to change them.

As far as drinking, most of her friends did the same. Lately she had woken from a few too many drunken stupors, losing hours of evaporated time. Her friends would tell her things that happened the night before and it was like listening to stories about another girl. This was enough deep thought for one day, she decided. She called some friends and headed out to the bar.

***

The next morning the glaring sun woke her. She opened her dry, crusty eyes and stared at a white wall, dirty near the bottom, with a grimy window in the middle. It was not her wall or her window. Alarmed, she turned over. Next to her lay a man with his back turned to her. Who was this man? Her clothes were strewn about the room. *What?*

Her heart pumped heavily as she slowly slunk out of the bed and quietly pulled on her clothes. How could this have happened? How could she have slept with someone and not remember? Despite her quiet efforts, the slumbering man awoke.

He looked sleepily up at her and smiled an intimate smile, indicating he remembered, even if she didn't. "Good morning, Anna."

"Uh, hi. I forgot, I have this thing. I'm late. I'll see you around." Which of course, she hoped, she wouldn't.

Anna realized that morning that things were spiraling out of control. She needed to talk with the person she trusted most in this world—her dad. It had been a month since her last visit with him. She drove home for the weekend, using the pretense of boredom and excessive laundry, to visit.

When she walked in the door, he hugged her. He pulled back and a look of concern crossed his face. It made Anna want to cry.

"Hey, you doing okay? You look tired or something."

"I'm fine, Dad. Hasn't anyone ever told you that you don't tell a girl she looks tired?"

"I forgot my manners. Come on in. Are you hungry?" he asked.

"What's that smell?"

"I'm cooking."

"I don't know if you can call microwave meals cooking. It's more like warming."

"Ha, ha! I've got stew cooking on the stove."

"What? You've never cooked a stew in your life."

"It's not every day I get a visit just because." This made Anna's eyes well up. She turned away.

"Wow, I'm impressed. I can't wait to try it. I think," she teased. *He must really be worried about me if he's cooking.*

Anna stirred her spoon around in the bowl of stew so it looked like she had eaten some, then feigned fullness. It tasted hideous. They decided to veg out and watch *Seinfeld* reruns—their favorite comedy. Hours into the marathon, they took a break to make popcorn. The smell of popcorn made Anna emotional. That smell always reminded her of the joy and sadness of her youth, all at the same time. It brought back the pure excitement of baseball games with her dad and the concurring yearning for her mother to be there and be well.

The full force of her emotions hit her like a train and there was no drunken stupor to hide behind. The tears finally fell. He reached out and hugged her while she released her tears and tension. Once she had gained control over her emotions, they sat down and ate popcorn and talked.

"What's going on?" he carefully questioned.

"I don't want you to be disappointed in me."

"Honey, you're my girl. You couldn't disappoint me."

It was all or nothing at this point, and she didn't want to throw her life away before it had even started. She was being sucked down a dark hole, and the light was quickly vanishing. Things had to change. She needed help. "I'm having a rough time lately. I just don't feel like…me."

"Who do you feel like, then?" he asked, not sarcastically, but in honest wonder.

"I feel like an imposter. I don't know. I've been screwing up at school. I'm not doing horrible, but my grades are down. I've been going out too much."

"You mean drinking?"

"Yeah."

They discussed moderation a number of times before she left for college. A few parties or a few drinks were not a big deal, but more meant trouble. That was her father's advice. "Everyone goes through a slump. Alcohol's not gonna make it better."

"I know. It's been too much. Too much drinking." She looked down, sorry to disappoint her father.

"Can you stop drinking? Do you need help?"

"I don't think I'm an alcoholic." The pressure in her decreased as she talked. "Remember Dr. Hamway?" Dr. Hamway was a psychologist Anna and Joanne had seen after the accident with their mom. It didn't help much because she either lied to him or sat silent during their sessions, but she was willing to try again.

"Yes."

"I think ... maybe I need some direction."

"Ok. We'll call tomorrow and make an appointment."

Anna looked down, relieved but embarrassed.

"How'd I get so lucky?" Trent asked happily.

"You seem particularly unlucky to me, Dad."

"I have two beautiful daughters. And baseball. What more could a man need?"

"I don't know."

The rest of the weekend they watched television and ate a variety of take-out foods. It was exactly what Anna needed: relaxation, a high-fat diet, and time with her dad. Her father grounded her like no other force. He wasn't perfect—he couldn't cook or keep house—but he was the one thing that stayed constant in her life, and she loved him for that.

Goodbye

Anna thought people noticed her father at first because of his height, but then because of his personality. Everything he did, he did with full force. He loved his family and cared for them the best that he could. He loved baseball and inserted it in his life in as many ways as possible by announcing, writing about, and watching as many games as he could. His enthusiasm for the Tigers ran so deep that he had their insignia tattooed on his arm. Nearly everything in life could be described with a baseball analogy for him, and he even wrote a book of famous baseball quotes and quotes of his own, although he never tried to publish it. He took life as a gift and made an effort to see the good and value of things.

Anna remembered the day she answered the fateful phone call that change everything. She drove to the hospital, the car silent except for the sound of her constant prayers for her father's recovery.

He suffered from a stroke, but he lived, although in a different way. Once he was stabilized, they transferred him to Blue Haven Nursing Home. He was a changed man. Most often, Anna found her father lying on his side in bed, curled into a shrunken ball. He seemed to cower from something, a trait he had never exhibited prior to his stroke. Like a radio on low volume, Anna heard him mumble the details of numerous Tiger innings. Over the weeks he remained in the nursing home, he must have announced a hundred games. Anna would ask him questions and whenever he tried to talk of anything but baseball, it came out in a muffled string of syllables. Sometimes Anna could glean a bit out of it, but usually she just let him replay the games in his mind. It seemed to offer him comfort, and she didn't want to take that away from him.

"So, how's our announcer doing today?" asked a nurse named Ellen.

"Same as yesterday," Anna answered tersely. Ellen was the third staff member that day to ask about Trent. He had attained notoriety at the nursing home. They seemed entertained by his baseball litany. They would often pause outside his door, even when he wasn't their patient, smile, and try to offer words of encouragement. Anna wished she could accept their comforting words with grace, but really it all just pissed her off. Not at her dad, of course, but at the situation.

The only thing that made her smile in that place was a patient named Bess. She was the tiniest elderly woman Anna had ever seen. Bess's under-five-foot stature and very petite body made people want to care for her until they heard her voice, which demanded attention and compliance. The mismatch of her voice and size startled Anna.

"What's there to eat?" tiny Bess boomed.

"Nothing here, Bess," Anna replied.

"I know they're hiding food around here. Tell me where it is."

"I don't know. Go to the nurse's desk and ask them. I think they know where the good stuff is."

It was the same conversation every day. Bess walked through the hallways searching for someone who would give her a snack. When food came, she ate like a bird, quickly satiated. Then her hunger soon returned and she spent all her time and effort in pursuit of relieving it.

Bess lacked a filter, saying whatever came to her mind, which was something Anna found interesting in people, except her mother. Sometimes Bess would sit for a while and listen to Trent's baseball ramblings. She watched him with extreme pity, then looked back at Anna and said, "I'm sorry, but that man is crazy."

Anna heard Bess say this dozens of times. This would set Anna into a short laughing fit, because she thought she knew crazy, and her father was about as sane as people got. No matter how much she thought about it, she couldn't understand her reaction to Bess's comments, so she decided to stop analyzing it.

Although she knew her parents had remained close through the years, Anna was surprised by her mother's level of loyalty to her father. Clare remained steadfast at Trent's side after his stroke. When Anna entered the room to visit, her mother would already be there, reading from a baseball book or chatting as though Trent understood. Clare would go for a walk when Anna arrived and give her time alone with her father.

Anna and Joanne did their best to avoid each other at the

nursing home. When circumstance forced them into close proximity, they exchanged only necessary words and talked through their mother otherwise. Since their early years when they first moved in with their father, they had stopped understanding each other, and nurtured a steady stream of hate.

Anna spent every moment she could with her father. She watched his decline like a silent spectator. She read to him, showed him pictures, and recounted stories of their life together. On rare occasions, he bubbled with random enthusiasm, which would result in a home run in his baseball announcing. Anna couldn't be sure if he responded to her in these moments or if she placed hope where it didn't belong.

Three weeks after his initial stroke, Trent had a final stroke. Anna went to get some lunch in the cafeteria downstairs and when she returned to her dad's room, she knew that he was gone by the looks on the faces of her mother and the nurses. They said it happened fast. Nothing could be done to save him.

**

Anna had known her father would die after his first stroke. She tried to prepare for it, but that didn't make it easier. The day of his funeral she felt a mix of emotions. She ached for her father to live, but she knew he wouldn't have wanted to remain in his crumpled state. Still, the finality of his body inside the coffin devastated her. The rock she depended on would soon be buried under dirt. Why him? Who would she turn to when she needed help? Certainly not her mother or Joanne.

At the services, Joanne and her mother sat close to one another, holding each other up. Nothing bound them to Anna anymore, which relieved her. She knew her father would be disappointed by her distance, but he had been the glue that kept their loose bonds from release. Now there was nothing.

Clare walked up to Anna during the service. "I wish I knew the right words, sweetie. I'm sorry. Your father was a good man." They stood looking at the casket for some moments before she continued, "I know this is hard. Just know that your dad loved you."

"Thanks, Mom." Anna accepted her hug somewhat stiffly. She wished she felt differently, but she didn't know this woman in front of her. Her mother and Joanne were like their own two-person family. She was glad Clare had Joanne; she didn't wish any ill toward her mother, but she felt little connection to her.

The words that severed what was left of Anna and Joanne's sisterhood came later. Their usual dance of ignoring and avoiding was unhinged by the emotions of the day. They found themselves in the funeral home bathroom, overwhelmed by the smell of too many flowers and confounded by death.

Joanne's eyes filled with contempt as she stood washing her hands, looking at Anna's reflection in the mirror.

"I bet you're relieved," said Joanne, her hands and voice shaking.

"Relieved? What are you talking about?" Anna hated her. Who says such things?

"Now you can skip Dad's holiday parties. You won't have to see us anymore."

"Fuck you, Joanne. That's really shitty."

Joanne ignored her and calmly continued. "I'll be glad too. I'm tired of pretending I can stand to be in the same room with you." Joanne stormed off before Anna could respond.

For the sake of their mother, Anna resisted doing what she wanted, which was to slam her sister's face onto the floor. She survived the rest of the day by keeping her distance from Joanne.

***

Anna's phone rang. It was her mother's weekly call, most of which Anna ignored. After her father's death, her mother called consistently once a week. They hadn't spoken in a few weeks so Anna decided to answer. Clare quickly moved to the point of the call.

"I hope you won't find this upsetting, but Joanne asked me to move to Indiana and I agreed."

"I didn't know she was even considering moving."

"Yes, she was offered a promotion, but it came with a move."

"Oh. Well. Good for her. When are you moving?"

"Two weeks. I think it will be good for me. All I can think about lately is your father. It seems like everywhere I go, something reminds me of him. I think a fresh start might help. I hope you understand."

Anna understood and approved. More distance between them meant more of a buffer zone and fewer visits, even though they rarely saw each other as it was.

"I think it's a great idea, Mom. I'm not upset at all." *I'm elated*, Anna thought guiltily.

"Thanks. I feel a little unsteady lately. I think this is what I need."

"Good. I'm glad then."

It got a little easier for Anna once Clare and Joanne moved away. She didn't feel as guilty for not visiting because of the distance. Her conscience was relieved until she ignored another phone call from her mother. When she did answer, the conversations confounded Anna. Sometimes her mom would be full of topics, almost like she wrote them out, about news, weather, and stories about people who lived by her. Other times, she would ask a few questions and that would be the extent of the phone call. Anna rarely had much to tell her mom, but felt obligated to at least attempt to hold up her end of the conversation.

The relief Anna experienced after Clare and Joanne moved away was short lived. A hole of empty sadness grew daily in her father's absence. Soon, it consumed all of her hours. Attending classes or work became too much effort so she chose to spend most of her time in bed. Her family, to her, was gone. She'd lost the person with whom she'd connected most in the world. Depressive darkness filled her days and she became immobile except when she arose to urinate or eat some bit of food. Her head grew dizzy when she stood because she had been horizontal so long. She cried so often that tears rarely formed.

Weeks or days passed like this, time could not be measured in her current state of existence. Then, one day, she heard an insistent knock at the door. Then the telltale rattle of a key twisting open the lock. It could only be Kate. No one else had a key.

Lights flicked on around the apartment as Anna heard the sound of approaching feet. Her eyes couldn't adjust to the brightness, so she pulled the covers over her eyes.

"Anna, why haven't you called me back? I've been worried." Kate sat on the bed next to her friend. Anna stayed silent.

"Well, I'm glad to see you're breathing anyway. I see you need some rest, so go ahead and sleep. I hope you don't mind, but I'm staying here for a while."

Anna pulled her head from behind the shield of covers. "What?"

"Well, as you know, those extra summer classes paid off and I'm done with school. I don't have a job yet and it looks like you could use a little help, so I'm staying here for a while. I'm between places anyway."

"You can't," Anna protested. The last thing she needed was cheering.

Kate stood up and looked down. "You wouldn't kick out a friend in need, would you?" She left the room before Anna could answer.

In moments, Anna heard the sounds of cleaning and sorting. She knew trash and dirty dishes littered her apartment, but she was too depressed to move or care.

Days passed and Anna stayed in bed. Kate brought her food and sat with her, but said little. Over the course of several weeks, Anna progressed to sitting vertical more than lying and finally ventured into her living room. It had never before looked that clean or organized. It made her cry.

"It's looks so good in here," Anna blubbered.

"You don't have to cry to thank me," Kate teased.

"I don't know what to say." Anna sat down on her couch. "You've done so much for me."

"I did exactly what you'd do for me. It's what friends do. No thanks required."

Anna smiled through her tears. Yes, Kate was a true friend, but she was more than that. She was family. Anna knew she wouldn't have made it through the spiraling darkness without her.

It took months for Anna to piece together all that Kate had

done, besides the obvious cleaning, cooking, and listening. She'd spoken with the school on Anna's behalf and convinced them to postpone her classes. She'd waited patiently for Anna's grief to recede enough for her to complete simple tasks and gently prodded her to move to more complex ones like returning to school and work. Kate put her life on hold for Anna with no complaint. In the haze of grief, Kate had lit a candle in the darkness.

Anna realized that she couldn't give up on life—even if she wanted to. Her father would disapprove.

New Beginnings

Anna loved the smell of fresh baking bread. When the rich, wholesome fragrance reached her nose canal, its wholesome smell made her feel complete. When she baked she was as transformed as her creations. She wanted everyone to be reformed daily by this scent. Anna's love of baking and that smell urged her to start a baking business that she named Savory Scents.

Opening Savory Scents was bittersweet for Anna. The dream of owning a bakery grew within her for many years, evolving with what she had learned at school and during her work at the bakery in East Lansing. She never thought that she would have the funds, at twenty-five, to start her own business. The funds came from her dad. He left the world at sixty-five and left his possessions and money with his daughters and Clare. Anna didn't know what Joanne did with her portion. She didn't care.

It took a year to research, plan, and open her business. She spent hours tweaking her recipes to perfection. When a small shop became available in downtown Royal Oak, she jumped at it, knowing a better one couldn't be found. When the inside of the bakery was expertly arranged with counters, mixers, ovens, and a cappuccino machine, she interviewed dozens of people. Bev was the third person Anna interviewed, but she knew on the spot that her feisty, energetic personality would fit well with what Anna envisioned for her bakery. Then she interviewed dud after dud, fearful she wouldn't find any other qualified candidates. But she did, and Sue was one of them. Anna trusted her immediately. Something in her gut told her these two women could be counted on.

Anna woke up daily at 3 a.m., and managed to arrive at her work kitchen thirty minutes later. She and Bev started their early mornings to the hum of mixers. The second round of coffee poured when Sue arrived for her 5 a.m. shift. The smells overpowered and uplifted Anna's senses by 6 a.m., and then the customers lined up. People left loaded with carbohydrates, coffee, and sweets. She hoped that they came back for the smell and comfort they gained from Savory Scents.

Mornings whipped by as the women worked to feed the customers. It amazed Anna how they worked circles around each other without an accident of flying coffee or bumbling bread. Savory Scents brought out the gracefulness in them all.

***

The table was loaded to capacity with plenty of baked goods at the third annual holiday dinner party that Anna held for her employees. There were also many serving plates with ball-shaped foods, including tiny rounded buns, cheese balls, pizza balls, and a plethora of dessert balls in many colors and sizes. Anna was slightly obsessed with how many recipes she could add to her ball-shaped repertoire.

Bev teased Anna about her obsession for ball-shaped foods. The teasing also was part of the annual festivities.

"Anna, your balls are delicious," Bev mischievously chided. Warmed by the wine, the women roared with laughter.

"Thanks, Bev, I have a lot of experience with balls. I'm glad you appreciate them." Anna lifted her eyebrows in mock sensuality. Further laughter ensued. Calm then reigned as the women refilled their drinks and filled their plates with more rounded foods.

"You should do something with those balls, Anna. Put them to work for you, so to speak. Why not have a store dedicated to balls?" Sue asked. The other women chimed in, in agreement.

"How vulgar," Bev said in a pretentious, mocking tone.

"I'm serious. Picture everything rounded—the foods, the chairs, all the décor. You could have a lot of fun with it," Sue added.

"Would we keep the names dirty or clean?" asked Anna.

"Clean on the menu and dirty in the kitchen," Sue laughed.

"You could have so much fun with this. You could make everything into a ball—brownie balls, cookie dough balls, cake balls, peanut butter balls, spinach balls, cheese balls, meaty balls … I could go on and on," mused Bev.

"Please don't," begged Anna.

"I think it's a million-dollar idea. I would definitely be in on it if you wanted to pursue it," Bev said seriously.

That was how the idea for Spherical Treats and Sweets came to life. Anna started by selling round sweets at Savory Scents from the recipes of her "All Things Round" recipe book that she had developed over the years. It was amazing to her how many things could be shaped into a ball. Customers loved them so much that the women started a new business. Bev and Sue were co-owners.

They named the treats they created with socially acceptable and proper names for the store. In private, they used more original and entertaining names. These women had never heard so many dirty jokes as they did the year they started Spherical.

The women spent nearly all their spare time working in their new store while Anna let other trusted employees run Savory Scents. Their sweat equity paid off—Spherical Treats and Sweets was extremely successful. It went so well that a year into it, the women were offered a deal by a well-known Midwest company to buy the rights to the name so they could create a national chain with it. They accepted it, grateful for their good fortune. They all went back to working mornings at Savory Scents. They didn't need to do so for the money as much as the joy of the work.

Anna had never dreamed that at twenty-nine she would have already owned two successful businesses. Her dad was right, she thought, life could throw some curveballs, but sometimes they were good ones.

***

David Montagna drove down Main Street on his way to work on a sunny spring morning. The beautiful weather teased of summer yet to come. A woman with long, black hair caught his eye. She was a slim woman, with curves where they belonged. He hated how so many women were rail thin these days. Men liked curves. The woman turned toward the woman next to her, laughing at something she said. Even at that distance, he could see that her eyes were incredibly blue, like warmth and ice simultaneously. He had no choice—he had to meet the woman behind those eyes.

He wasn't a stalker, but he did something that shamed him at the time. He parked his car in the first street spot available and, meeting be damned, followed the pair of women from a distance.

In his life, he had been attracted to plenty of women, but he had never done anything quite so bold. Thought didn't even enter into his actions that day. Some unidentifiable force compelled him to follow that woman. *This is not what normal people do*, he thought. *I can't believe I'm doing this.*

Five minutes after the women walked into Savory Scents, he followed. Four people stood in line before him. The beautiful woman took order after order, moving gracefully as she cut bread or poured coffee. Finally, it was his turn. His breakfast pushed up his throat in his nervousness. Another woman walked up to the blue-eyed beauty and whispered something to her before dark-haired woman walked out of sight through the kitchen doors. He had missed his chance, and a good thing too. He heard his voice quiver as he ordered a bagel and coffee.

As a boy, when David was nervous, he would become tongue tied. Letters and sounds would shift senselessly of their own accord and incomprehensible, jumbled sound would come out. It had first happened in second grade. He stood in front of his classmates, reporting what he had learned about animals of Africa, filled with nervousness, and his syllables mixed and mashed until the whole class laughed. It cemented in him a fear of public speaking.

A kind, patient speech therapist helped him learn to control his tongue. By the time he was out of middle school, he had mastered the proper relaxation techniques to help him avoid disrupting his phonemes.

Law might have been an odd career choice for a boy with a speech issue, but he was passionate about it and fought hard to become comfortable speaking in front of people. He suspected his colleagues would be surprised to know these parts of his past. It never happened in court, where confidence burst from him. It had been so long, he rarely thought of the time when he stumbled with words. Until now. His voice hadn't quivered like that since he was a boy.

He left Savory Sweets dazed from the experience, but

determined. David knew how to work for what he wanted. He noticed no ring on her finger so he would be back. He would break the ice somehow so he could talk to the beautiful woman. If he tried to talk to her with his words twisting in the wind, she was liable to run away.

***

Very little distracted David from his work, yet lately, he didn't quite feel like himself. Something had changed in him. At first he suspected that someone at work, maybe Dillon down the hall who loved to play jokes, was messing with him. David kept misplacing and losing things. He would set a stapler or file down on his desk only to turn and find it missing. One day he sat confounded for minutes, trying to analyze what was wrong with the printer, when normally it would take him only a moment to realize the paper drawer was empty. It took some time, but he finally realized the woman was distracting him. He thought about her all the time.

He made it his new habit to walk to Savory Scents most days for some coffee and a sandwich for lunch. The aroma of coffee lingered on his clothing after he left, and he treasured it. Although he wanted to go more often, he worried about being interpreted as a stalker, which he was on the verge of becoming. Impressions were crucial, and he had to make the right one.

Each day David noticed something else he adored about this woman and fell for her a little more, even though they hadn't even been properly introduced. Her easy smile, intense energy, and striking beauty mesmerized him. He tried to hear every word she said while he pretended to work on his laptop or look at his phone. Sometimes he thought about how ridiculous and cheesy his crush would seem to others, but he couldn't help himself.

He managed some words with her finally: hi, yes, regular coffee, breakfast bagel, nice weather, thank you, and have a good day. At least it was start, he thought, and thankfully he had maintained control over his voice, although it took effort.

After a few weeks, the thought of walking up and asking her

The Nature of Denial

out still intimidated him. He decided to try something different, something bold. He would start sending her anonymous gifts to give her the hint that someone was interested. Eventually, he'd let on that it was him. How could she refuse a date with him then? He started his gift giving that afternoon with flowers. Over the next few weeks he sent her flowers, fruit, and chocolates.

He overheard her name one afternoon when the shop was unusually quiet.

"Anna, have you been to a game yet?" a woman who worked there asked.

"No, I haven't had any time," Anna said.

"Don't you usually go to opening day?"

"Almost every year. There's been no time. Jan's been sick, so we've been short. She should be back next week, so I'll get to one soon."

"Go Tigers!"

"Yeah, hopefully this will be a good year."

Baseball? A woman who liked baseball? He had to ask her out soon!

Two days later, David sent Anna an envelope containing four Tigers tickets. He overheard the conversation when she opened her gift.

"What is it?" a woman he'd heard them call Bev asked.

"Tickets."

"To...?"

"To the Tigers."

"Who are they from?"

"It's signed David. Again."

"That is so romantic. I wonder who this David is? Flowers, chocolates, tickets. I didn't even know guys could be romantic anymore."

"Yeah, I guess," Anna said before walking toward the kitchen with Bev, continuing their conversation out of David's hearing.

David watched Anna wash her hands, take off her apron, and hang it on a rack. She walked into the back of the bakery and emerged from the kitchen doorway with her coat in hand. She spoke with a woman at a nearby table, another regular whom David recognized, then turned to leave.

She stopped when David asked, "'Tuse me, have mint?" He

heard the irregular words come out and winced. He slowed down, calmed his racing heart, and tried again. "I mean, excuse me, do you have a minute?"

The woman stared at him for a moment too long. *She must think I'm crazy*, he worried.

"Sorry about my slurring. I'm not a drunk or crazy person, I'm just a little nervous."

Anna smiled at David. It seemed a practiced, empty smile, probably reserved for customers she wanted to placate.

"What's going on ...? Ah, sorry, I don't know your name. I should though. I've seen you here before."

"It's David. And you're?" he asked, pretending not to know.

"Anna."

"Nice to meet you, Anna."

If he didn't do it now, David knew he might lose the nerve. A motor of nervousness revved up inside him, "I was hoping we could together the game." Her smile faded, and it took him a moment to realize what he'd said. He laughed nervously. "I mean, I was wondering," he paused and breathed, "if we could go to the game together." Anna stared at him with a look he couldn't decipher, and he worried she was contemplating how to deny him. "Sorry, I'm just a little nervous."

"Are you *the* David?"

He could feel his face burn red. "I am."

"Wow, I don't know what to say. Thank you for the gifts."

"I hope it's not too much. I wanted to ask you out a while ago, but I was ... well ... nervous."

An awkward pause stood between them.

"Did you get the tickets? Would you like to go with me?" David tried to resuscitate the conversation.

"Um ... why *four* tickets?"

"I thought you might want to invite a friend or two since you don't know me from Adam. I thought it might make you more comfortable."

"Oh," she said and looked off into the distance. Was she trying to think of a way to turn him down, he wondered?

"The weather is supposed to be nice that day."

"Well ..."

"I will spring for popcorn, hotdogs, whatever you like. If you don't have a good time, at least you'll be well fed." He sent his most charming smile across his lips. "Come on, it'll be fun."

"Okay. I'll invite my friend Kate to come. I'll tell her snacks are on you." Anna smiled.

"Do you want to invite another friend?"

"No. Kate will be enough. Trust me."

***

Michigan Avenue, which led up to Tiger Stadium, was like an old friend to Anna. She had traveled it many times with her father on their trips to see the Detroit Tigers. He would often imitate Ernie Harwell's trademark baseball phrases as they drove to games. This year would be the last year the Tigers would play at Tiger Stadium. Comerica Park would soon be finished and then they would play there. A part of her childhood would be lost.

The immense walls of the stadium before her enclosed more than baseball players and fans—they were also where Trent taught Anna about baseball and life. Everything could be boiled down to a baseball metaphor for her father. As a child, her behavior was either on or off base, according to him, and when she fought with her sister, he called it a no-win situation. As a teenager, it drove Anna crazy, but standing there before those walls now made her crave to hear her father's litany of philosophical baseball.

Anna felt she had her bases covered, as Trent would say, having Kate with her. For all she knew, David could be some freak who wanted to cut her to pieces. He seemed trustworthy, or at least that was Anna's impression of him, but you never knew. Now at least she understood why he had stared at her all those times in such a peculiar way. Although she saw him daily at Savory Sweets for weeks, he had said very little, unlike other guys who tried to hit on her. All that time he sent her gifts. Anna never would have guessed it was him. It intrigued her, but the intensity of it frightened her as well.

Anna and Kate waited for David on the north side of the stadium.

"So, tell me about this guy," Kate said.

"I don't know what else to say. I've told you he sent the gifts and asked me out. That's all there is to tell."

"Is he hot or not? I haven't heard that, and that's what matters," Kate laughed.

"He's good looking. I don't know. It just seems a bit over the top—the anonymous gifts, tickets to the game. It's a little too perfect, like a romantic comedy before you find out the guy's married or something."

"Come on, Anna. Give it a chance. Don't be so dramatic."

"Here he comes," Anna said and looked over in David's direction.

"The guy with the brown coat?" Kate asked.

"Yeah," Anna said.

They watched David walk toward them. Anna appraised his looks. He was tall with dark brown hair, warm brown eyes, and a face chiseled in all the right ways. His smile was contagious. Yet she knew from experience that looks didn't mean anything. People could be attracted to the absolute wrong type. It didn't tell you much about a person's character. Even rapists and serial killers could be attractive. What if this guy wanted to hurt her?

After introductions were made, they walked in, purchased drinks and snacks, and found their seats. The familiar aromas of the stadium, popcorn and peanuts, calmed Anna. Even if David turned out to be a nut, she was determined to enjoy her afternoon of baseball.

"So, David," Kate said, leaning forward to look around Anna, who sat between them, "tell me about yourself."

"Well, I work at Haynes, Reynolds, and Associates. I'm a lawyer."

"Oh, you know what they say about lawyers," said Kate.

"What do they say?"

"They can't be trusted."

"Who's spreading misinformation?" David joked. "What do you do?"

"I'm a chemical engineer at Envirotech. What made you decide to become a lawyer?"

Anna interrupted the interrogation to say, "Look, guys, we're up."

Kate couldn't be stopped so easily, however, and she continued to ask David about himself. She found out that he had no children or ex-wife, experienced speech issues as a child, loved sports, and most of his family lived out of state.

Kate's behavior embarrassed Anna, but she was used to it. Kate made no apologies for her directness—she was looking out for Anna, and if he didn't like it, too bad, was what she'd say. Anna knew if she was quiet, she'd learn a lot about this man during Kate's interrogation—like if he was patient or not, and his threshold for annoyance.

When Kate finished, Anna apologized to David for her friend and escorted her off to the bathroom like she was going to scold her, which she was not. As soon as David was out of earshot, they pored over details like he was a new species under study.

"He seems very nice," Kate concluded.

"Don't you think the gifts might be overcompensating for something weird or little?" Anna asked.

"Just because a guy is romantic doesn't mean there is anything wrong with him, or small. You've just had a few bad experiences is all."

Anna didn't want to think back to her short string of bad relationships, every one a disaster. From her relationship with Ben to a few after, they all ended up being more trouble than they were worth.

"You're right ... I guess."

"Anyway, he's hot. If you don't want him, can I have him?" Kate asked joking.

That comment surprised Anna. It sparked some kind of possessiveness in her which she dared not share with Kate or she would be teased relentlessly. This man had put in a lot of thought about how to earn her attention, and it worked. She would at least give him a chance, she decided.

"No, you can't have him. You don't want my leftovers," Anna said.

"Ha, ha. Well, what do *you* think of him?"

"I agree, he's hot. I'll just have to take it slow and see what he's like. He seems nice, but it's too early to tell."

"What else do you want me to find out about him?"

"Nothing! Give it a rest. I already know he's patient for

putting up with all that!"

When they walked back from their girl-talk session, Anna couldn't help but notice David's good looks. He stood up for her as she squeezed by to get to her seat. His eyes were so warm. When she brushed past him, she felt some kind of warm spark.

***

Anna's suspicions about David being too good to be true slowly receded. They'd gone out on a handful of dates and jogged together weekly for the past month. Each time they met, her doubts washed away a little more, like a river working on soft earth. Generally, when she dated she kept things superficial and light. Her carefully constructed walls that kept men from getting too close soon began to crumble.

She learned the most about him when they jogged together. Not many people could run at Anna's pace, but David kept up and had enough breath to talk. They traversed the neighborhoods and cityscapes of the area. He introduced her to a trail that twisted through the forest of a local park.

"Have you ever been backpacking?" he asked.

"No, I haven't. You?"

"I went on some amazing backpacking trips during college. I mostly backpacked in the Upper Peninsula. Have you been there before?"

"Only once, when I was a kid," said Anna.

"We've got to go, then. You'll love it. The scenery is magnificent. I'm planning a backpacking trip in two weeks, a long weekend. Would you be interested in coming?"

Enthusiasm emanated from David's voice, but Anna couldn't share it. She was not an outdoor girl. Anna didn't want to start their relationship by pretending she liked something she didn't, even though it would probably be easier.

"Sorry, but not really," Anna said in a voice she hoped didn't offend David.

"Why not? It's not like I'd expect anything." Anna assumed he referred to their slow pace in the sexual realm. "We'd just be hiking." David had been a perfect gentleman so far. Although they shared many passionate kisses, he kept his hands from wandering to other regions.

Anna laughed. "That's not it. I just don't like the outdoors."

David slowed his jogging and stopped. He caught his breath for moment and looked quizzically at Anna. "What do you mean? We're outside right now."

"I like running and I'm not *against* the outdoors. It's just that being outside for an extended time is not my thing."

"Have you ever tried camping or anything?"

"No, but I don't intend to either. Sorry."

"Ok, ok. Message received. No backpacking." They resumed jogging. "Yet," he continued. Anna gave him a sideways glance and smiled.

They ran out of the short woodsy path and toward the downtown area. A man pushed along a rusty bike that had garbage bags dangling off the sides. One was filled with pop cans and bottles. David stopped and pulled a twenty dollar bill out of his pocket and gave it to the man. The man looked surprised and thanked him. Then David and Anna jogged on.

"That can be dangerous, giving money to homeless people. Have you done that before?"

"I have. I know a lot of people disagree, but ..."

"Don't you worry they might spend it on alcohol or drugs?"

"I don't really think about it too much. I just do it."

"Maybe you should give that money to a place that gives them food instead."

"I do that too. Once a month I serve food to the homeless with my church. The way I see it, no one should go hungry. You should come with me next time."

Anna agreed. A good-looking man who cared about other people too? Now Anna worried again. It was too good to be true. Something must be wrong with this guy.

***

David invited Anna to his apartment after their fifth official date (not including the handful of times they ran together). The large two-bedroom apartment was somewhat sparse for Anna's taste. It needed a woman's touch, she thought.

It looked clean at first glance. They stayed in that night to make dinner and watch a movie. David's movements in the kitchen informed Anna of his lack of proficiency as a cook, but she withheld comment on it.

As he opened cupboards to search out items, Anna noticed the massive disorganization within them. She knew how kitchens should be organized, and this was not it, not even in the ballpark. Boxes of pasta and dry goods were haphazardly arranged, and many of them couldn't be clearly seen. Dishes and glasses echoed the same lack of organization and care. When she opened the fridge, she quickly closed it. She'd learned enough.

Curiosity got the better of her after that. As David prepared food, Anna looked around his apartment, peeked in closets and glimpsed under his bed. As she suspected, this man was a slob! She knew men often paid less attention to organization and cleanliness than women did, but she'd never met anyone this bad.

They sat down to a dinner of overcooked pasta and rubbery chicken. Anna tried her food. She cut it up, pushed it around her plate, and took incredibly small bites.

"How do you like your dinner?" David asked.

"It's good," Anna lied.

"You know what?"

"What?"

"I've learned something about you tonight," he smiled.

"What's that?" she asked.

"I've learned that you're a terrible liar. Actually, it's a relief. Good liars, now those scare me, and I see quite a few in my work."

"Oh. I didn't want to hurt your feelings."

"I know, and you're sweet for that. But this," he pointed toward his plate, "is awful!" I can't believe you ate more than one bite!" he laughed.

Anna smiled. "You tried anyway."

"What do you say we order some pizza or something?"

"That sounds great. I'm starving!"

They ordered pizza and watched the movie *Big Fish*. They

snuggled on the couch after they ate. David's embrace warmed and comforted her. It made her yearn for more from him, but she knew the power of intimacy and sex to make women blind. She wasn't ready for that. She wanted to know all she could about David before she lost control over her feelings. It spoke volumes to her that he didn't push her for sex, but part of her wished he would.

***

Anna sat on David's bed and kept him company while he packed for his trip. Random items tumbled out of his closet along with his backpack. She watched, amazed at how a person could be so disorganized.

"I'm embarrassed to have you see this," he said.

"It's very entertaining. I've never seen anything like it."

"I know. It's something I have to work on. It's awful."

"I never would have guessed your closet would look like that, based on your car. I mean, your car is immaculate."

"I hide my messiness. You can see it out in the open in a car."

"Oh, I get it," Anna said, but didn't.

"Are you sure you won't reconsider coming with me? My friend Nate would love to meet you. It's going to be so beautiful."

"I'll take your word for it. I'm sure there will be lots of bugs and few toilets. No thanks."

"I've heard it's beautiful at South Manitou Island. Lots of beach, amazing forests, sand dunes. Toilets, too—well, the no-flushing kind."

"No thanks, but you have a good time."

"I'll try, but it'll be hard without you." David stopped packing and walked to Anna and kissed her cheek.

***

The next day, David called on the ferry ride over to South

Manitou Island.

"You are not going to believe this." The phone sputtered with static. Anna could barely make out David's voice.

"What? Is everything okay?" she asked.

"Yeah, but Nate couldn't make it. His son got really sick and he didn't want to leave. He was nice enough to make some calls to a few friends of ours for me while I drove out and ..." Static filled the phone. Anna pulled it away from her ear.

"... Ashley lost ... phone ... dropped it in the water .... unbelievable."

"Who's Ashley?"

"A friend of ours Nate found to take his place. Not as good as having you here, but better than being alone ..." The phone went silent for a moment, and then the call was lost.

The phone rang. "Hello?"

"Sorry about that. Something is wrong with .... not much charge left. I won't be able to call again until I'm back at my car ... save the rest for emergencies."

"You're breaking up. I can barely hear you."

"Ok, well. Ashley and I will take lots of pictures. Wish you were here. Miss you."

"Have fun," Anna's voice trailed, "bye."

Who the hell is Ashley? What kind of friend is Nate, sending a woman with David when he just started dating someone? Well, here's the imperfection. Obviously, he's a womanizer. And he doesn't even bother to hide it? What a wasted two months. What an asshole.

***

The next week David couldn't reach Anna. He left four messages with no response. He went to Savory Scents, but she disappeared to the kitchen and her employees told him she'd left. What happened, he wondered? Things were going so well. Was she the kind of woman who expected a man not to do things without her? He *had* invited her.

David drove to her apartment that afternoon. No answer. Obviously, she didn't want to see or talk to him.

The Nature of Denial

This required swift action. He would not let her go that easily. Anna was the right woman for him, he knew it, although he knew enough not to tell her that yet. It would frighten her. He drove to the flower store and pulled out his credit card. He would get to the bottom of this, but he needed to talk to her in order to accomplish that.

She should be leaving soon, since the place closed thirty minutes ago, thought David as he placed roses on and in her car. He heard the door opening and hid on the opposite side of Anna's car.

"What is this shit?" he heard her say. Not the response he was hoping for. He stood up, realizing this wasn't the most romantic way he could have done this.

"Hi, Anna."

"These are from *you*?" she growled.

"Yes. I've missed you. How are you?" He couldn't imagine what he'd done to make her mad, but clearly she was furious.

"Keep your flowers." She pushed the flowers away from the car and opened the door.

David put his hand on the door, holding it steady. "What is going on, Anna? Why are you mad at me? I haven't even seen you since I got back. I called as soon as I could. My phone died at the island. Did you hear that part of the conversation?"

"I heard plenty. I hope you and *Ashley* had a grand time. Call *her* when you want a date. I'm done."

David started laughing. He put his hand in front of his mouth to stifle it, but he couldn't. He bent over, catching his escaping, snickering breaths.

Anna continued, "I don't see what's so funny. You get my hopes up that you're a normal, nice guy and then throw them under the bus? Is that your idea of fun? Do you get your kicks that way? You're a sick person. Sick, sick, sick. Now leave me alone!"

"I will leave you alone, if you listen to me for one minute."

"Fine," Anna said as she folded her arms over her chest and sighed.

"I have known *Ashley* since college. Nate and I told Ashley long ago that he should go by his middle name—Thomas. We told him no woman would want him if she had to call him Ashley. Needless to say, he didn't listen."

"What?"

"Ashley is not a woman! He's a man with parents who didn't give him a very masculine name."

"Are you kidding me?"

"I have the pictures to prove it, Anna. I can't believe you thought I would just go on a weekend trip with another woman on a whim. Is that what you think of me?" *The last months have been a disaster if that's how highly she thinks of me.*

Anna looked at the pavement, speechless. Moments passed and all David heard were city sounds—cars passing, people talking in the distance, a siren far away.

David moved closer to Anna and touched her arm. He put his hand gently on her cheek and directed her gaze up toward him.

"Hey. I wouldn't hurt you like that."

Anna's eyes welled up with tears. "I'm sorry. I can't believe I thought ... it's hard for me to trust, David. It just is. I'm sorry."

"Don't be sorry. Next time, if you have a problem, just come to me. You may not believe it yet, but you can trust me."

He kissed her gently and then more firmly. Weeks of pent up attraction and desire exploded in him. He had to have her. Now.

"Let's go to my place," he said. Her hands were all over him, urging him on.

"My place. It's closer" she said. They climbed into her car. His hand rested on her knee, then gently moved up and down her thigh. She pushed down on the gas pedal.

They parked abruptly and hurried to her apartment. Their hands explored each other's bodies and their mouths moved with urgency. In moments, their clothes lay in a pile on the floor and they were in bed, making love. David worried it would last only a moment, because he'd never been so excited, but he managed to prolong their connection until both were satisfied.

***

Over time, Anna realized that she trusted David. She tried to hold back her feelings until she was sure that David was genuinely what he claimed to be. She didn't want to pretend that this man she was falling in love with was infallible because she knew better. All she'd found lacking in him was his unsightly morning appetite, which caused him to shove food down like he was preparing for hibernation, and his messiness, despite his attempts to be otherwise.

Eventually, Anna stopped worrying and just went with it and let the river of emotions guide her. Her walls came down, dissolving to nothing. Anna and David became inseparable, except during their working hours. When they were apart, a strong yearning distracted her from day-to-day functioning, and lust made her watch the clock. Their schedules were quite different, Anna with early hours and David with later ones. She took naps so she could stay up later and spend time with him in the evenings. They reunited daily like lovers separated by months and seas instead of hours and blocks.

Six months after their first date, snowflakes and holidays approached. David asked Anna to meet his family for their pre-Christmas holiday celebration. His parents lived in Florida now. He explained that after he and his two brothers had moved away from home, his parents became snow birds who flew down south during the cold Michigan winters. David's mother, Linda, had bad arthritis and living in a warmer climate helped, so they decided to move there permanently.

On the flight down, Anna twitched with nervousness. David mistook it for fear of flying, but Anna set him straight: "I am terrified to meet your family!" she confessed.

"They'll love you, just like I do." He kissed her cheek softly.

"So tell me more about them. What are your parents like?"

"Well, my mom is the glue of the family. She moves slowly because of her arthritis, but her mind is quick. She's always finding new ways for us to keep in touch. She learned how to Skype before I did and made my brothers and I use it for family chats. Without her, we'd probably only get together at Christmas with Todd in California and Bryan ... even though he lives in Michigan too, I just don't want to talk much with him."

"She sounds amazing."

"She is. I'm always getting letters, emails, and now texts. It's just the right amount so we can keep each other updated."

David explained that he and his brothers all visited Florida more often the over last few years because his father, Tony, was in the early stages of Alzheimer's disease. Tony had always been a man of few words, and more so now, so Linda did most of the talking, which seemed to suit him fine.

"Each time I see him, I notice more forgetfulness in him. My mom always makes it seem normal that anyone would forget the news they heard the day before or constantly lose things."

"I'm sorry to hear that." Anna reached for David's hand. She didn't know the right words to say.

The sunlight reflected beautifully over the water. What a contrast to the blasting snow they left behind.

They sat quietly for some time. David stretched and leaned back in his seat.

"We'll arrive a full day before my brothers. That way you'll have a chance to visit more with my parents and less with my brother Bryan and his wife, Natalie."

"Are they really *that* bad?" Anna asked.

"They are. Bryan used to be a laid-back sort of person. He never judged people by their money or lack thereof before he was with Natalie. Now, he's different."

"That's unbelievable. How did she do that?"

"I don't know. Sex? Brainwashing? I'm not sure. I noticed it on their wedding day. They dropped names of designers and party planners, and talked about cost like it was a contest instead of a wedding. It was disgusting. It didn't get much better after that, so I don't talk to him much. It's too bad, but what can you do?"

"Have you tried talking to him about it?"

"Honestly, I don't know how I'd touch that one. Do I say, Bryan, you're stuck up and your wife's a bitch?"

Anna laughed. "No, I guess that wouldn't go over too well. I hope they're tolerable during the visit."

"Oh, it'll be fine. You can block them out, and you'll like Todd and Beth, they are fun. Too bad they live on the other side of the country. My parents are going to love you, too. Don't worry."

***

The Montagna's house was a modest ranch, well kept on the outside, and Northern Michigan-like on the inside. Anna wasn't sure why she had expected seashells and ocean décor, but instead she saw black bear decorations, moose, and country furnishings. When she walked in the door her nervousness grew exponentially. She didn't know how normal families were supposed to function, and she worried that she'd be found out. When David's mom, Linda, hugged her, she noticed in Linda's eyes the same hue and warmth that she noticed daily in David's. Linda welcomed her like they'd known each other for years. Tony stood back from the group, obviously less exuberant than his wife, yet he looked happy to see them. He gave Anna a warm handshake, and they all sat down to coffee and appetizers.

"David tells me you own a bakery. What is that like?" asked Linda.

"I like it. My mornings start early, but business has been really good."

"David's lucky to have found a woman who can cook. My son is skilled at many things, but cooking? Not so much."

"Anna knows, Mom. I've tried to cook for her before." They all laughed.

"Do you miss living in Michigan?" Anna asked Linda.

"I do. The weather here is lovely, and the ocean is beautiful, but I miss the snow, even though it makes my body ache, and I miss the seasons. We like it here too, though. Especially when our boys come to visit." She smiled at David. "Would you like to play a game of Rummy?"

Anna agreed, and David shuffled the cards.

Luckily for Anna, Linda didn't immediately shower her with questions, as Kate had done to David those long months ago. The conversation flowed around the news of Saddam Hussein's capture, Anna's recipe secrets, and childhood stories of David.

The conversation eventually quieted, and they focused on their game for many hands. Tony picked up a long line of discarded cards and arranged them in his hand. Then he rearranged them. Minutes passed and then more passed. David kept the conversation going, but Anna saw him shoot a look of concern toward his mother.

Finally, he looked at his dad and said, "I need a break from

Rummy. What do you say we go outside?"

Tony looked down at his cards, and confusion crinkled his eyebrows. David said, "Let's go outside, Dad. Anna hasn't seen your garden yet."

"Oh, yeah. The garden." He looked at Anna. "You've got to see our lemon tree." He smiled proudly.

***

Later that night after Tony had retired to bed, Anna sat with David and Linda in the sunroom, which overlooked the garden and the lemon trees.

"So how is Dad doing? It seems a little worse," said David.

"Oh, you know your father. He's a trooper. He's hanging in there."

David stared at his mom for a while. "Mom, you don't have to sugar coat it for me. How is he? How are *you*?"

"It's like watching a turtle climb down a hill. He's making a slow but steady descent. It's not easy. Your father is handling it better than I am."

"He's lucky to have you. You're good to him."

"Funny, I think I'm the lucky one."

"If you need anything, let me know. I know I'm far away, but I'll do whatever I can to help."

"I know, honey. Being here, now, that's a help."

Anna thought about how David treated his parents. She remembered the expression "watch how a man treats his mom and you know how he'll treat you" and now she knew why. He was attentive toward his mom, engaged in what she had to say, willing to give. His patience with his father and respect for both of his parents spoke volumes about his character.

***

The next afternoon, Todd and Beth showed up. They were tan

and fit, California style, and extremely relaxed. Todd looked nothing like David. His blonde hair and green eyes were unexpected. Beth was warm and talkative. It took the pressure off Anna to let Beth do most of the talking. The day progressed pleasantly.

That all changed when Bryan and his wife, Natalie, arrived. The air in the house changed and grew thick with unpleasant energy as they walked in the door. Anna had never experienced such obvious tension, except in her own family. David hugged his brother and sister-in-law, but his eyes told a different story. Anna realized that he wasn't skilled at dishonesty. Anna was a little more practiced in this and smiled fully as she watched Natalie look her up and down, assessing her attire, hair, and quality in one sweeping look.

As the day progressed, Anna equated talking with Natalie to spending eternity in a hellish, fluorescent-lit department store where you walked around endlessly and never found what you needed because the shelves were stocked with thousands of the same incorrect item and you couldn't find a bench to rest your tired feet because there weren't any. How could anyone talk so long about blinds, paint colors, fixtures, and hardware for cabinets for the house they were building, Anna wondered? Who could even care so much? It would be one thing if Natalie were genuinely excited, but she seemed to talk most about how she found the most expensive, name-brand, and exclusive items. *I hope she leaves or shuts up soon,* thought Anna, who literally made her tongue sore by biting it to keep from scolding Natalie. It wasn't that Anna didn't care about decorating and clothing; it just wasn't the most important thing to her. She had a hard time with women who tried to play high school by elevating themselves falsely with the items they owned. She thanked God when Beth saved her and said she needed help in the kitchen.

Being a newcomer, Anna wasn't going to mention how annoying she found Natalie, but Beth said it all for her. "You have to have excuses ready when Natalie's around. Otherwise, you could get stuck for hours," she said, then winked.

"Thanks for rescuing me. What can I help with?"

Beth directed Anna to the vegetables, which needed to be chopped, then turned her attention to the spinach dip. The men were all outside, grilling steak and chicken. Anna heard Linda, stuck in the living room with Natalie. The woman continued to ramble on, to the refrain of Linda's consistent response of, "That's nice, dear."

The family sat outside on the deck to eat the abundance of grilled foods, salads, and garlic bread. Words were sparse at first, except to request that someone pass a dish or to compliment the food.

"So, how was your flight?" David asked Bryan.

"It was fine. Except that I had to wait forever for any service. First class isn't what it used to be. I sometimes wonder what you're paying for. How was your flight?" he asked David and Anna.

"Fine. I loved stepping out of the plane into sunshine," David responded.

There was a lull in the conversation. Natalie turned to Anna. "I hear you're in the bread business."

"Yes, I am."

"How did you end up doing *that?*" Natalie questioned, distaste in her voice.

"I always wanted to own a bakery. I started working at one in college and I knew it was what I wanted to do. I enjoy it."

"Well, how interesting," Natalie said, although clearly, she didn't feel that way.

"I think it's amazing," Beth commented, "to own your own business. David says it's always busy there. You had another business too, David told me?"

"Yeah. We sold that one. I owned it with two other women, and a company basically bought the idea and the name."

"What was that?" Natalie questioned.

"It was called Spherical Treats and Sweets. All the products were round, from desserts to appetizers."

"And someone wanted to buy that?" Natalie said in disbelief.

"Mm-hmm," Anna responded. She took a bite of her food, hoping the focus of the conversation would turn elsewhere.

Natalie continued, "I think it's absolutely charming. How good of you to be in the helping profession. I mean you are feeding people, and making them fat, but that's beyond the point. Very noble profession."

Anna was tired of this pretentious woman. Everything she said seemed to mean something else entirely. She wanted to be left alone. "What do you do, Natalie?" she asked, hoping that this would take the focus off her.

"I am an interior designer. I am hired by the who's who of Michigan to show them how to spend their money. It's a natural gift I have. I create things, like you, Anna, but instead of creating what people eat, I create rooms that bring them happiness. What they eat lasts a day, but a redesign lasts for years. I change lives."

Anna could see the room deflate as Natalie's description of herself went on a little longer. She didn't get it. Natalie seemed to think that people enjoyed her self-appreciating banter, but it was quite grotesque.

Thankfully, David broke into the conversation and steered it toward Todd and Beth, asking them about life in California. Seemingly chastised, Natalie kept quiet for the rest of the dinner.

The next day the whole family visited the beach in the early afternoon and spent the rest of the day in the Montagna's beautiful backyard. Anna made a point to avoid Natalie and Bryan.

Besides the delusions of grandeur from Bryan and Natalie, the visit was successful. What she remembered most was David's compassion toward his father when Tony forgot something or became confused. She knew David's kindness was genuine. This trip confirmed what she had already suspected. She wanted to spend her life with David.

***

Never in his life had David done a romantic thing for a woman—until he met Anna. He had failed to think that far ahead with his previous girlfriends. He wanted to impress Anna from day one. He hoped to marry her, and he thought it would take something special to accomplish this.

Valentine's Day was always a holiday he scoffed at: a fake holiday developed to sell flowers, chocolate, and jewelry. Yet he vowed that this year, and every year he was with Anna, he would do his best to celebrate her on any occasion that allowed him. His mom had taught him that even if a woman said she didn't care about gifts, she did.

Their first Valentine's Day, he purchased enough roses of various hues to fill Anna's apartment. He picked her up from work for a date. He gallantly opened the door to his car for her.

She leaned her head back and sighed.

"What's wrong?" he asked.

"We were so busy today. I'm exhausted. Hey, do you mind taking me to my apartment so I can change before dinner?"

"No time," he said. "I brought some clothing options for you." He pointed to the bag in the backseat of his car. "Would you like to change here or at my apartment?"

"You're acting strange, my dear. How about your apartment?"

They drove to David's apartment, where Anna used the bathroom to change her clothes. She asked through the closed door, "Where are we going?"

"It's a surprise."

"Ok. I hope I'm dressed alright. But if I'm not, I can just blame you, right?"

"You'll be stunning as usual," he said.

They drove thirty minutes out of town and arrived at Antonio's Restaurante on the outskirts of Detroit. The small restaurant served the best Italian food that Anna had ever eaten. *I can't believe he remembered.* Many months ago, Anna told David that her dad took her to Antonio's sometimes as a teenager. The savory foods and rich scents brought back fond memories of her father. They discovered the restaurant after Joanne had moved to college, so the comfort of the place was bolstered because her sister wasn't there to ruin dinner.

Anna was intrigued. She and David both agreed that Valentine's Day was a commercial racket, but now he was taking her to a special place.

They ate a romantic dinner by soft candlelight. The place looked the same with its red tablecloths, rich dark-wood walls, and Italian-inspired pictures. The pasta brimmed with delicious basil and tomato flavor. It seemed at that moment that her dad's spirit surrounded her, and he offered his blessing on Anna's relationship. It filled her with calm.

After dinner, they drove to Anna's apartment. When she opened the door, the smell of roses wafted out to greet her. Brightly colored roses in beautiful vases covered every table in her apartment. She walked from flower arrangement to flower arrangement, appreciating them in all their glory, stupefied that the man she loved would do something like this. No one had ever done anything so romantic for her. *Am I worthy of this kind of attention?* When she turned to thank him, he bent on one knee and held out a small black box.

"I know I am not deserving of you, Anna Cromley, but I will try my best to be. You are everything I've ever wanted." David paused, his brow glistening with perspiration, then continued, "I know it's only been six months, but would you please be my wife?"

Anna's feet were rooted to the floor, her mouth empty of words. She hadn't anticipated this turn of events. Her heart pounded so hard that she feared she might faint.

"David … I … I can't believe it."

Anna stood for a moment, breathing, trying to regain her equilibrium. David's face fell as he waited. Then she ran at him, slid down onto the floor, and hugged him, saying "Yes," over and over.

Parenthood

Anna stretched her feet out on the soft, blue quilt that covered their bed. Her feet were swollen like overstuffed sausages, so she sat propped up by pillows while she looked at her wedding album. She shifted her hips so the baby inside her wouldn't push uncomfortably on her bladder.

As she turned the photo album pages, she thought about how quickly five years of marriage had passed. *Time is a fickle thing.* They had a whirlwind romance and married six months after David proposed. Their cozy end-of-summer ceremony included family and close friends. She remembered the sand tickling her toes as she said her vows on the Lake Michigan beach. As the sun set, it lit the sky with an orchestra of blues, pinks, and oranges as they made their promises of forever and always. Inside the beautifully decorated white tent that billowed with the breeze, they celebrated by the soft light of covered candles far into the night.

When there was no baby a year later, doubters like Natalie realized they had married quickly for love, not for pregnancy. Anna never considered motherhood before David came along. The thought terrified her. There were too many ways to mess up parenthood. David knew Anna's concerns. He said he hoped she would change her mind in time, but he didn't pressure her much. He claimed that he would accept their life with or without kids, but Anna worried he would resent her if she denied him children.

After they had been married three years, something like a maternal itch started in Anna. She would see mothers come into Savory Scents with their babies, and their loving interaction tugged at an emptiness within her. One time she even ran to the bathroom to hide the tears that threatened to show themselves. Soon after her thirtieth birthday, she told David she wanted to try. He was elated. It took two years before Anna became pregnant. They were considering in vitro fertilization when she missed her period.

Right after the pregnancy test showed a plus, Anna went to the bookstore and bought an armful of books on babies. She read them all and immersed herself in all things baby. Knowing that life grew inside her lightened something in her soul.

Part of her believed that she should reach out to her mother and sister right away, but she resisted, out of fear and habit. At the end of her first trimester, she knew that she'd better tell them the news. She didn't want to shock them one day with a baby in hand, although the thought did cross her mind. Joanne responded, "I hope you are a better mother than you are a daughter." Clare offered to stay with Anna to help for a week or so after the baby was born. Anna politely declined the offer. The last thing she wanted was the unpredictability of her mother amidst the joy and uncertainty of new motherhood.

Reading books didn't prepare Anna for the assault on her body that pregnancy would cause. In the beginning, she vomited so much that she lost weight. After a month of that, things settled a bit, and she hoped it would stay that way. They didn't. She experienced intense fatigue and her early morning schedule became close to impossible. Following weeks of this, she had another short reprieve. In month six, her body began to balloon. She imagined if she looked close enough, she could watch her belly expand.

Month seven came with killer cravings. Until this, she had always thought the Hollywood portrayal of pregnant women's cravings were ridiculous exaggerations. Now her body would scream for hamburgers, strawberries, or sundaes at odd and unpredictable times. If David hadn't been so obliging, she didn't know what she would have done. Her cravings were demanding, like a basic need, not a want.

"Hey, honey, how are you feeling?" David asked now as he opened the bedroom door and came inside. Anna could smell the hamburger in the bag he carried with him.

"Thank goodness you're here. I'm starving. And swollen! I feel like a beached whale."

"Well, you look like my hot pregnant wife."

"Hot? Huh! That's funny."

"I know you don't feel it, but you look beautiful."

Anna scrunched up her eyebrows in disbelief. "Okay, now can I have my food?"

"Sure." He handed her the bag and brought a tray for her to

put her food on. She tried to place it over her belly, but it wouldn't fit so she sat it next to her. David stared at her with a peculiar expression.

Anna swallowed some desperate bites of burger before taking the bait and asking what was going on.

"Why are you looking at me like that?" she asked.

"I have some news."

"Good news, I hope."

"Well ..."

"Ok, out with it."

"Natalie offered to throw you a baby shower," he said.

"What?" Anna choked on some beef.

"I'm sorry. I know you wanted to skip it, but it looks like it's a done deal."

If it were up to Anna, she would have avoided a baby shower entirely. She didn't relish being the center of attention.

"Why couldn't Kate do it? I mean, I can't imagine why Natalie would even *want* to, except to torture me."

"I guess she's been planning it for some time. She told my family, yours. I just found out. She was going to make it a surprise baby shower. I've never even heard of such a thing, but I put a stop to that part anyway. Maybe her heart is in the right place."

Anna didn't say anything; she just looked at David with skepticism. "You're right. I'm not sure what the deal is," he said. But it's *one* day. We can get through it, right?"

"I'm not sure if men are allowed at baby showers."

"Oh, I'm not going to leave you alone to the savages. I'll be there as your shield." David smiled and gave an old-fashioned bow.

"At least it won't be boring. I guess," Anna said, and she leaned back into her pillows with a deep sigh. She wished it could already be over and hoped for the best.

***

Anna felt like her stomach was stretched to full capacity the day of the baby shower. *What will I look like two months from now?*

An image of her head atop a giant rounded bus of a belly came to mind.

Natalie chose the most overpriced, pretentious restaurant in town. As Anna walked in the door, stress emanated from every pore. She hated these kinds of places, with all white linens and walls, no character, and no welcome unless you were rich and liked to flaunt it. She pictured an uptight server giving them looks of disapproval like they didn't belong—which they didn't. David and Anna did well financially, but they liked to be humble about it.

Natalie rented a private room in the restaurant for the party. Anna saw friends sprinkled between people she rarely saw. The women from Savory Scents and Kate stood off to the side, munching on appetizers. Anna decided she would try to stick by her friends and make the best of it. Hopefully the shower would end before she had to pull her shoes off her fast-swelling feet.

David agreed to run interference with Natalie and Bryan. Anna wouldn't have to deal with them any more than was polite. After he said hello to Anna's friends, he started making his rounds to thank everyone for coming. Anna admired his ability to slap a smile on his face and engage in small talk with anyone.

After everyone sat for lunch, Anna realized with relief that things had gone smoothly so far. She had only an hour to go and nothing catastrophic had happened. Natalie stood up and congratulated David and Anna and said soon they would play a few games.

Games? That doesn't seem to fit into Natalie's elite list of acceptable activities, Anna thought.

At first the games were innocent enough, with guests trying to identify the baby food and unscramble possible baby names. Then the games took an unpleasant turn as the guests tried to guess the size of Anna's belly. *What an evil game. Who made this up?* Groups of people took rolls of toilet paper and unrolled them to indicate the size of Anna's belly. Natalie grabbed a toilet paper roll, asked Bryan to hold the end, and walked all the way across the room. If anyone else had done this, it might have been funny. Natalie gave Anna a sly look, implying that she thought Anna was fat. When she reached the door that opened to another area of the restaurant, she said, "I would go further, but I'm out of room," and then laughed innocently for the benefit of the rest of the guests.

After her toilet paper display, Natalie came over to Anna and said, "I was just joking. I hope you didn't take that the wrong way. Obviously you're not that big, but you do seem to be popping out now," she gestured toward Anna's belly.

"No, it's fine," Anna lied. She wanted to keep the peace and get out of there as soon as possible. *Is she bitter because she and Bryan have been trying to have kids unsuccessfully, or is she just mean?*

"Don't worry, you'll probably lose the weight ... eventually," Natalie smirked.

"Thanks," Anna said. She refused to bite.

"I do hear, though, that even once you lose the weight, things aren't quite as ... firm as they once were," she said, pausing to look at Anna's breasts and stomach with a smile, "but it's nothing a little nip and tuck won't take care of."

"Thanks for your encouraging words," Anna said and walked away before she beat the woman.

She joined David and Kate and described Natalie's latest rudeness. "We're almost out of here," David said. "We'll open presents and then go for the I'm-tired-because-I'm-pregnant fake and we're outta here."

"Do you want me to take care of her for you?" Kate teased, fists up.

"No, just don't let her near me again!" Anna told her. "It wouldn't look right with my pregnant ass kicking hers, but I'll do what I gotta do." They both laughed at the ridiculous image.

***

Anna's mother didn't make it to the shower. Anna didn't mind; she could handle only so much stress in a day. Joanne said she couldn't get the time off work. Clare insisted that they visit Anna the following weekend.

Usually Anna and David went to Indiana to visit Clare and Joanne. That way Anna could control the length of the visit. Her sister and mother had stayed at Anna's house for the night only one other time. Anna remembered how she and Joanne had exchanged heated words after their mother went to bed. The two sisters couldn't be in a room for longer than five minutes before sparks started to fly.

When Anna's mother and Joanne arrived, Clare glowed with joy while Joanne glared at Anna, contempt filling her eyes.

Clare embraced Anna as best she could around her daughter's growing bump.

"I am so happy for you, Anna banana. I have waited so long for this day. I wondered if I would ever be a grandma." Anna saw her glance at Joanne. *I doubt you can expect one from that spinster.*

"Thanks, Mom."

"I'll take your things upstairs, ladies," David offered when silence filled the room.

Joanne remained stiff and wordless. She made herself comfortable in the living room, which was fine with Anna, while Clare bombarded Anna with excited questions and comments.

"So, have you picked a name yet? Joseph is nice. What do you think? Have you been eating right? They say what you eat is very important. Do you—"

This reminded Anna of manic mom and immediately made her anxious. "Let's sit down. My feet are swelling again. Would you like anything to drink?" she asked.

"I'm fine," Clare told her, and they joined Joanne in the living room.

"We're still working on a name. We—"

"You need to choose it soon. When the time comes, you'll have other things on your mind."

"Don't worry. We'll pick one soon."

"Do you have everything you need? Bassinet, changing table, diapers?"

"Mom, don't worry. We'll have everything ready."

Her mom leaned back in her chair and took a long breath. "I'm sorry. I'm just so excited for you. Being a mother is the best thing in the world. You'll see."

Anna noticed that Joanne rolled her eyes at that comment.

"I'm excited too. I can't wait," Anna said.

"I know you'll be a great mom."

"Thanks." Anna tried to hide her growing frustration. If

Joanne rolled her eyes again or her mom didn't calm down, she might explode.

"I am so happy for you, Anna."

"Thanks, again, Mom."

"So, have you started on the baby's room yet? Can I see it?"

"No, we haven't gotten it set up yet. David's going to paint it next weekend."

"Let me see what you've gotten done so far."

"Not much, Mom. Really."

"Let's go have a look."

Anna walked her mother upstairs to the room her child would inhabit one day soon. The talk of paint colors made Anna think about the fateful spring when her mother's symptoms showed and she painted the walls with color.

Clare walked over to the crib and caressed it gently. "The years go by fast. Make sure to enjoy it all. That's my advice," she said as she faced the crib. "You've got to get this painted. Get David moving. You've got to hang your pictures up, and your changing table…" she paused and looked at the picture of the changing table on the outside of the box. "You've got to put this together. You need to be prepared."

Clare's energy made it hard for Anna to maintain her composure. *Why am I so angry?* she wondered. *I've got to calm down. She's just excited.*

"We'll get it, Mom. Don't worry. It's for us to worry about, not you."

Her mom looked at her then, injured.

Anna quickly added, "I mean … aren't grandparents supposed to have the fun part?"

"You're right," Clare said. "I'm just so excited and happy for you."

"I know, Mom."

They walked back downstairs, where Joanne and David waited. Clare walked behind Anna, bubbling over with excitement and more advice. Anna saw Joanne roll her eyes at her again. Anna looked at the clock. *Less than twenty-four hours to go.*

As the day progressed, Anna did her best to avoid Joanne altogether. She didn't want to indulge her in another fight, which she knew her sister wanted, or upset her mother. By evening, her mother and sister were upstairs getting ready for bed and Anna sat on the couch in the living room, her puffy feet on the coffee table, her head leaned back, breathing a deep sigh of relief. They would be gone soon.

Joanne came down the stairs. "Do you have an extra pillow? Mom asked for one," she said with a sneer on her face.

Anna sat up and put her feet down. "Sure, let me—"

"Oh, no, I'll get it. We don't want precious to have to move."

"Come on, Joanne, let's not do this."

"Do what?"

"All you've been doing all day is rolling your eyes at me and giving me dirty looks. Can't we just be civilized for one day?"

"Maybe I could be civilized for one day, if you could, in your life."

"What do you mean?"

"You know what I mean."

"No, I don't," said Anna. "You are always so angry at me, and I have *no idea* what your problem is."

"You're an asshole for even saying that," Joanne snapped.

"What did I do that was so bad that you are boiling over in hate?"

"You want me to spell it out? Fine. You are a vile person. You can't even treat your own mother with the kindness she deserves. You tolerate her and you think she doesn't see that? It's a good thing she has me to take care of her, because who knows what would happen if it were up to you. You—."

"Don't blame me because you've insisted on mothering her. She's a grown woman. I have never treated her badly."

"Who the hell are you kidding? When she gets off the phone with you, she's sad. Most of the time, you don't even call her back. It's obvious that you don't want to be around her," said Joanne.

"That's not true!" Anna said. But was it?

David walked in at that moment. "Everything okay?" he asked, looking at Anna with concern.

"Yes. Fine. Can you get Joanne an extra pillow for my mom?"

"Sure, no problem," he said and walked up the stairs with Joanne.

Anna couldn't believe how angry Joanne was with her. It seemed only yesterday that Anna had been the one caring for their mother while Joanne denied the problem. Now Joanne was obsessed with their mother's illness. She barely let Clare out of her sight. That couldn't be healthy for either of them. Anna guessed it must have started when they moved in with their father. Joanne would drive over and stay with their mother often. Even if Anna could have driven herself, she wouldn't have gone. After the accident, she had a hard time being around her mother, even when she was stable with her meds. Maybe Joanne was right, she hadn't been a good daughter. At this point, she didn't even know how to be.

***

The first time Anna felt the baby move, it startled her. It was like an alien inside, trying to take over her body, poking its elbows and knees around as it pleased. Once she adjusted to the feeling, Anna looked forward to the baby's movements. A relationship grew between them. She would talk to the baby, and sometimes the baby would respond with movement. After she ate, he would do a dance of appreciation and an occasional somersault inside her belly. She could barely wrap her mind around the idea that life grew within her and would soon be in her arms.

As the delivery date approached, she decreased her work schedule. She decided with the women of Savory Scents that she would consult, and fill in occasionally, but otherwise take a year off of daily work. It would be a huge change, but the place nearly ran itself with the staff she had, and she wanted to stay home with her son.

The delivery day finally came. Her body was stretched to capacity and she was ready to reclaim it and meet her baby. It took eleven hours of painful labor and countless screams of agony before Anna held Andrew Trent Montagna. He had Tony's middle name and Anna's father's name. David suggested that his first name be Trent, but Anna thought that would be too painful.

The hustle of nurses settled down. David and Anna were alone with their son, who was lying against his mama's chest, asleep. The one who had moved within her all those days finally within her arms. His eyes were like David's and he had a black puff of hair.

"I can't believe how beautiful he is. I mean ... wow. It's amazing," David sighed, a bit tongue tied, and gave Anna his what-are-you-gonna-do smile.

"It doesn't seem real."

"I know what you mean. I'm glad he's not so red anymore. That was scary."

They sat in silence for a while.

Anna broke the quiet. "It seems like with everything you do in life you have tests to pass, but with a child, you just make it, take it, and go. I mean, I could be totally crazy." She immediately regretted her choice of words.

"Well, you're not, and I think requiring parents to pass a test to have their baby would be against the law."

"I know. It's just weird. I don't even feel like a parent, but here I am."

"I'm sure it takes practice to feel it. I know what you mean, though."

Andrew started to fuss. Anna unbuttoned her shirt. David stared, apparently mesmerized at her new, expanded chest size. "A little privacy, please," she laughed.

"Of course," David said and looked away. Anna situated her son at her chest, as the nurses had taught her. He didn't latch on. Anna sighed as she tried again.

"Do you want me to get the nurses? They can help."

"I don't want anyone else looking at or touching my body for a long time. Just give me a minute." Moments passed as she rearranged the baby against her breast.

"You can turn around now," she told him.

"You may not feel like a parent yet," David told her, "but you look like you've been doing it for weeks."

She looked at David and was caught off guard by her overwhelming emotions—love and gratitude for her new family.

After all the papers were signed and the wheelchair was delivered, David escorted his sore wife to the passenger seat of their car, parked outside the hospital. The late-September air had a crisp feel. It took him—a well-educated lawyer—fifteen minutes to figure out the arrangement of the car seat, even though he had practiced at home. Anna pretended not to notice. He carefully placed Andrew in the seat and buckled the harness.

"We came as two, we leave as three," he said as he sat in his seat. He cupped Anna's cheek with his hand and kissed her.

"I just can't believe it, David. I'm so happy," she said. Then they drove their expanded family home.

***

Anna wasn't prepared for the demanding job of caring for a baby. She read all the books, and they helped, but she was overwhelmed. The moment she caught up with her duties, ready to sigh with relief, a stench in need of attention would saturate the air, or Andrew would cry for something. Breastfeeding itself consumed hours of her day. Although the work exhausted her, she loved it and her beautiful son.

Babies are powerful beings, thought Anna, *they change a home so drastically.* Baby paraphernalia was strewn everywhere, as if a bomb of baby gear had exploded. The smell overpowered the visual change—a mix of baby ointment, powder, and the innocent smell of Andrew himself infused the house. If Anna went outside to get the mail, the smell greeted her at the door when she returned. It filled her with a sense of pride, responsibility, and incredible love.

Anna loved Andrew in an all-encompassing, primal way. She had known that she would love him, but she hadn't expected to be blown away by its intense fierceness, unlike any love she'd ever known. She sat with him, staring at his face until she etched his features into her heart, mind, and soul. One day as she held his sleeping body in her arms, she realized that she would do anything for the little precious bundle in her arms. Absolutely anything.

Holidays

David glowed like a young boy at Christmastime. His eyes reflected the small white lights he tested. Even before Andrew came along, he had gone a little over the top for the holidays, in Anna's opinion.

"You remind me of Chevy Chase on *Christmas Vacation*. Is that movie your inspiration?" she asked.

"No. You can never have too many lights, you know," he answered.

Anna imagined the electric meter spinning faster with each string of lights. Usually, she closed her mouth and left David to his joy.

This holiday season seemed different for Anna, infused with bitterness and disappointment, when it should have been filled with excitement and joy. Anna let loose. "Who are you doing this for? We are so behind with basic stuff: cleaning, laundry, and everything. Don't you think you could just keep it simple this year? It's not like Andrew will remember the lights."

His face fell like that of a boy who'd lost his favorite toy. "What do you mean?" his brown eyes were bewildered. "It's Christmastime. Don't be a Grinch. So what if the house is a little more disorganized or dirty? It will get cleaned up."

"Yeah, it will. When I do it. You're never fuckin' here. Who are you kidding? And when you are, you don't do shit."

He looked hard at Anna. "You write down what you need from me and I'll take care of it. You spend a lot of time complaining lately, but you don't tell me what you want me to do."

"Okay, I'll get to that right now," she said, her sarcasm flowing. "I'm sure my lack of a list is the problem and not your lack of initiative." Then she stomped off and locked herself in their room. The Christmas movie played to half-emptied boxes of decorations and a hurt and angry husband.

Joy became a stranger to Anna. As she lay on her bed, she realized that the goodness in her was being sucked away by some dark, featureless phantom. One minute she knew that David caused their problems, and the next she accused herself. *Was it her or David?* The answer depended on the moment.

When she had worked at Savory Scents, she hadn't noticed how little David did at home. His messy nature had not changed since the day she saw the overflowing closet in his apartment. She had never really stopped to think about it, but rather just did what needed to be done. Obviously, Andrew's birth changed everything, but David still did the same chores as he had before. *He acts like I'm supposed to clean up after him. It's not the 1950s.*

Hours later, Anna woke to Andrew's needy cries. Guilt consumed her once she realized that she had locked David out and fallen asleep. *Why didn't I just talk to him? I can't take my problems out on him. But he just doesn't get it. I've got to control myself. I'm so tired. Maybe some extra sleep this weekend will help.* She headed off to tend to Andrew.

***

Christmas Day wasn't much better. They decided to have Natalie and Bryan over, against their better judgment. They were the only family they had who lived close by, but Anna wished they lived the farthest. Natalie had never spent a day in her life thinking of anyone else's feelings, unless they were directly related to her own. Life occurred *for* her, and everyone else was just a spectator. The worst part was Natalie's obliviousness to other people and to reality. Whenever she gave a compliment to other people, a verbal slap followed. *Torture would be less painful than talking to her,* thought Anna.

Natalie had chided Anna for things she ate during her pregnancy, evaluating the judiciousness of each calorie. "You'll be spending more time getting that brownie off than it took to go through you," she had said with a misleading, sweet smile on her face. Anna knew Natalie would be ecstatic if she never lost the baby weight.

Soon after their guests arrived, David and Bryan went out front to fix some troublesome lights. Anna heard the hum of the furnace. Andrew napped upstairs in his room. Anna wished she could use the rare quiet time to rest herself, but seeing no way out, she sat with Natalie for some tea.

"So," Natalie said with a quiet voice of confidentiality, "what doctor did wonders for *you*?" She accented her syllables in a way that produced the snobbiest tone possible.

"What are you talking about?" Anna asked.

"It's obvious you've had some work done, you're so trim. I'm just wondering where you went for it."

"I didn't have anything done. I guess I'm just lucky, genetically speaking." Anna sighed with annoyance as she got up under the pretense of finding sugar, which she actually hated in tea.

"Ok, our little secret," Natalie winked.

Anna tried to tame her boiling anger, but her blood threatened to beat out of her veins. *Who does this bitch think she is?*

Natalie went on, "I would do it too, if I had a baby. I mean, why wait a year in miserable fatness when you can just get a little nip tuck. You don't want David's eyes to wander while he's waiting for his wife to shrink, right? I'm sure that's how many affairs start," she said, laughing.

Anna whipped around, fired up. "Since we're having secret *girl* talk, there *is* something I've been dying to tell you."

"Do tell," Natalie said, cautiously.

Anna couldn't control the eruption of anger from within. Her voice rose with each word. "You are quite the pretentious bitch most of the time, and I can't stand you. How can you stand yourself? You are nothing but a bitter, angry person. Why are you even here?" Then Anna walked away. She couldn't spend another moment, holiday or other, with this woman. Bryan was difficult enough to deal with, but Natalie was impossible.

***

Natalie and Bryan left in an angry whirlwind soon after. When Anna described her heated exchange with Natalie, David's reaction surprised her. She thought he would be angry and disappointed. Instead, he laughed so deeply that his face turned tomato-red, tears spilled down his face, and he bent forward, toppled by his chuckling.

Finally, when he could breathe, he said, "Thank goodness. I couldn't take it anymore either. I hope my brother divorces that woman. Maybe then he'll be somewhere near normal again."

"I'm sorry? You're not mad?"

"No, it had to be done. I mean, I couldn't take anymore either. You did us a favor. Then you added what she deserved on top. That's the best part. Thanks!" He sat down. "Besides, do we really want those kind of people around Andrew? I love Bryan, but I can't take all their bullshit anymore. You just made it easy and took the pressure off me, thank you very much."

Throughout the rest of the night, David would break out in fits of laughter from time to time. He even called Todd and relayed the story to him. They spent a good half hour laughing about it. It didn't seem so humorous to Anna. She prided herself on controlling her temper, most of the time. It didn't make her feel good that had she lost it, even if Natalie had deserved it.

***

On New Year's Eve, Anna planned to paint a smile on her face and get along with her husband. They had been bickering for weeks and needed a good night. Usually, New Year's Eve included a party or two for them. This year, however, they wanted a quiet night and weren't ready to leave their infant son.

Anna made a special dinner for her and David to enjoy late in the evening after they put Andrew to bed. Her eyes drooped as the evening progressed, but she drank extra coffee and tried to fake her way through. David had been working extra hours, and when she wasn't angry with him, she missed him.

Marriage had its ups and downs, and she knew things would improve, but it didn't make it any easier. They hadn't been intimate since before Andrew's birth, and she decided that this would be the night. As the evening progressed she found the urge passing her by, but she knew from his hints that it pressed at him.

Dinner was pleasant enough, and they engaged in

conversation, yet something gnawed at Anna. She suddenly saw herself from the outside, and she didn't like what she saw. It was as if she had been replaced by an imposter, who smiled and doted on David. The disconnect between how she acted and how she felt inside—empty and cold—jarred her.

She tried to block out her confused thoughts as she brought out dessert—peach pie, his favorite. She hadn't baked much lately, and this comfortable habit had brought her pleasure, like visiting an old friend. Feeling some release of tension, she took a bite, but found that the pie tasted like a lump of nothing.

***

Later in the evening, while others were counting down the minutes to midnight, Anna and David were making love. As David moved within her, Anna looked up at the ceiling. She wanted to enjoy David's efforts, but she felt nothing but pressure.

She wanted to yell at David, "Don't you feel this emptiness?" Negative thoughts immediately consumed her. *You should be ashamed of yourself. You are an awful wife. Look at his eyes. He loves you and you are cold.* Then she thought of Andrew. *Is he ok?* Too many thoughts spun around in her head, mixing with the movement of David's busy hips. It was as if with each thrust her anxieties became stronger and stronger.

When David finished, she kissed him and immediately ran toward Andrew's room to make sure her son was safe. She tiptoed into his room and stood next to his crib. He lay peacefully on his stomach, and she could hear his tiny breaths.

Satisfied, she walked back down the hall to David. He lay sprawled comfortably on their bed, naked and relaxed.

He turned toward her when she sat down on the edge of the bed. "I've missed you so much," he told her. "Did it feel okay? It didn't hurt or anything, did it?"

"No, it was great." *Fake smile, fake Anna.*

She moved up next to David on the bed, and forced herself to lie next to him and hold him. *There is something so wrong with me. I love David. Why do I feel so cold toward him? He's a good man. I'm just tired. Things will look better in the morning.*

Broken

Anna read in one of her books that new mothers tended to fit into different categories of mistaken notions of motherhood. Many mothers began motherhood with naive notions of what motherhood entailed. Some expected that their lives would go on much the same, just with a swaddled baby in hand to occasionally feed and change. Others thought that the love they had for their child should bypass all the other frustrations—a June Cleaver version of sorts. Some mothers had no idea at all what to expect and feared that they would somehow make a mess of it all.

Anna fell into the first category. She believed that she would have all this time now that she wasn't working at Savory Scents to get every closet organized, paint over the putrid color of the guest room, and dote on her baby. It astonished her how much time it took to complete all the baby tasks. She would feed, change, soothe, hold, and burp Andrew, only to turn around and do it all again. This became the play-by-play of her life, as her dad would have said.

Initially, she thought it would change, but gradually a new idea took seed, rooting in the darkness: maybe it would never change. Worry slowly consumed Anna. She was drowning in it. She worried that she might never again have more than three minutes in the bathroom. She worried about the well-being of her son. She worried that her needy son might suck all the energy and life from her.

Everything became a heart-pounding, standing-naked-in-a-crowd kind of worry. It became difficult for her to get her heart to beat in a normal rhythm; it preferred a wild, unpredictable mix instead. When sleep should have been a respite from all of her anxieties, it was interrupted by worry that woke her and eliminated the only peace and quiet she could find.

It didn't start out this way. The first few months were happy, albeit exhausted, ones. Then, day by day, it seemed, her anxiety and frustration grew. In moments of clarity, she feared that she was becoming a monster. She could hardly recognize this fearful, angry woman in the mirror. As the days progressed, her thoughts spiraled deeper into darkness.

This was supposed to be a sunshiny part of her life, beautiful and filled with wonder and love, everything new like an opening rosebud. Baby smells were supposed to awaken her mothering instincts. The touch of her son should have brought warmth to her heart, and watching him grow should have filled her with wonder. Instead, she would sit and wonder why babies were made so helpless. *What are we supposed to do with them?*

In the middle of a late-night feeding, she would stare at the sitcom reruns and ache for Andrew to finish so she could return to soft slumber. Resentment would fill her as Andrew sucked her milk dry. Angst over her angry thoughts would soon follow—a vicious cycle with no end in sight.

Anna soon had a hard time feeling anything at all, except aching exhaustion, which her friends claimed was normal, but it seemed the walls were closing in around her and that didn't seem normal. She wished she could tell someone, but she felt that her thoughts were too evil to share. When anxiety claimed her, it took all of her strength to maintain the outward appearance of sanity. *Now I know how Mom feels. What if I'm becoming like her? Please, God, no!*

***

Andrew cried red with rage over whatever ailed or irritated him at the moment. Anna rocked him in the special mahogany rocking chair, chosen with love before Andrew's birth. She sat in his calm, blue room, rocking him endlessly, a slight squeak announcing her struggle. His angry crying stopped only when he paused to breathe. *I wish he could just tell me what the fucking problem is.* The crassness of her thoughts made her cringe. *I want it to stop. I would give my life for this. I can't handle it.* She gently placed Andrew in his crib. She needed a break, but Andrew wailed in protest. She walked out of the room and ran down to the basement. The moment she reached the bottom step, she unleashed a tirade of screams and a string of swear words.

I feel like I'm going crazy. I refuse to lose it. Why do babies cry all the time? Did I finish the laundry? Is something wrong with my baby? Her heart started to pound like it had the time she had taken caffeine pills in order to pull an all-nighter to finish a college essay due the next day. Her breath eluded her. She slid to the floor and tried to catch her breath before the dark spots that settled across her vision took her to complete blackness.

Finally, after slow minutes that felt like hours, her heart calmed and her breathing regulated. No longer focused on herself, she noticed that Andrew's crying had stopped. In a panic, she ran up the stairs. Tears raced down her cheeks as she opened his door and saw him lying peacefully. He looked angelic. She could hear his breath, his calmness a contrast to her own frantic state. Exhausted, she flopped onto the couch and tried to forget about the frustration, confusion, and anger. She quickly fell into a fitful, disturbed sleep.

***

She looked at her clock. 5:00 A.M. *This is what it feels like to be a zombie. Everything in you dead, but your body still moves.* The image of zombies on the Michael Jackson video from her youth circulated in her head, briefly entertaining her. She heard Andrew whimpering through the monitor. *Please go back to sleep.* He grew more alert by the minute. *He is not going back to sleep.* He started to fuss for a feeding. Anna went to him, a ghost of a person, like a guest in someone else's body moving down the hallway. The sensation was surreal.

The morning routine was typical—change diaper, feed, burp, change diaper. Anna touched Andrew and interacted with him. *Maybe faking it will make it real.* A numbness ran though her veins, but where the numbness hadn't yet reached, her love for Andrew ran deep. Yet distance grew between her and her son, making it more impossible each day to feel anything. *What is going on? Am I crazy? Not now. Why now? I can't let him go through that. Crazy mom. I know what that feels like. Stop thinking like this. It's fine. Relax.*

Andrew took his morning nap, a brief deliverance. He woke up wailing. *Red-faced monster again.* Feeling dizzy, she went to him. With a resigned sigh she lifted him up and held him close. Her heart beat erratically, but she cooed to him and swayed with him, gently patted his back. He seemed to grow angrier with each action, as if he knew his mother's true feelings.

Anna went outside and brought in the stroller from the garage. Desperate to make the wailing end, she walked for an hour through the house with Andrew in the stroller, wearing wheel marks in the beige carpet. He grew calm and his eyes became heavy with sleep. Anna stopped to sit on the leather couch and rest her aching feet. The screaming returned, so she pushed the stroller through the house again. This time it didn't calm him. Nothing did. Back to basics, she thought as she tried to hold, burp, feed, and sing to him. He had no fever or other obvious problem. Anna lacked any further ideas on how to help her adorable, screaming devil.

The pressure intensified, and like a balloon filled to its maximum, she felt like she was ready to pop, but she was not quite sure what this meant. Only that it pushed on her from all directions. *Deep breaths. Count to ten. Inner peace.*

The wailing continued, now at a higher decibel. The balloon burst. Anna squeezed his arms as hard as she could, screamed, and shook. Then she put him down roughly and screamed some more, the words too wrong to repeat. She closed her eyes. An image emerged in her mind of Andrew on the floor, bloody, limp, and quiet. Her skin jumped to ward off the image. She looked at the red spot on his arm, soon to be a bruise. Deflated, she went limp. Folding down into herself and onto the floor, she cried along with her son because she knew that she was evil. Crazy. She realized at that moment that she must leave her son in order to protect him.

God, forgive me, I have to leave. I don't want to, but I am out of control. I will not put Andrew through this. What if I hurt him? What if he ends up hating me because I'm crazy? I can't do this anymore. I need to end it or leave. I need lots of money to get settled. I can't take any kind of credit cards, or I will be traced. I need clothes and my car. I can't keep the car long, either, or it will be found, along with me. She continued to plan her escape while her son wailed on. She thought of it as the one great act of her life—saving Andrew.

The knowledge that she would soon be gone and Andrew

would be safe energized her. As he finally slept, she researched on the computer how to get money. Fast.

Loss

On Wednesday when David got home from work late, the house didn't look right. The lights were all on, which was unusual—Anna turned lights off to save energy. The rounded side of their house, like a castle turret, was lit up, reminding him of a lighthouse, warning of the rocky shore ahead. He opened the garage to an empty, gaping spot where Anna's car should have been parked to greet him.

He felt heaviness in the air while struggling to properly fill his lungs as he walked through the door and into the house. Melissa, their neighbor of six years, looked at him with alarm.

"She asked me to babysit," Melissa said as soon as David walked inside.

David barely nodded, his jaw tightening as he listened. Melissa shook slightly, then continued, "She called me this morning and asked me to come over after lunch. Said there was a family emergency. She said she'd be back by dinner. I had to feed Andrew more formula because he drank all the milk she left. She's three hours late and hasn't called or answered her phone."

Numbness overtook David, time changed, each second ticked like a minute. Something told him Anna was not coming back. *I cannot crack. Andrew is depending on me.*

"Everything's going to be ok. I'm sure she's running late. Maybe her phone is out or something. How long have you been here?" David asked, faking a lack of concern.

"Since 2:00," Melissa answered.

Where the hell is she? As they walked to the door, he thanked his neighbor and reassured her that all would be well.

He found a note on his pillow. It read, "*Dear David, I am so sorry. I don't know what else to say. I am not made for mothering. I need to go. Please forgive me and be good to our son (I know you will). I wish I could explain, but I barely understand myself. All I know is that I have to go. Please don't try to find me. Forgive me. I love you and Andrew so much. --Anna*"

Shock overtook him and immobilized his body for long moments. A jumble of thoughts raced through his mind.

Suddenly his body started to move of its own volition, his mind a few steps behind. He marched ahead like a robotic version of himself. He watched as his fingers dialed and listened to his voice beg his wife to call.

Over the past few weeks, David had sensed a problem, but couldn't put his finger on it, like an itch under the skin that couldn't be reached. Everything had looked right—Andrew beamed with health and happiness and Anna seemed joyful, although distant. They had waited so long for this miracle yet David never anticipated how Andrew would change his life. His love for Andrew knocked him over emotionally and left him breathless. Despite his joy, he remained concerned.

He realized that the transition must be hard for his wife. He wondered if she missed work or needed help. When he asked her about these things, she had brushed him off. In fact, she said very little at all. A wall grew between them. He tried to jump over it, pound through it, but it stood impenetrable. He loved his wife deeply, yet even when she was home, he missed her. Maybe she needed time, he decided, but it was hard giving it to her. He kept pounding at the issue, and asked her too many times what was wrong with no response except finally anger. He now wished he had acted differently.

Andrew lay in his arms, content, then started to fuss for sleep. After David fed him another bottle, he walked him to his room and sat in the rocker that he and Anna had chosen for their son. Soft cries accompanied the small wooden squeak of the rocker. David wondered if Andrew sensed his stress. He tried hard to hold it in, but his eyes denied him. Andrew eyes grew heavy and he surrendered to sleep.

David walked downstairs, once Andrew fell asleep. His eyes burned with tears. The pressure threatened to destroy him. He needed to talk. He called Kate and told her the news. Kate told David about Anna's strange call earlier asking her to tow her car.

"I would have called earlier. I assumed you knew. If I had known…"

"Do you think that she is actually at the cabin?" David asked.

"I'm going to leave in a few minutes and check it out. I doubt she's there if she doesn't want to be found, but it's worth a shot."

"I should come with you."

"You have to stay with Andrew. He needs you. I will call you when I get any news."

"Alright," David exhaled.

"This doesn't make any sense. I mean, Anna hasn't seemed herself lately, but I can't believe she'd take off like—" David heard the thump of a dropped phone followed by a rustling sound. "Sorry, I'm putting on my coat and my phone fell," said Kate. "Do you think she's depressed or something?"

"I don't know what to think. Every time I asked her how she was doing, she would get mad, but I couldn't help but keep asking. She seemed so distant."

"At least you've talked to her. She's been ignoring my calls. We haven't talked in a week, which is a long time for us."

"I can't believe she's gone. What the fuck is going on? She has to be depressed—what else could it be?" asked David. He sniffed deeply and cleared his throat, trying to hold back the tears.

"I'm sure we'll find her by the end of the night. Maybe it's lack of sleep or hormones. Don't worry, we'll find her and figure this out," Kate said.

"God, I hope so," David said.

"Have you called the police yet?"

"They said to call tomorrow, after twenty-four hours have passed. Like that's any help."

"We won't even need them. She'll turn up before tomorrow. She wouldn't leave you and Andrew for real. She just wouldn't."

Four hours later, Kate called David to report that there were no signs of Anna at the cabin. No tread marks impacted the snowy driveway but her own.

***

When Anna didn't come home or call that first night, David knew she wasn't dead or hurt, or at least he convinced himself so.

The police were little help. They said they were searching and even had a blip on the news about Anna, but no solid leads came from it. Her phone didn't send any signals for them, so she must not have turned it on or maybe she didn't even have it with her.

David tried to busy his mind with daily tasks: work, Andrew, household chores, dinner. The pain and worry would sneak through the cracks, not to be hindered or ignored. *Nothing is worse than not knowing.*

He called her phone several times a day and left messages or texts with half of those calls. Then he started to send pictures of Andrew so maybe pangs of guilt would bring her home.

The only good news for David was Andrew's continued healthy development. He grew without constraint. He squealed in delight when David came home from work, oblivious to his mother's abandonment. It seemed everyday Andrew did something new. Without him, David knew he would have succumbed to hopelessness.

Finding a suitable caretaker for Andrew proved difficult. Andrew visited five daycares and interviewed several nannies—none of them good enough for Andrew. His neighbor suggested Amy, a college student in the neighborhood. She took night classes and had four younger siblings, which meant she had both time during the day and experience. David interviewed her at the house. During the interview, Andrew started to fuss. Amy didn't hesitate, but picked him up, calmed him, and made him smile within minutes. She was a natural. David felt comfortable and secure with her care, which offered him some relief. He worked much less now, but he still had to work.

Each night while Andrew slept, David went through a ritual. He pored over pictures of his life with Anna, looking for clues as to what went wrong. He allowed himself a stiff drink or two of whiskey while he sent messages to his wife. He watched sports and sometimes cried. Hollowness grew within him.

Anna's friends occasionally broke his routine with visits. They kept him supplied with various casseroles, soups, and breads. They tried to offer hope as well, but it wasn't as well received. He became tired of their voices filled with false hope. Some even sent messages to Anna and encouraged her return.

Kate showed up most often. He knew that sometimes Anna went to Kate first with concerns, and in the past this had fueled a slight animosity which David tried to keep in check. Now he was thankful he had someone next to him who shared in his abandonment. Sometimes Kate and David would talk in circles trying to solve the mystery of Anna. Often, they would sit and stare at the television, no words necessary, sharing their pain.

***

When the phone rang and David saw Joanne's number on his phone, he thought she must have found out about Anna. Kate and David had decided not to tell Joanne or Clare about Anna's disappearance yet. Part of him suspected that it wasn't the right thing to do, but they didn't want to cause Clare stress.

"I have been calling Anna's phone all day. I need to talk to her. Now."

David could hear the tension in Joanne's voice. "What is it? What's wrong?"

"My mom ... oh God ..." Joanne choked out between sobs, "has been in a crash."

"Is she okay? What happened?"

David heard some muffled sounds through the receiver. "Uh ... no, she's not okay," Joanne cried, "she didn't make it." David felt the earth shift. It didn't seem possible. How could this have happened?

"I ... I'm so sorry ... my God ... I can't believe—"

"--Is Anna around? I need to talk to her."

"I should have called you. I don't know how to explain this, but ... Anna left me about a month ago."

"What?"

"She—"

Joanne's sobbing ceased and her voice became cold. "I heard you, I just don't get it. What about Andrew?"

"He's here with me."

"She just up and leaves her baby and husband? She's always fuckin' running away. That is her M.O.," Joanne sighed. "I will call you when I have the arrangements worked out. I guess I'll have everything here, since Anna's not around. It's not like Mom has anything left in Michigan anyway."

***

The moment David got off the phone he burned with anger toward Anna. He exhausted his patience with her, and now a sour, bitterness filled the hole that Anna had left. *How could she be so irresponsible? How could she not tell me what was going on or what she was going through? After all this time, I deserved that much.*

Clare's death threatened to break open fissures in David's carefully constructed, but crumbling, composure. He had conflicting emotions when it came to Clare, and it confused him. Anna had kept Clare at a great distance since David first met her. They visited Clare only a handful of times a year when they drove to Indiana for the obligatory holiday visits, and even those Anna kept short. Whenever he saw Clare, he felt nothing but warmth for the woman who had brought him Anna's blue eyes, and sorrow for all Clare and Anna had been through. He didn't express his thoughts to Anna because he understood that the topic was off limits.

Telling Anna of her mother's passing by voicemail or text message seemed so wrong, yet David knew he had to tell her somehow. He worried what this would do to his wife, but she should know. Maybe it would even bring her home. He decided on a voicemail.

Moments later, he received a text. When he saw Anna's name on his phone, he knelt down and gave a prayer of thanks, briefly ecstatic on a grim day — Anna was still alive.

I am ok. Tell Joanne I'm sorry. Please find happiness and peace. I'm not coming back. I love you and Andrew forever.

***

Kate and David drove to Indiana together. Andrew fought the pull of sleep and remained fitfully awake in the car seat until they were five minutes from the funeral home.

"I'll stay with Andrew while he naps in the car," Kate said.

"Are you sure?"

"Joanne doesn't want to see me anyway. I don't think she cares for me much. I don't think I'll bring her much comfort. Anyway, the last thing you need is Andrew to be fussy because he's tired."

"I don't know what to say to her."

"Just be there for her. There aren't any good words at a time like this."

"I feel so bad for her. Her family's all gone except for Anna, and she's not even here."

No one should be alone in their grief, and David knew this. The sisters' extended family consisted only of Trent's two brothers, and they hadn't spoken to the family for years before Trent's death and didn't attend his funeral either. Clare's only sibling had died many years ago from cancer. David felt he was a poor substitute for what Joanne deserved at the moment, yet he would offer his best.

Kate stayed silent. David looked back at Andrew. "Ok. If you need anything, come in or text me."

***

The clouds hung low in the dark and gloomy sky. They hinted of rain or snow. Many people commented on the lack of sunlight as they walked in the funeral home. Joanne hadn't even noticed it until she heard the words. It could have been eighty degrees and sunny on that first day of March and she would not have noticed. She had wrapped herself tightly in her grief, her family all gone. Sure, she had Anna, but that didn't count. In her mind, she disowned her sister years ago, and now, as far as she was concerned, it would be official.

David walked in, said something, and stood by her side, a comforting, silent presence.

An hour later he ushered her to the sitting lounge. "Would you like some coffee or something to eat?" he asked.

Joanne bristled at his question. He had awakened her from a sad trance, and his pretense of a relationship between them that didn't exist annoyed her. "You don't have to pretend we're close or that you care. I'll be fine. In fact, you might piss off your missing wife by being nice to me."

"I know you and Anna have issues. They're not *my* issues. I think it's sad and ridiculous you *both* can't get past them. We may not be blood, but we're family. I don't want to make you mad, I just want to help. If you want me to sit across the room and not talk to you, then that's what I'll do."

"I think that would be best. No offense."

"That's fine. I'll be here if you need me." David drifted back into the viewing room.

Joanne later followed, but sat a few rows behind him. She watched as he talked with a group of women from Clare's women's group at church. They had worked together to orchestrate food drives and activities to earn money for their local food bank. She overheard him say, "I had no idea that Clare was so involved in her church." *Of course he didn't. Because Anna didn't know anything about our mother. All she did was try to brush Mom off.*

The church ladies ambled on, and others took their place.

"How did you know Clare?" he asked.

"We're part of her art group," a lady named Reva answered.

"She was an amazing artist. She painted incredible watercolors."

I bet he didn't know that either.

"The last few years, she taught art classes at the community center. They were very popular."

Joanne began to feel remorse for her behavior, a soft spot for David grew by the moment as she watched him talk to her mother's friends. She did not want to do this alone, and even with all these people around she stood isolated by grief. He was, after all, the last of her family. *He must get it a little since he lost his father not long ago. Damn Anna for checking out yet again. When it counts, she is never around. I will never forgive her. Her husband, though, I can deal with him.*

Joanne walked past the chairs separating them and sat down next to David. "I apologize for my rudeness. Forget what I said," she said, then paused. "There is something uncomfortable I have to say, though." David remained silent. "I do like you. You're right, we're the only family here—we should stick together. I am just so angry at Anna that I directed it toward you. This is probably the final straw for us. Her and I. How can she not be here? What is she thinking?"

"I honestly don't know. I'm worried though."

"I'm not worried. She's just where she always is when there's trouble. Gone."

David's lips tightened, and he looked down. He took a deep breath. "I don't think we should talk about Anna right now. I understand why you're upset, but let's just keep off that topic. Deal?"

"Deal," Joanne agreed.

Joanne realized that without some sort of assistance she might have just found a quiet place to hide until the wake was over. David served as a buffer when she could no longer talk to people about her mother.

Later, Kate walked in the funeral home holding Andrew in her arms.

"I'm so sorry for your loss," Kate said.

Joanne looked at Andrew. She felt a connection to him. They had both lost their mothers. "Can I hold Andrew?"

"Sure." Kate handed Andrew to her, and Joanne moved across the room.

"Hi, little guy," she said to her nephew. "Your mom is awful, but you're adorable." She hugged him and sat down. He bubbled with energy. He burst into a loud litany of baby talk, oblivious to the sadness around him. People looked her way and smiled the smile that babies generate. For a brief moment, Andrew pulled her out of her drowning sadness.

***

Joanne remembered little about the day of her mother's funeral. She knew that, like a curtain, the clouds withdrew and revealed the bright sun, which offered no warmth. David sat by her, and Kate next to him. People stood and said things, but what words were uttered she didn't remember. Lips moved, but all she heard in her head was her mother's voice, saying things of no importance, but a treasure just the same.

The unseasonable, extreme cold encouraged a brief graveside service. Joanne wanted nothing more than to go home, alone. *Why do people insist on being together after such horrific events?* She followed David wordlessly through the rest of the afternoon. When he offered her food, she ate a bite and pushed around the rest. When others talked, she nodded, while inside her head she hoped they would soon leave.

Joanne never imagined that her mother would be taken so suddenly. She had put such care into her mother's health and longevity, making sure she ate properly, took her pills, and saw the doctor, that she assumed Mother would have a long life. All those years she had worked to keep her mother safe from her illness, only to have her taken by the recklessness of a driver paying attention to a phone instead of the road. What would her life be about now that she didn't have her mother to care for?

David insisted on staying with Joanne for at least few days after the services, depending how things went. Joanne reluctantly agreed. She knew she needed help, although she didn't want to admit it. Kate left in a rental car soon after the service.

David made himself busy when Andrew slept or played. Joanne had him help with things she couldn't deal with alone — sorting through her mom's belongings and organizing and freezing the casseroles that kept coming to the door.

They developed a friendship, and by mutual agreement, they didn't speak of Anna, although Joanne thought of her often. Joanne fumed over Anna's absence, although she would have fumed at her presence just as easily. *How could she be so cold as to abandon her husband, son, and grieving sister? What kind of woman does such things?*

Andrew provided the distraction and comic relief that she needed with his loud and boisterous ways. Joanne helped care for Andrew during their two-week visit. He was the only bright spot in her dark world. She couldn't help but fall in love with Andrew and his contagious smile. He was a lifeline for her, keeping her afloat, and she would forever be indebted to him for that. *How could such an angel emerge from such a devil of a sister?*

***

Midway through David's stay with Joanne, he helped her empty Clare's closet and waited while she painstakingly decided the fate of each item left behind. The day physically and mentally exhausted David, and he wanted a beer or two to unwind. The fireplace blazed with a fire he had started. The shades of orange and yellow calmed him. Andrew slept in the spare room.

"I don't usually drink, but this tastes good," Joanne commented. "You know, if you weren't here to help, that stuff might have stayed there ... maybe forever. Thanks for staying."

Joanne's sincere gratitude shocked him after she had teased him all week about kicking him out. "No problem. I'm sure you would have done the same."

"I doubt that," she said, drinking deeply, "but now I would." She stared into the fire. "I don't know how Anna did it, but she found a decent guy, although she doesn't deserve you."

Joanne had broken their agreement not to discuss Anna. David let it slide. He hoped she would say no more about his wife, his Achilles heel.

"I know you've had your difficulties with her, but she's a good woman, Joanne." He wished he understood the troubles in the sisters' relationship. "I know one thing," David said, changing the subject, "Andrew adores you."

"The feeling's mutual. He's got personality."

After a long silence the conversation turned to Clare. "Did your mom ever want to live on her own?"

"Yes. We talked about it a few times over the years. The problem was I think she would have blown off her meds. She'd think she was better and want to stop. I had to make sure she kept taking them."

"It seems like if she was feeling ok, she'd want to keep taking them."

"That's not how it works. There were unpleasant side effects, and I think she just wanted to think that she was normal and didn't need them."

"You took good care of her, Joanne. You're a good daughter."

Joanne couldn't respond, as her eyes welled up and threatened to spill over.

When Joanne opened up to David, he realized how trapped, yet comforted, she'd been by caring for her mother. He wondered how Clare would have functioned living alone if she had been given the chance. From what he heard from her friends, she was feisty and independent. Joanne seemed to have feared that if she didn't control things, Clare's illness would swallow her up again. Right or wrong, she had sacrificed much for her mother. No wonder Joanne looked at Anna with such bitterness.

They sat in silence and watched the fire. Many topics hung between them that David wanted to talk about but lacked the courage to breach.

David's devotion to helping Joanne wasn't a completely selfless act. He gained blessed, although brief, distraction from his troubles. An added benefit was what he learned during his stay. He learned more about Joanne (whom his wife never spoke of except to berate) during his visit than he had in all the time he'd known her. He glimpsed deeply into Clare's life too. He was sorry it had to happen too late, but grateful to know her better nonetheless.

Come Home

At home, without as many distractions, David became even more obsessed with trying to contact his missing wife. He captured and sent images of Andrew while he smiled and played, showcasing his adorable moments. Hours passed as he wrote and rearranged words in an attempt to find the sentences that would bring his wife home. Occasionally, he would flat out beg her to respond. More than once, he boiled over with anger at what he could not understand. He needed to hear his wife say that she would reconsider her decision to abandon their family.

Day after day he hoped, and night after night disappointment crawled in. One night he cracked. Without thought, he charged into the garage and broke everything he could wrap his hands around—wrenches, screwdrivers, and golf clubs didn't yield to his anger, but the windows to his car succumbed to it. By the time he had finished, glass littered the garage floor like broken ideas and hopes. He didn't realize his muscles ached with tension until they released in a moment of respite, only to find more misery waiting when he realized the mess he'd made. He pulled himself together, walked back inside, and tried again to compose the words in an email that would stir his wife to respond.

Dear Anna,

I've decided that I can't have our son not know how beautiful, intelligent, and wonderful his mom is, so I am going to write about our story so when he's old enough, he can read it. Remember the first year we were together? We were inseparable. I never told you this, but the first time I saw you, you were walking down Main Street and I followed you into Savory Scents. You were so beautiful. I'd never done anything like that in my life, but it was the best thing I ever did. You and Andrew are the best things that have ever happened to me.

It would be better for Andrew to hear the story from both of us. He deserves to have us both. He needs his mom as much as I need my wife.

Before Andrew was born, I longed to see your features in our child's face. I've seen that and more in our son, but I need to see you. Whatever has happened, don't be scared. We can work through it. I will be here when you are ready to come home.

I can't live like this, wondering every day where you are and what happened. I want to be there for you and help, but I can't if you're not here. Please email me or call or something to let me know that you are okay. It's torture not to hear your voice. If you ever loved me, Anna, please call.

Your mom is at rest at Peaceful Pines Cemetery. It's a beautiful place.

Joanne was devastated and couldn't understand when I told her I didn't know where you were. I know you won't believe this, but she needs her sister right now.

Please let me know you are okay. I need to know. Please give me that much.

Love Always,
David

Words were effective, but only if they are read. David doubted that Anna would read his words. After the initial text from Anna after David told her of her mother's death, the police tracked the call and said it came from the U.P. Their forces north investigated, but found nothing. Maybe someone had stolen her phone or maybe they were wrong, but David was done with words. If they couldn't figure it out, he'd find someone who could.

All this time he believed that she would come home of her own accord. With a sinking sensation, he realized his miscalculation. Anna must be confused. He would find her, no matter what, and bring her home — kicking and screaming, if necessary.

He decided to hire a private detective.

***

The office of Grendal Moore spoke of a man who spent little time there and didn't worry about its state of cleanliness — dinginess reigned. David could be messy, too, but never in his office. Grendal looked to be somewhere in his sixties. He had a scruffy gray beard and thick gray hair which stuck out in various directions from his head. He had a gruff and direct demeanor.

David's first impression of Grendal wasn't a good one. Yet he was there, so he might as well have a conversation with the man. After all, he came highly recommended by a colleague of his.

"Hello, I'm David Montagna," David said and held out his hand.

"Yes, that is what it says on my calendar," Grendal laughed. They shook hands. Grendal pointed his large hand at a chair and said, "Sit down, David. Let's see what I can do for you."

"What kind of experience do you have in finding missing persons?"

"A lot." Grendal settled back in his chair, wove his hands together, and proceeded to give David an education. "There's three kinds of missing persons. The ones who don't want to be found. Those can take a week to a month to locate. The ones who haven't really tried to hide, but took off. Those are quick. Then there are missing people who are, well, how to put it .... missing because they're dead. Which one you think you got?"

"Um ... I have the first kind. My wife, Anna, is the first kind. I'm not sure what happened, but I know she doesn't want to be found."

"You love each other?"

"Of course. I wouldn't be here if I didn't."

"Sometimes, men come to me because they want to find the one who left so they can teach 'em a lesson. Is that your motive here?" The detective's puffy gray eyebrows lifted in an accusing manner.

"No!" David said, louder than he meant. "I mean no," he said, more calmly. "Sorry. These weeks ... I don't know what happened to my wife. We had just had a baby, everything seemed fine. Then she was gone. I need to bring her home. I know she's alive. She sent me a text about two weeks ago."

"A lot can happen in fourteen days," Grendal said, his eyes wandering around the room. He looked at David, tilted his head to the left, and said, "That is good news, though. That could be helpful. We'll just go through this list of questions," he nodded as he picked up his clipboard, "and I'll start looking for your wife."

Part Three

Senses

From day one Leena knew that Anna existed in a fragile state. It seemed a strong wind could break her carefully constructed house of lies. Leena dutifully nodded at the sentences Anna spewed about her life and wondered all the while what purpose they served. Anna's fabricated story unfolded one evening at Bart's, when there wasn't a single customer in the bar. Leena had asked Anna a number of times since they'd met what brought her to Mikamaw, and finally an answer came.

Anna said, "My husband beats me. If he finds me, he will kill me. I don't know what I'm going to do, but I'm going to lie low for a bit until I figure it out. He won't find me here."

"Did you ever call the police? Or buy a gun?"

"I ... it wouldn't have worked. He would have finished me. But I'm safe now. Just don't say anything to anyone," Anna insisted.

"Course not. Your secret's safe with me," Leena assured her.

Anna's eyes exposed her lies, though, try as she might to veil them. They twitched slightly and looked at everything but Leena while she told her tale. *What is she lying about?* Leena wondered. She knew that stories had to come out in their own time, like a good wine needs to age, or they ended up spoiled. She decided to wait to ask Anna the truth, since she was obviously not yet ready.

Over the weeks that Anna worked at the bar, Leena observed her like a painting or puzzle, trying to decipher the mystery, but few clues came her way.

Anna's chest and waist size had decreased since her arrival, and Leena suspected that Anna had recently given birth to a child. Anna's Bart's Bar t-shirt originally stretched across her chest so snugly that the first B and last R were hidden from view, which Leena never wanted to notice, but couldn't help. Now the all the letters were readable with fabric to spare. *Where is the child?*

Despite the mystery and the lies of the newcomer, Leena found herself liking her. She suspected that behind the walls Anna put up, there existed a decent woman in trouble.

The Nature of Denial

***

Leena had a special knack, or curse, as she called it, for knowing things before other people did. The strange sensations, indicating doom, would strike her body suddenly. The hairs would stand up on her arms, her heart would race into overdrive, and there would always be some telling smell.

In the fifth grade, she had known Sarah Stark would break her arm when she reached the top of the monkey bars. She smelled dirt, felt pain in her arm that she knew was intended for Sarah, and then watched her fall from her perch. It happened too fast for words to form on Leena's lips to warn her friend, and then time cruelly slowed as Sarah fell to the ground, like a slow-motion video with no stop button, her face covered in dirt, her arm twisted at an odd angle.

On June 12 of Leena's twentieth year on this earth, all the hairs on her arms stood up and she smelled sawdust and gasoline, compounded by a crushing sensation that stretched the length of her body. She knew before the phone rang that her father had died, a victim of a logging accident, killed by the work that he loved. That's when she decided that her premonitions were a curse.

Only once did her gift give Leena comfort. Years before, when her mom was diagnosed with cancer, Leena waited for the sudden knowledge of her mother's death and after some time, realized that the lack of uncontrollable sensations signaled hope. She knew her mom would survive and guessed that she had many years ahead of her.

Two years before, she had experienced her most intense premonition. At first, she feared a heart attack as she stood doubled over the kitchen counter, unable to breathe. Then her body hairs stood up and she smelled burning rubber. She could feel heat coming from somewhere other than her own body, and she watched her skin turn red from it. Try as she might to keep the truth from her mind, she knew Frank wasn't coming home. Ever. When the police came to inform her that her husband's soul had left the good earth for the great beyond, they saw that she was already in the grip of grief.

Leena hoped to never experience those dreadful premonitions again; she prayed for it with each nightly prayer. She did her best to move forward, to practice sisu, as her mom had taught her. It meant to persevere, to be determined not to let life bowl you over. In other words, giving up was not a viable option. All her life, her mom had reminded her of this word from their Finnish background and how it applied to all things in life.

On a snowy evening at Bart's, over a week after Anna started working with her, Leena smelled the fresh, dirt-churning, fish-laden smell of large waves over the smell of grease and beer at Bart's. The hair stood up on her arms, and she saw Anna floating in the water near the pier, face down, moving with the force of the fierce waves. Then she saw a ghost-like vision of Anna walking down a snow-laden First Street.

"Toward the lake!" She screamed as she ran to the kitchen. "Lloyd, we got a girl to save, grab your coat." *Please don't be too late. Please, God, let me save her. Let this curse do some good.*

"Hurry, Lloyd," she yelled as she jammed her feet into her boots, grabbed her coat, and ran out the door.

"Where are we going?" Lloyd yelled after her as he rushed to follow her out the door.

"To save someone. Run!" she yelled as she bolted toward her Suburban. She hastily scraped icy snow off her windshield, leaving a small hole of visibility to guide them to the lake. The wind howled in protest as they drove. When they pulled into the small parking lot of what the locals called Rusty Pier on Lake Superior, Leena prayed that she was not too late as she hurried out of her truck.

The wind pushed against them as they ran to the shore. The last of the daylight dimly lit the pier. They struggled through the misty, snow-swirling wind and splashes of angry waves toward the pier.

Leena slowed her pace slightly to accommodate the sheet of solid ice when she reached the pier. A figure lay motionless at the far end of the pier. Anna. Leena feared the worst, angry at her curse of sight for not warning her sooner. She cautiously moved over the icy surface to her friend's oddly postured body. Freezing blood pooled around Anna's head. Leena reached out and touched her body. Warmth. "Be careful, Lloyd," she urged as he picked up Anna's limp body.

"My God, Leen...how'd you? She's lucky she's not frozen. What the hell happened here?" he asked over the wind as he carried Anna's limp form.

Leena yelled to be heard over the elements. "I don't know, Lloyd...We've got to get to Marquette Hospital. Quick!"

**

Leena drove quickly but carefully. She didn't want to kill them all in a race to the hospital on the slick roads. Lloyd propped Anna up against him, his arm awkwardly around her, looking uncomfortable as he held up her limp body. Minutes passed like hours as they slowly proceeded to the hospital on treacherous roads. Silence pervaded the vehicle.

Anna stirred against Lloyd's arm. Her eyes opened and she expelled a slurred string of syllables. Then her words started to coagulate into comprehensible chunks and words. "Oh, my head. What happened? We were going to go swimming." Leena and Lloyd shared a concerned look in the rearview mirror.

Anna squinted her eyes. She blinked. "How'd *you* get here?" She pointed a shaking finger at Leena, then jumped a bit when she noticed she wasn't alone in the back. "Why are you touching me?" she asked as she pushed Lloyd's arm off of her. "What are you--"

"It's okay, Anna. You fell, and we're going to get you looked at. Just relax until we get there," Leena reassured her.

Anna said nothing more for miles. When they approached the Marquette Hospital, Anna became frantic. "They will find me if I go to the hospital! I can't go. I can't!"

"We'll figure something out, Anna. I will keep you safe, but if you don't get looked at, you could die. We have to make sure your head is okay."

"What's so wrong with dying? I'd rather take my chances." The words were barely audible, but Leena heard.

Leena abruptly stopped the vehicle. She turned back to look at Anna. "Look at me." Anna's eyes seemed troubled, and her focus wavered from Leena to somewhere behind her. "I don't give a damn what you're running from. You will *not* put your death on my conscience. We're friends, and friends don't pull that kind of shit. So, kindly get off your ass and do something unselfish—get your head looked at, whether you want to or not!"

Leena didn't wait for a response. One door slammed shut, another opened as she helped Anna out of the car.

"He's going to find me if I go to the hospital."

"They have laws about that stuff. Privacy laws. You won't be found. Trust me." Leena hoped that she was right as she helped Anna to the hospital doors.

***

Hours later, Anna lay in a hospital bed, her hands and ears defrosted and bandaged. A deep itch and ache in her fingertips begged to be violently scratched. Leena told her that the MRI had revealed no bleeding from her brain—she was lucky. She had mild frostbite, bruises, and cuts from a concussion-inducing fall on the ice—not to mention a killer hangover and headache. She wordlessly went through the tests, and she slept intermittently. Leena stayed by her side like a mother bird. The doctors decided that Anna needed to be observed. Too exhausted to fight about it, sleep began to claim her. Before it did, she looked up, droopy eyed, at Leena and said, "You didn't have to do this."

"Please, don't mention it. I'll be here in the morning to pick you up. Get some sleep. I've got to go home now." With that she touched Anna's shoulder softly and left.

Anna didn't have the energy to correct Leena. She wasn't thanking her—she meant that Leena didn't have to *save* her.

Release

Leena and Ron had known each other most of their lives. His friendship had anchored her over the two hellish years while she wrestled with grief for her husband. She was stronger now, but still needed his help and friendship. Ron never failed her. Last year when the snow came up to her roof and she needed to see sunlight out her windows for sanity's sake, Ron dug a path. When her toilet clogged because her youngest threw a rattle in and flushed, Ron fixed her plumbing. He never questioned or admonished her. His steady, calm demeanor relaxed her at intense moments.

When she called him at the last minute and asked if he would relieve her mother from babysitting while Leena waited at the hospital with Anna, he didn't ask why, he just said, "Okay." Leena couldn't ask her mother to stay late into the night. Jewel wouldn't admit it, but her chronic back pain only gave her so many good hours, and chasing Hank around too long would wear away at her back and leave her in intense pain. Leena wouldn't have asked her to watch them for so long to begin with, but her regular babysitter had the flu and Ron was at work.

The last thing Leena thought she wanted when she pulled into her driveway from the hospital was a long conversation, yet, that's what transpired, and she was grateful for it. Talking to Ron about the tense night eased the stress within her.

"I didn't realize Anna was in so much trouble. Are you sure she was trying to commit suicide?" asked Ron.

"Without a doubt. I don't know how it went wrong, but thank God she didn't succeed.

"Why didn't you tell them it was a suicide attempt? What if she tries it again?"

"I don't think she will. I'll keep an eye on her here, and if she seems a threat to herself, I'll send her back. The shorter her stay in the hospital, the better, just in case she is telling the truth about her husband."

Leena absentmindedly held Anna's phone, which she saved from the icy pier. She looked at it and said, "I guess this is probably junk."

"Try it out," Ron suggested.

Leena turned on the phone. The screen lit up with a picture of a handsome man and a baby. "That must be her husband. Is that her baby? You know, I noticed, and don't think I'm weird ... but I noticed that since she's been here her boobs have shrunk."

Ron laughed. "I didn't know you were a breast woman. What *are* you talking about?"

"Ok, female health 101, after women have babies their boobs grow to feed the babies milk. When they are no longer feeding them, their boobs shrink back over time."

"You think she has baby? Do you think it died or something or the husband is hurting the baby too?"

"I'm not sure what to think. I'm just going to try to help her and not question too much."

"You're a better person than me." In the pause that followed, Ron looked at Leena in a way that unnerved her. "I couldn't do that for someone and not ask them what the hell was going on."

"You did that for me when I called. You didn't ask a word. You just came to my aid."

"Well, that's different. I'd do anything for you." Ron said the words full of serious emotion. Leena looked up, expecting him to make a joke, but his eyes shone with intent that she didn't recognize.

Leena stood up, frightened by the affection in Ron's voice. "Thanks again for helping. I've got to get some sleep and get over to the hospital in the morning."

"Why don't I come by first thing and watch the kids while you're gone?"

"Thanks, but my mom agreed to come out. It shouldn't be too long."

"I'll just come and assist her. Sometimes it takes forever to get out of the hospital."

After they said their goodbyes, Leena went upstairs to bed. If she hadn't known better, she would have thought that Ron had a crush on her. He wouldn't do that to her, she decided. He knew better.

***

Anna slept deeply, as if she, like the world outside her window, were blanketed by the sleepiness of the snow, resting through a long winter. Hospitals sometimes keep people awake, but no interruption kept her attention long. Sleep carried her worries away. When the light woke her in the morning, she felt like she had slept for days. Her body ached from it, and her mind was restless.

Should I have been nicer to Mom? Did I treat her wrong? Will God be mad at me? Is there a God? What are Andrew and David doing? No, don't think of them! Why am I alive? I should have fallen into the water instead of on the pier. Her mind vacillated between thoughts of her mother, sister, David and Andrew. Snapshots from her life appeared in her mind in random order.

She thought of how her mother had too many sides to her. It was as if she were more than one person. One Halloween, during a manic phase, her mom had energetically allowed Anna and Joanne to walk farther than they should have, not calculating the length of the walk back, and then she became furious when the girls complained that they were tired. She began to throw their candy to decrease the weight they had to carry until the girls shrieked for her to stop.

One time when Anna was sick, her mom let her watch her favorite movie, *Neverending Story*, over and over while they snuggled together under the quilt. Anna felt so loved that day. Her mother had a very loving side, punctuated by an unpredictable and sometimes harsh side. Anna realized that she had blocked out the pleasant memories, focusing on her mom's insufficiencies. Until now, Anna never fully considered that her mother didn't control the illness that snaked through her brain and emotions. When her mom had stopped taking meds, Anna took it as a personal assault. Forgiveness rarely entered her heart, and this left a hole for bitterness to fill. She wished she could turn back time, treat her mother differently, and beg for her forgiveness.

Anna could almost see why Joanne hated her. Joanne had made it her life's mission to care for their mom, while failing to live her own life. Joanne had found her own kind of bitterness. Anna's head started to ache with the immensity of her thoughts. She asked the nurse for more pain medicine.

***

Leena showed up at 10:00 to pick her up. Anna didn't know what to think of Leena. Yes, she emanated warmth and assuring determination, but her eyes looked *through* Anna. *Was she friend or foe?* She worried that her secrets might come tumbling out.

Silence flooded the air for most of the drive back to Mikamaw. When they turned down Latson instead of First Street, Anna became agitated. "Did you hit *your* head?" Anna asked, trying to make joke out of her concern. "You're going to your house, not mine."

"Doc's orders are that ya not be alone for a bit with the head thing. *My orders* are that you aren't alone until inside your head — and by that I mean your emotions — are better. I got some stuff from your place. Ron let me in. Only thing is … you'll have to put up with my kids. I'll try to keep 'em quiet until your head feels better."

This is worse than being dead. I want to be alone. Snow-covered trees passed by in a blur outside the window. She wished she were on the other side. "I think I'll be fine. You've got enough to do."

"Listen … I didn't tell them about your suicide attempt. We can go back if you'd like and they can deal with it. Or you can stay with me." She paused, then asked, "What'll it be?"

"I guess I'll stay. It doesn't sound like I have much of a choice."

***

Leena's two-story house was her paid-in-full pride and joy. Frank's life insurance had paid her enough to cover the mortgage, but she'd much rather have her husband. They had been the rare kind of couple who were still in love after fifteen years of marriage.

Not a day went by that she didn't think of Frank. He was taken too soon. He didn't even get to witness the birth of his youngest son, Hank. It had been the strangest agony of Leena's life, childbirth surrounded by the sorrow of death.

From the outside, the saltbox house didn't look like much. It screamed for paint and landscaping, yet, inside it radiated a warmth Leena spent a good amount of time and effort to achieve. Within its country charms, the various signs of children's play were strewn about like abandoned ideas.

***

Anna had heard Leena talk of her kids, but she tried not to listen, so she couldn't remember if there were two or five kids living at the house. One toddled up to Anna, his cheeks covered with some gooey substance, followed by an older, slightly bent woman, who ambled behind him.

"Thanks, Ma," Leena said. Anna could see the resemblance in the discerning brown eyes of Leena's mother, although they were nearly hidden by tired, worn lids.

"Little Hank here's been on a rampage, my girl. He dumped all the toys out of his toy box and won't let me clean his face. Little stinker," she said with obvious love.

Hank ran over to his grandma, laughing the whole while, and put his sticky hands around her legs. "Wuv gama!" he screamed and ran out of the room without even stopping to notice Anna.

Leena and her mother laughed at Hank's antics. "That's Hank, my tireless one. This is my mom, also known as Jewel."

"Yes, my parents were ahead of their time in new-age names. I like the more traditional ones myself. Anyway, nice to meet you," Jewel said and smiled at Anna with her worn teeth and tilted her head of thick, gray, curly hair. A slight grimace crossed her face as she started to shuffle toward the door. "Got to go. I need some drugs and a nap."

Leena helped her mother with her coat and held open the door.

"I'll see you later for dinner, Ma. Get some rest, and thanks for watching Hank."

"Ok. No need for thanks. Oh, by the way, Ron stopped by but I sent him out. I'm not helpless, you know."

After Jewel left, Leena explained that her mom's back was as crooked as a question mark and despite surgery and years of other therapies, she suffered from chronic pain.

"Sorry to hear that."

"Me too. Thanks. I guess you've got to deal with what life gives you and do your best to move on. You've got to have sisu."

"What's that?"

"I forgot for a minute you're not from here. It's a Finnish word. It means a lot of things, really. My mom lives by it. It means sticking it out, no matter what, being tough, resilient—that sort of thing."

"Oh. I've never heard that word."

"I think it's what's got her through these painful years. Otherwise, you're stuck in the "why me?" mentality. I have been there, and it is no place to be, let me tell you." She paused with her thoughts and then seemed to snap out of them. "Don't mind me. Sometimes I rant, as everyone else calls it. Let's get ya settled."

Leena led Anna upstairs and showed her the guest room. "It used to be our study, but now it's a playroom. For now, it's your oasis."

Leena tidied the toys. Anna's things were neatly stacked on the futon and the table beside it. "I just picked up some basic clothes until you have a chance to decide exactly what you need. I hope you don't mind. Let me know if you need anything."

"Thanks. I hope you don't mind, but what I really need is some rest."

"I understand. I will shut the door here so Hank doesn't bother you. Feel free to watch TV if you'd like."

Finally, Anna sat alone with her thoughts.

She was interrupted by a knock at the door. The door opened and Leena walked in. "I forgot ... this was at the pier with you. I plugged it in, and it looks like it charged, so here you go." She handed Anna her phone and left again, closing the door behind her.

Anna couldn't bear to deal with the phone. She hid it under her clothes and stretched out on the futon. Emotions mixed and mingled and images danced together senselessly as she slumbered through the pain.

Water permeated her dreams. She heard waves and felt a sloshing sensation on her mouth. *Am I drowning?* She woke with a start to a golden retriever licking her face. Hank stared at her with a smirk on his lips. "Spks like you," he laughed. Her face betrayed her thoughts and she smiled at Hank's contagious merriment. "Wat dink?" he asked, offering her his sippy cup. She sat up.

"No, thanks."

"Who wu?"

"I'm Anna."

"Wu sick?"

"No, I just bumped my head. I'm okay."

"Ight back," he said and walked away holding up one finger. He came back with his doctor kit. The dog stared at her longingly, wanting something.

"I make beddo." He opened up his kit and took out an oversized, blue toy thermometer. He put it under Anna's arm and turned it to the sad face. "Wu still sick. Ight back." He made the minute sign again and came back with toilet paper trailing behind him. Anna thought of her and Kate decorating Tom's house with toilet paper. It made her smile, briefly. Hank proceeded to wrap her head in toilet paper, but mostly he piled it on her head. He stepped back to survey his work and looked pleased. "West now," he said and then he and the dog left. She felt compelled to follow, but the feeling quickly dissipated. Isolation and quiet called to her.

Rest

Five days passed while Anna lay attached to Leena's futon like a lifeline and endured the occasional visit from nurse Hank. His cute smile, often accented with sticky goo of one sort or another, grew on Anna, although she tried her best to deny it.

Leena gave Anna space. She offered her food, a place to stay, and friendship. Anna appreciated it, but preferred solitude.

Anna's health gradually improved, though she feared to acknowledge it. Her headache faded away, and the anxiety abated enough for her to remain calm for longer periods. She had mastered moments of denial over the thoughts that most wanted to infiltrate her mind.

All of the rest caused her body to scream for movement, lest her full anxiety come back. In all her life, she had never been one to sit around much—she preferred to be with people, do things, keep busy.

To escape a growing claustrophobia, she finally walked outside. Leena stood beside the house, smoking.

"Sneaking smokes, I see?"

"Yes, I know, it's awful. Sometimes I come out here when Hank naps." She held the baby monitor in her hand. "My kids don't know I'm a closet smoker. I will quit one of these days."

Anna looked into the woods that sprawled behind Leena's house, a seemingly endless forest. "Don't you miss *people*, living here?" she wondered aloud. "No offense or anything. I just wouldn't be able to handle all the quiet."

"We all need quiet, whether we know it or not. I just know it," Leena said with a slight smirk. "This," she said while motioning with an open hand toward the surrounding woods, "is my grounding. My connection to God. I couldn't live without it. Nature is a part of me."

"Sorry, I guess I was kind of rude. I'm just feeling cranky." Remorseful, Anna added, "Thanks for all you've done for me. You didn't need to, but I appreciate it."

"No problem. I should thank you. Hank's been so busy doctoring you that it's given me a chance to get a few things done." Anna smiled at that. They sat in silence for a while, looking at the woods beyond.

Leena said, "I know you're having a rough time, and if you want to talk—"

"I don't, thanks."

"Well, at some point you will, and when you do, you can talk to me."

"I appreciate it. I'm feeling a lot better now. I just need to move around. My body is achy from all the rest."

"Or, if you want me to find a professional—"

"Can we talk about something else?" Anna insisted.

"Sure. Speaking of movement, how would you like to go for a walk in the woods tomorrow? I know this beautiful hike that's not too far a walk, if you're up for it."

Anna wondered if she was only imagining it, or if Leena talked like a philosophy professor. She pushed the thought aside. She owed her host a lot and her body needed some movement, so she accepted the invitation.

***

Leena noticed a crumpled pamphlet in a pair of Anna's pants that she emptied to wash. It read …

The Upper Peninsula of Michigan offers unique splendor due to its violent geological past and the travels of glaciers over its surface. There are many different microcosms of beauty there, each with unique features. From the rugged Porcupine Mountains, to the vast shorelines of the Great Lakes, continuing to the Mackinac Bridge, there are many wonders to see. Rocks rich in varying color and type, swift changes in elevation, miles upon miles covered with thick forests, and ever-present water reveal the vastness in which land can be formed and altered on earth.

The brochure went on to discuss seasons. The description of winter caught her eye.

Winter is a near-permanent condition in the Upper Peninsula. It occasionally breaks for the other seasons, but it lingers in the shadows—waiting to return. A certain hardiness of character is required in those who endure her magnificence. For the most part, Yoopers make peace with winter and work to find the splendor in it through their appreciation of the recreation and beauty it offers.

The brochure went on, but Leena reread that part. She liked it how it described the Upper Peninsula and the character of the people. The people had to have sisu to endure the winters here. One thing it failed to mention, though, was the spiritual element of all that natural beauty. It could transform people. Leena wanted to share the healing power of nature with Anna. She prayed that the spirit of nature might fill Anna with hope.

So many questions about Anna revolved through Leena's mind. She sorely wanted to ask them, but she knew better. When you poke at a cornered animal they lash out to protect themselves, and the same is often true with people. Leena guessed that Anna had experienced something that could be shared only in proper its time.

Leena had spent more time than she'd care to tell on the trails of the U.P. She backpacked with her husband Frank on numerous trails before their kids were born. Their longest backpacking trip was outside of the U.P., in Canada, at Lake Provincial Park. It was a difficult hike. They spent seven days on trails that alternated between swift assent and descent for hundreds of feet. A mile could take an hour to traverse. In a way, it was pure hell. Leena pushed her body so hard, she broke down twice, sobbing over her exhaustion. Her muscle mass seemed to grow daily, albeit with some pain. She lost seven pounds that week, although some of it was water weight.

Frank and Leena learned about each other through that trip — the maps of their personalities were laid out through the trail they traveled. Frank teased Leena about how she frightened him when she got over-hungry. He learned to stop and set up camp before ravenous hunger kicked in, and often offered her snacks. He told her he wished they'd gone hiking sooner when he realized she would stop and make love nearly anywhere outdoors. That might, in fact, have been where they conceived their first child, Jeff.

Leena found out how gentle and patient Frank could be. Leena's excellent physical shape could not match Frank's endurance. He never begrudged her this, but let her set the pace. It was during that trip that she discovered Frank's intense fear of bears. Most Yoopers make their peace with the bear. Bears are around, and people have to accept them and take appropriate precautions. Frank would go nowhere without his bear spray in hand — not even to the privy (when there was one).

Leena wondered if other couples felt a deep, spiritual connection to the forests. When they had kids, they talked about how they wanted share this love of the outdoors with them.

Hiking with kids had its own set of difficulties and rewards. Leena's kids grew up in the woods. When they were too little to walk, Frank carried them. Once Jeff, her oldest, could walk some distance, they followed his pace, which was surprisingly brisk by the time he was five. Frank followed with baby Molly in the backpack, her chubby cheeks pushed against her carrier while she tried to glimpse all the magic of the wooded world. Hank hadn't been deep in the woods yet. Since Frank's death, Leena hadn't gone much into the forest; it made her miss him too much. She decided that maybe the time had come to change that; she would still miss Frank and be reminded of him, but maybe it wouldn't break her now, to remember her husband.

Leena found it odd that Anna didn't seem excited to go snowshoeing, yet owned an expensive hiking backpack. Sure, snowshoeing and hiking were two different things, but usually if someone liked one, they liked the other as well, or would at least be happy to try it. She didn't say anything, but added it to the growing list of Anna's inconsistencies.

Leena kept what she'd learned from Ron to herself. He said the state police had come into town a few days before and asked people if they recognized Anna. Her hair was long in the picture they were showing around, and the people who had seen her had decided to stay quiet since word had gotten out that a wife beater was searching for her. Luckily, the women's bowling league had taken a trip out of town that weekend, or surely Nelly would have run to the police with the news.

***

Anna tried to prepare herself for ultra-boredom as they

prepared for the hike. She loved exercise, but running was more her style. The world whirled by and she didn't have to focus on much besides her breathing and body when she ran. Her mind would go blank, like a machine following a program.

I have got to be nicer to this woman. I should at least try to pretend I'm enjoying myself. It's the least I can do. If it weren't for her, I would be dead. Anna tried to approach the hike with an open mind and ignore her heavy heart weighted with stress.

It took Anna half a mile to adjust to the snowshoes and the motions required by her legs to effectively use them. Once her movement became automated, she began to look around. The more she looked, the more she noticed visual gifts everywhere, like how the slant of winter light bounced through the branches of the few pine trees that dotted the hardwood forest, lighting the snow like diamonds, each bare needle highlighted in a light show of praise. Anna had never paid much attention to nature. The beauty of nature that came from careful observation evaded her until now.

She took a deep breath. It smelled different in the woods, unlike the smell of car exhaust that she'd grown accustomed to during her walks and runs at home. The air smelled pure, like warming earth frosted by snow, like pale gray-blue. Except for the sound of their snowshoes against the crusty snow, all was utterly quiet, as if the whole forest, even the trees, was at rest.

Peace and calm found Anna in the woods, much to her surprise. They filled her so thoroughly that for a moment, she didn't even hear the snow crunching beneath her feet. Everything else in that moment was secondary. She'd never experienced anything like it.

Slowly, however, worry began to peck away at her peace, and then it took over. Delightful peace was cut short by sudden panic. The anxiety that had plagued her for months would not be so easily relinquished. Her anxiety found a target when she saw a pile of rocks that resembled a cave. "Are there bears in these woods?" she asked.

"Only if they're insomniacs," Leena answered.

Anna laughed. *Idiot! Bears hibernate!* "Don't you worry during the other seasons?"

"I don't. I've spent a good part of my life in these woods and have seen bear only three times. When hiking, I mean. And they were more scared of me. They don't want anything to do with us. Unless ya dip yourself in peanut butter and honey or you get between the mamas and cubs, nothing's gonna happen. Better chance of winning the lottery."

Leena's words calmed Anna, but a small part of her refused to relax.

As they walked, the forest slowly changed, and pines took the place of hardwoods. The wind picked up, the smell changed, and hints of blue glinted through the forest. "There's the big, cold lake," Leena announced.

They changed direction and forged their own trail for a while to walk closer to Lake Superior. Anna noticed how the landscape looked different here than it did near Mikamaw. The shoreline consisted of red rock with slashes of cream color for as far as she could see, disturbed only by large, dark-colored boulders. The water looked bright blue and inviting, despite the frigid temperatures and the huge blocks of ice, which stood like bricks pushed up in a pile by the water.

"This is amazing." The words astonished Anna, even though they came from her mouth. She meant them. The abounding beauty touched her heart in a profound way. It made her feel as though maybe hope still existed for her. Maybe it was good that she didn't succeed at the pier that night. Maybe there was more for her to do in this life, even if her life no longer included Andrew and David. Maybe.

The wind grew fierce, so they opted for lunch back in the shelter of the forest. The women had ravenous appetites after their long walk, and they devoured the chicken wraps, pretzels, and cookies that Leena had packed. They washed it all down with water and then sipped hot coffee poured from a thermos.

With the last filling bite, Anna leaned back against the base of a tree to rest. "That was the most amazing lunch ever!"

"Thank you. Food's always better in the woods, or after you've been in them for a while. I remember when Frank and I spent five days backpacking at Pictured Rocks. The first thing we did afterward was stop for Pepsi and candy bars. I thought I was gonna reach climax." Leena laughed, "But honestly, they were the most amazing things I've ever eaten."

"Wow, I've got to go hiking more often!" Anna joked. Their laughter filled the woods.

After they finished their coffee, Anna felt the call of nature. "Is there a bathroom nearby?"

Leena pointed toward the woods. "Yeah, just past that tree and to the left," she snickered. "The bathroom is wherever you want it to be. I've got t.p. if you need it, but bury it some, if you know what I mean."

"Oh, okay." That was not the answer Anna had hoped for, but she didn't expect to see facilities around the corner, either. "I shouldn't have drank all that coffee," she said, hesitantly moving in the direction Leena had pointed.

"You act like you've never peed in the woods."

"It's just been a while. And it's so cold, that's all."

"Try to go fast, it won't be bad."

Anna found a private spot where Leena couldn't see her. She worried she might have an accident by the time she took enough snow gear off to squat. The small length of t.p. oddly reminded her of Kate. *What would Kate think if I told her that toilet paper made me think of her?* It hurt to think about Kate, so Anna brushed the thought aside and focused on the task at hand.

Communication

Leena was a patient woman. As a single mother of three, she rarely raised her voice—she had learned early on that it didn't do much, except make her feel guilty. She gave Anna all the patience she had to offer, knowing that she needed a safe, judgment-free environment. Leena did everything she could for Anna in the weeks she stayed at Leena's house. Her charge improved daily, and Leena hoped that Anna would soon divulge her secrets. It would help them both. Curiosity about her guest nagged at her.

Leena didn't mean to invade Anna's privacy. It started as an accident. Anna's phone lay on the pier, abandoned, the night of the incident. Leena found it and wanted to return it in working order. On the way to the hospital, she dried it with her shirt. That night she and Ron saw the picture of the man and the baby. Later that night, she scrolled through more of the pictures on Anna's phone. A picture of Anna with the baby in her arms, smiling as the man kissed her, confirmed her suspicion—that was Anna's husband and child. She didn't look like a woman stuck with a miserable husband, and even if she was, why would she leave behind her child? It made no sense. Even so, Leena refused to give Anna up.

Two weeks had passed since Anna's suicide attempt. The women grew closer as they chatted more each day, but Leena grew no closer to knowing what really brought Anna to Mikamaw in the first place.

On the fourteenth day of Anna's stay, Leena needed space. It seemed the walls were closing in on her. It could have been the winter weather or the lack of sunlight bothering her. Maybe it was hormones, or that her children had been particularly difficult that day, or the stress of caring for her mysterious guest. Whatever the cause, her body writhed with tension. She had used all the patience she had to give for that day and needed a night out alone. Anna thwarted her escape, however, and invited herself along. Leena wanted to say no, but didn't.

After Leena's teenage babysitter, Paige, arrived, Anna and Leena left to go out to dinner. Things started out better than Leena had anticipated, and her agitation subsided. Anna's sense of humor surprised Leena. Her impressions of George, some of his workers, and the customers at Bart's Bar made tears of laughter spill down Leena's cheeks. The laughter died down and comfortable silence followed as they devoured their burgers and drank beer. The smell of fries and sound of football filled the emptiness left behind.

Later that evening, alcohol tingled and pulsed in Leena's veins. She decided on an impulse that the time had come to ask Anna some questions. *If she doesn't answer, there won't be any harm. But if I never ask, I won't ever get to the bottom of this.*

"Anna, we're friends, right?"

"Yes."

"I don't mean to pry, but—" said Leena.

"--Then don't," Anna stopped her, her smile disappearing, though she quickly replaced it with a warm, although fake, smile.

"Good one," Leena said and tried to laugh off the awkwardness. The Redskins played on TV, and Anna feigned interest.

"You know, you can tell me what happened. You can trust me. You know a lot about me."

"I didn't ask you to share. I would have respected your privacy."

Leena stared at Anna, until Anna looked down. She fidgeted and then sighed. "Okay, ask me one thing. I'll answer and then let's move on to making fun of George."

With only one question, Leena knew she'd better make it a good one. One question burned most in her mind, "Whose baby is that on your phone?"

"Have you been going through my shit?" Anna roared, her face instantly red.

"I didn't do it on purpose," Leena said. "I wanted to make sure your phone worked. I was gonna have it fixed if it wasn't. I was trying to help."

Anna looked into Leena's eyes, anger emanated from her. "The baby, anything on my phone, and anything about me, is none of your fuckin' business." She sat, arms crossed, looking down, her eyes wet around the edges.

Even if we never speak again, I need to say my piece, Leena thought. "God didn't put us on this earth to sit on our asses, watch sunsets, and drink margaritas. Everyone has their bag to deal with." She paused and tried to think of the right words in the haze of alcohol. "I mean their bag of shit. The stuff they have to overcome to find happiness, and even that is only for a while, until the bag fills up again."

Anna rolled her eyes and tried to interrupt, but Leena continued with determination. "Life isn't all carnivals and lollipops. We've got to earn our place with God. I don't even think he creates these tests. It's just a matter of the human condition. It's life. You've got to pull yourself up and deal with whatever's in front of you. Stop trying to shove it under; it's not going to save you, it's gonna drown you."

Exhausted of words, Leena took a drink. As the liquid poured down her throat, she realized that the drowning metaphor was a bad choice.

"Can you get off the philosophical soapbox bullshit? You think you know everything, but you don't know shit," Anna snarled.

Leena refused to let Anna see how her words stung. "I do know you need to start living life, because before you know it, it's over. I know *that* for a fact."

"That's quite a nice speech and all, Leena, but who are you to talk about *dealing* with things?" Anna's voice quivered, and her lips curled in a snarl. "When I look around your house, it looks like Frank still lives there. How long has he been gone? He's not coming back, in case you didn't notice."

Leena gasped with anger. Anna's words were like a slap in the face.

Anna continued, "You have Ron following you like a lovesick teen and you don't even see it for what it is. That man is in love with you. If you dealt long enough with your own issues, you might find out how you feel. So, until your shit don't stink, stop getting into mine." The last words rang in Leena's ears as she watched Anna leave.

Leena sat immobile with shock. *I don't know if I hate that woman or love her spunk. I do know I need a break from her.*

It took an hour before she could move. She was stunned by the turn of events. When Leena got home, Anna's things were gone. She called Ron to ask if he would change her schedule for a few days so she didn't work with Anna.

***

Back at her apartment, guilt consumed Anna in the night, snaking through her defenseless subconscious as she slept. She dreamt a lifetime worth of dreams. The psycho with the truck who wanted to rape and maul her chased her through the woods. Her sister lovingly called to her, wanting her help. Her mother drifted in and out wordlessly, a ghostly apparition. Andrew stretched into manhood before her eyes. "Why, Mommy?" he whispered, the words coming from the mouth of a man but in the voice of a toddler. Suddenly the scene changed. The smells of Savory Scents touched her nose before the sight of it. She walked through the door to the shop that was her pride and joy. Loaves of bread rose on the counters and bagels baked in the oven. David and Joanne groped each other on her favorite workbench, in a lover's embrace. She woke to the sound of her own scream. Her body was sweaty and depleted.

Loneliness gnawed at Anna. She hadn't realized the space Leena had filled in her life. For three merciful days their schedules didn't overlap at Bart's, either by accident or design. Anna regretted the fight, but Leena had pushed too far. Now Anna had nothing but time when she wasn't at work.

Nighttime was the worst. It became nearly impossible for her to ignore the ache. She missed David and his ways more with each day—his raunchy humor, intelligent banter, and insatiable appetite for her were the essence of the man she loved. It was hell not having him next to her at night.

One night, her defenses weakened by loneliness, she turned to her phone for refuge and comfort. It was bittersweet. She knew that she shouldn't look at the pictures, each one like an ax in the heart, but she had no will left to resist. The pictures of Andrew were painful to view but impossible to ignore. She watched Andrew change vicariously through David's photos. His eyes reminded her of her father, while his black hair was a tribute to her.

She read David's words about their past together. He wrote about his favorite memories of their life. He rehashed their early courtship, when they were physically inseparable, driven by their insatiable sex life. He said he admired her drive and accomplishments. He placed her sense of humor and forthright ways upon a pedestal. His words were toxic comfort, tempting her resolve.

He examined his deficiencies in detail—working too much when Andrew was first born and not doing enough to support Anna in her new role of motherhood. She agreed with his assessment, but felt bad that he found blame in himself. He wasn't perfect, but what had transpired was not his fault.

The pictures and David's updates temporarily relieved her pain, yet intensified it soon after, with the knowledge that she would never see them again. Discontent flowed through her body like fire. Then the sobs came and she promised herself she would stop looking at her phone.

She wanted to write to David and tell him the truth—she was a monster and a danger to their precious son. She had shaken and bruised Andrew, yelled foul words at him, she could have done worse. He deserved better than that. They both did. She wanted to tell David this, but she couldn't. No words could explain the depth of her failure. David needed to move on and so did she.

Anna walked through town, down Rusty Pier, and threw the phone into the waves.

***

At Bart's Bar, Anna and Leena danced around each other silently, eyes down, mouths closed. It lasted for days. They each tried to pretend that the other didn't exist. If one was in the kitchen to drop off or pick up an order, the other stayed out. If communication was required, they did so through whichever third party stood near.

Leena wasn't sure how to feel about Anna. The way she saw it, they were either friends or they weren't, and if they couldn't talk honestly by now, then they probably weren't friends. She regretted encouraging Anna to work at Bart's. If she could go back in time, she would undo it. This relationship had caused nothing but stress for her and now bitterness followed, which was a condition that she abhorred. Leena had worked tooth and nail to earn peace in her life, and her relationship with Anna had disrupted it. *Damn this woman and her secrets.*

How could Anna leave behind a child? It was an unthinkable act, especially if she'd left him with an abusive father. When Leena left her kids for too long, it felt like pieces of her were missing, parts of her heart rented out, not to be felt again until her children returned. In her happiest moments with her family, Leena sometimes experienced an ache in her heart, always mindful that these beautiful creatures would one day leave to live their own lives. She never wanted to be the kind of mother who held back her kids because she needed them too much, so she let them grow, prepared them as best as she could for the future, and carried around a deep happiness with a hint of sorrow, for they grew incredibly fast.

Despite the lingering confusion, Leena's anger decreased as the days passed. She could see Anna regressing from the progress they had made, slipping back into herself. In spite of her misgivings about supporting a woman who would leave behind her child, Leena realized that she didn't have the whole story. There must be some reasonable explanation. Anna seemed depressed and tight lipped, but not cold and uncaring. Leena decided to wait for the truth, to forgive. She decided to reach out to Anna again and accept that Anna would open up only on her own terms, if at all. Leena left Anna a note on top of a plastic container filled with conciliatory pasta covered with tomato-basil sauce, and left at the end of her shift.

***

Anna regretted her quick tongue. Leena didn't deserve it. Her anger abated moment by moment, but she didn't know how to bridge the gap that was growing between them. Maybe too many angry words had been said. Maybe she needed to leave town and start over again, but she didn't have the energy for it.

When Anna saw the note, it broke something inside her — something that needed breaking. The bathroom stall banged behind her, and she sat on the seat and shed pent up tears until her eyes were empty and her heart was calm. *How can this woman do so much for me? How can she forgive? How could she even give when she's lost so much herself?*

Anna needed a peace offering. Ron approved her use of the kitchen and helped her find the appropriate supplies. The mixer squeaked as it turned ingredients into dough. While she waited for the first batch to rise, she mixed another batch, and so on until countless wads of dough dotted the counters, in different states of rising, in all kinds of oiled containers. Finally, she returned to her first dough ball, smashed it down, and released her aggression on the floury mass. When it submitted to flatness, she brushed it with milk, sprinkled it with sugar and cinnamon, rolled it up, and moved to the next batch as the dough rose once more.

Her fingers and wrists tingled with soreness by the time she finished shaping the last of the cinnamon bread and cinnamon rolls. The tasks of baking relieved her from a tangled web of indecisive thoughts.

Ron walked in and took a deep breath. "That smells so good. Where'd you learn to bake like that?"

"I worked at a bakery once."

"You should open a shop," Ron said as he ate a cinnamon roll. "I've never tasted anything like it. Incredible."

"I hope it does the trick on Leena."

"That woman has the biggest heart of anyone I know. You two fought—so what? Move on and it's done. Just remember next time to hold your tongue when she irritates you."

Is he chastising me? She looked up at Ron's face. He looked like he wanted to say more. "Ok, boss," Anna said.

"Anything else I can do to help?"

"No, I'm good. Thanks."

Ron left her to her work.

In the end, she made a dozen loaves of cinnamon-raisin bread and dozens of cinnamon rolls. The smell of cinnamon overtook the long-entrenched smell of salty fries and stale beer. Anna took some to deliver and, as agreed, left the rest for Ron to sell the next day.

***

The stars lit the sky when Anna knocked softly on the window near Leena's living room. Leena stood up from her restful roost on the couch and walked toward the door. Relief flooded Anna when Leena opened the door, smiled, and invited her inside.

They sat in the dining room, drank decaffeinated coffee with Bailey's, ate cinnamon rolls, and talked. The wholesome smell of cinnamon enticed Anna to relinquish part of her past. *It won't do any harm to tell her about my mom. I could use someone to talk to. David and Andrew are off limits though.* Anna told Leena about her mother's passing. They sat for hours as she rehashed her mother's battle with bipolar disease and how Anna had abandoned her mother. Anna painted a picture of her early life and that of her sister and the distance that had grown up between them in the years since.

"Now that my mom's gone, I can't believe how awful I treated her. What kind of person ignores their mother when she's sick like that? She tried to reach out to me, but I never reached back. No wonder Joanne hates me."

"I'm sure that your mother has found peace with it all, Anna. Mothers forgive. Maybe it's time you did the same. Maybe even reach out to your sister?"

"I wish I could tell her I'm sorry ... that I should have been there."

"Why don't you call and tell her?"

"I can't."

"Have you ever tried praying over it? Maybe God can send the message for you."

Anna shrugged, unsure. She sighed and wiped her eyes before standing to stretch. Talking about her family exhausted her.

"Well ... I should head back and get some sleep. Thanks for

the coffee ... and everything."

"What are friends for?" Leena said as she moved to clear the dishes. "I could use some fresh air. How about an outdoor adventure tomorrow? We could get out of town for the day. There's this place you've got to see."

"Okay, that sounds nice," Anna said, and she meant it.

***

The sun had not yet risen as Anna and Leena drove toward their next adventure. At first Leena kept the destination a secret, except to say that Anna should dress as she had for their last outing, which meant thermal undergarments and snow gear for full body coverage.

As they drove east, she told Anna about the rocks they were visiting. "They are known by many names to Native Americans and known as Pictured Rocks to others." She described how the Ojibwa thought the spirit of Paupukkeewis, a serious troublemaker, lurked among the jetting rocks in the form of an eagle. The Chippewa believed the gods of thunder and lightning resided in the carved-out caves.

"Is it scary at these rocks? I've got to admit, you're freaking me out a bit."

Leena smiled. "It's awe-inspiring. And if you were hunting there, as some Native Americans did, I'm sure it was dangerous."

"How do you know about Native American legends?"

"Over the years, Marianne has taught me. You know, the photographer who hangs out at Bart's? She's got a little Chippewa blood, and when she gets the pictures, she likes to learn the lore."

They traveled two hours before signs for the Pictured Rocks hinted that they were close. Leena had packed enough snacks to feed them for days, although the trip would last only one.

"We'll cross-country ski to the trailhead because the road is impassible."

"What's the point of having a road if you can't use it?" Anna asked.

"It's a seasonal road. There just aren't enough people to

justify the expense of plowing. If it's somewhere you really want to go, you can find other ways."

When the Suburban stopped, it looked as if they were parked in the middle of nowhere.

"Are you sure this is the right place?"

"Absolutely."

"I feel like we're in the middle of nowhere. If someone were hurt or attacked by a bear with insomnia, it would take hours for help arrive."

"You worry too much. It's going to be fine."

Anna began to boot up. She stuffed tissue near the toe for a better fit. The women filled their backpacks with a canister of hot coffee, lunch, water, protein bars, and extra socks.

They skied down a long, straight road topped with layer upon layer of snow made flat by snowmobiles. It seemed the road went on, straight, into infinity. Anna wondered why they had driven all this way for such a trail when there were much better ones in Mikamaw. Just as she had resigned herself to disappointment, however, the trail veered to the right. The women hid their skis behind some trees and donned snowshoes. The trail started to twist and turn, adding uncertainty for some time as they headed toward what Leena called Miner's Castle. The woods opened up and the smell changed to one that Anna recognized as that of Lake Superior's waters. The view was unlike anything she had ever seen.

A huge tower of sandstone stood sentinel in the distance, hundreds of feet tall, guarding Lake Superior's stunning, icy blue waters far below. It looked like the turret of a sandcastle made by a giant.

"Its two spires are now down to one," commented Leena.

"What do you mean?"

"I think it was in 2006 that the piece that looked like the one on the left side fell off and into the water. There were people below, but luckily not too close."

"That's too bad. I mean, it's too bad part of it fell, not that the people weren't hurt. That would be something to see, though, from a safe distance."

The cliffs and stones displayed a variegation of colors; hues of yellow, brown, and red adorned the rocks, which contrasted pleasantly with the vivid blue water. Much of the rock looked as if it had been blasted by sand and then painted with color. The water had transformed the rock face over time, leaving some parts smooth and others jagged and unfinished. In odd places, trees grew at seemingly impossible angles, trying to get a view of the beauty below.

Many kinds of ice adorned the shore, from large, boulder-sized chunks, to thin shale-like sheets of it. Small mountains of ice pushed against the shore. The blue-green water smashed at it with its waves, trying to reclaim her frozen waters. The color of the water and waves changed moment by moment with each passing cloud. When the sun briefly shone, the result was blinding blue. Anna and Leena stayed for a long time, speechless before the immense beauty.

Anna realized that nature could unhinge you with its vast power and splendor, if you chose to let it in. It was a force like no other, restorative to the soul, if allowed. She felt renewed by it. Being a part of nature's beauty, at that moment, created peace within her.

As they walked on, Anna noticed that there were caves near the shore.

"Walk by me and stay far away from there," Leena said, pointing. "The ice looks reliable, but it's not."

They kept their distance. The cave nearest them looked like a torture chamber. In warmer times, the waves of Superior frequently blasted it. Now, it rested with her frozen waters captured inside, and ice daggers three or more feet long hung from the top of the cave back as far as the eye could see.

As they continued their hike, Leena described the summer boat tours that ferried people to parts of the Pictured Rocks shoreline that couldn't be viewed by land. Anna made a note to see that over the summer. *Will I be here in the summer?*

They continued on quietly for some time.

"Frank and I backpacked the whole North Country Trail before the kids were born. Absolutely amazing."

"What was Frank like?" asked Anna, surprised that Leena had brought up her husband.

"He was an amazing man. Always there. Not just in body but in mind. We had a good marriage."

"It must be hard without him."

"It is. But I guess ... I need to move on. I just need to find a way to do it that keeps him near. Know what I mean?"

"Of course." Anna paused, hesitant to ask, but curious, then said, "What do you think he'd think of Ron?"

"He knew Ron. We all went to school together. They got along well enough when they saw each other. I know Frank wouldn't want me to live like a nun the rest of my years. But it doesn't make it any easier."

They continued to walk wordlessly for a long while. Anna started to giggle. Leena stopped and turned around. "What's so funny?" she asked.

"I hope you give Ron a chance someday because he may look like a hard ass, but I'm convinced he'd break right in two if he knew you weren't going to give him a chance."

"Anna, you think too much of my womanly powers," Leena snorted.

"All I know is that Ron would like to know your womanly powers a lot better." They both burst out in laughter as they continued on.

"There is a dirty mind tucked away under all the black hair. I know you try to hide it, but it's there!"

"That's not the first time I've heard that."

They found a dry log with a good view where they could stop for some lunch. Leena's food was delicious. They ate sandwiches, apples, and homemade cookies.

"I can't believe how good this food tastes. I feel like I haven't eaten in days."

"Food tastes better when your body earns it. When Frank and I backpacked, the food was one of the best parts. Especially when you're done and you taste something you haven't had all week, like a cold beer or pop. I think I told you what pop almost did to me!" They smirked at Leena's excessive enthusiasm about carbonated beverages. "You've got to see all of this in another season. You wouldn't believe how different it is in the summer. Will you be here in the summer?"

"I haven't thought that far ahead. When I do, you will be the first to know."

"Okay, I will count on that," Leena said and grinned at her.

They explored the shoreline before trekking into the woods on their way back. They found several small waterfalls, frozen in time. Anna wondered if there were as many names for ice as there were in certain cultures for snow. She noticed how water could be transformed in so many ways. It was not as simple as frozen or not, she thought; there were many states in between.

Most of the day had passed by the time they returned to Leena's yellow Suburban. Anna agreed to let Leena show her one more thing on their way home. They drove through Munising and stopped at the Munising Falls parking lot.

"It's only going to be a five-mile walk to see this amazing sight," said Leena. She looked hard at Anna.

Anna remained speechless. Her legs had been burning before she got into the truck, and now that she had sat for a while, they felt like rocks, incapable of movement. Anna tried to think of a polite way to decline this woman of amazing strength. "Um ... I'm not sure ... I ..."

"Speechless, eh? I'm just kidding. It's just a little walkway back to the falls. You'll be glad you went. We can't pass it by when we're out this way. It wouldn't be right."

Anna gave Leena a squinty-eyed look and a half smile. "Very funny! Five-mile hike."

They walked along a snow-covered wooden walkway. A deafening sound thundered in the distance and increased its authority with each step they took toward it. When they reached the end of the walkway, they were greeted by a fifty-foot-high waterfall. The pure power of the waterfall demanded immediate respect.

The rocks that surrounded it reminded Anna of the Pictured Rocks. The water rushed down upon an enormous sword of ice which pointed toward the cliff, defying gravity. She wondered what it would sound like if the waterfall wasn't half frozen.

Small evergreens and sleeping deciduous trees sprawled in all kinds of unimaginable positions along the cliff. It seemed they were all impervious to gravity.

No matter what, life moves on. Like the water, it will move forward, Anna thought. She started thinking about her life, and what her future should be. *Did I do the right thing? Will Andrew always wonder why I left without so much as a word? He'll never remember me.*

No. I'm being selfish. I want to be a part of his life, but his life will go on. He'll move forward, without all kinds of memories of how his mom frightened him or forgot about him. He'll be safe and happy without me.

Regulars

Bart's regulars earned their name. Anna tried not to notice them because she didn't want any attachment to people, no matter how trivial. Yet they were as much a part of Bart's as its beer or fry smell, a part of the ambiance not to be ignored. Their presence—faults, gifts, and all—grew on her.

One of her favorite regulars was Harold Jones, the trucker who drove Anna to Mikamaw those many weeks ago. Most people, especially women, found him irritating. He rarely spoke, and when he did, he generally hurled an unpleasant complaint or insult. Without a doubt, Anna had never met anyone so grumpy. He sat there many afternoons while he ate salty fries, followed by beer after beer, an angry stump of a man who constantly fumed over one opinion or another and made everyone around him miserable. Despite his nasty temperament, Anna was grateful that he never said a word about driving her to town.

He wasn't around often, because trucking took him great distances. When he was, though, everyone teased that Harold had a crush on Anna. A distinct struggle could be seen on his face as he vacillated between his urge to grimace, his usual presentment, and a desire to smile at Anna. What resulted was an uncomfortable mix of the two, which made people want to either giggle or run. After two beers, he would alternate between scowling at people and watching Anna.

"That man looks at you like a Rottweiler does a meaty bone," Leena teased one day.

Anna didn't think he looked at her with lust, but rather wondered about her secret. They never spoke of that night, and Anna trusted that Harold never would.

He was notorious for his small or entirely absent tips, but he started to leave Anna proper tips. Leena fumed, "I knew that bastard knew what a tip was and was holding out. After all the years I've served his grumpy ass."

Many of the other regulars were pleasant enough to talk to, and helped Anna burn empty moments by chatting about the weather, news, or gossip. She avoided Nelly and Alice and their gossip at all costs, however. They constantly strummed up drama with their words.

A few regulars had a special status, like Bill Fisher, who could barely walk or see, but said hello to everyone and handed out lottery tickets. Anna noticed that people seemed a little nicer after he left, at least for a bit.

Others regulars, like Gary Dell and his wife, Patricia, were remembered for their draining presence. They were an older couple who came in every Friday for the fish fry. They always started their visit jovial and happy, but by the time their meals arrived they were engaged in ugly, intense arguments. Anyone unfortunate enough to be around would be asked to take sides. Each employee developed a different way of dealing with the dilemma. Anna always said she had food to deliver and left. She watched as Leena matter-of-factly told the couple that she had enough arguments at home and didn't get involved in them at work.

Dalia Hornsby, a local writer, came in often for lunch. The staff flipped a coin over who would serve her because of her grotesque way of eating. When her mouth full of food she would ask questions or make comments. Anyone unlucky enough to be close to her while she ate might experience a spray of her chewed food or the site of it in her mouth.

Marianne Abner became Anna's favorite regular. She had the longest hair Anna had ever seen which flowed silver down her back or sometimes she wore it up, twisted in intricate knots that disguised its length. Marianne often arrived late on weekend nights, red faced and hungry from her nature exertions. When the bar emptied, she would ask Leena and Anna to sit with her and look at the pictures she had captured. By day she worked as an accountant for the few clients she could muster up, the rest of her time she spent pursuing her passion: photography. She traveled all over the U.P. with her dog, Peanut, to photograph what she called "nature's wonders."

Leena always welcomed Marianne warmly and offered her honest commentary on which photos she thought were the most striking. Marianne seemed to value Leena's opinion.

One day Marianne brought her laptop with her. She couldn't decide which photos from a group of twenty she should enlarge for an art show in Marquette. Anna learned to truly appreciate Marianne's art that day. The small LCD screen of her camera did no justice to what Anna saw on the larger screen. Marianne caught every shimmer of light and juxtaposed it to the most vivid and striking colors possible. It was inspiring.

"Marianne, you've got to print all of these for the fair. They are amazing. In fact, I want to buy some of them myself," Anna told her. These were the first nature photographs Anna ever bought. She preferred modern abstract art and had never grasped the attraction of nature photography, until now.

Marianne looked at her for a long moment, then said, "Thank you for the compliment. I believe the spirit of nature has touched you." Marianne often spoke of her Native American culture, which she had learned about from her mother.

"Oh?" Anna asked.

"The spirit of nature is part of us, but sometimes we lose it. I think you have found it again," Marianne said.

"Thanks," Anna said, not sure of how to respond.

***

Anna made peace with the waters of Lake Superior. She stopped replaying that snowy night when she tried to jump to her death. Now she thought of other things when she gazed at Superior's waters. She noticed how the water radiated moods and thoughts of its own. At sunrise, the water would mix and mingle with the pinks, purples, and blues of the backlit clouds, often making it difficult to discern the sky from the water, the colors coalesced in such an intimate way. The sunsets over Superior seemed more fiery, as though the sun resisted leaving this part of the earth.

When Anna wasn't at work and the weather wasn't too cold, she'd make her way over to Rusty Pier. Sometimes she would see Marianne there, camera in hand, so immersed in her work that it would take minutes before she noticed Anna's presence. Marianne contorted her body in odd angles and bounced her camera from one tripod to the next as she moved in a frantic hurry to catch the sun's setting rays or the changing afternoon clouds. Oftentimes when the mad chase finished, she would struggle to sit down, her layers of long underwear and snow pants impeding her bend.

On such days, Marianne shared her photographs with Anna. They discussed her successes and failures in converting natural beauty into digital display. Today was just such a day. They sat in Marianne's truck and reviewed her shots from the day before. Anna recognized the frozen waterfall in Munising. Marianne captured nature in such vivid detail—the Munising Falls in their partially frozen glory, the Pictured Rocks abutted with chunks of ice, and quiet wildlife eking out a living in the harshest of seasons.

Anna took a break from the pictures and looked around. Mikamaw had grown on her. It felt comfortable, now, almost like home. She had come to this place absolutely broken, but had begun to find comfort in the familiar faces around her. *Is this going to be my new home? Or should I move on?*

Before she could come to an answer, she saw images on Marianne's screen she didn't recognize. The water looked vast like Lake Superior, but the shore consisted of what looked like miles of sand. Sprouts of beach grass covered part of the area, and the sand glimmered in a glowing sunset.

"Where are those from? I haven't seen them before," asked Anna.

"It's some of my work from last summer when I had some time to travel. I went to the western side of the mitt. That's the Sleeping Bear Sand Dunes."

"On Lake Michigan?"

"Yep. Have you spent any time there?"

"No, I haven't. It looks beautiful. Are there lots of bears there?"

Marianne laughed. "No, ironically, there aren't many bears. Not like there are up here."

They continued looking through the pictures, which captured vast dunes against forests and the shores of Lake Michigan. Something nagged at Anna, and she asked, "Why do they call it that?"

Marianne told Anna the story of the Sleeping Bear Sand Dunes. A mother bear and her two cubs swam across the lake to escape a forest fire on the other side of Lake Michigan in

Wisconsin. The mother bear swam all the way to the shore of Michigan, but when she turned to find her cubs, they weren't there. She climbed to the top of a tall hill and waited. The cubs had not made it, but the Great White Spirit, a guardian of sorts for the animals, saw their struggle and turned them into islands. The mother bear saw that her cubs had been transformed into North and South Manitou Island. She sat down to watch over them. The Great White Spirit covered her with sand to protect her from the cold, and she watches over her cubs now and forever.

Anna wiped wetness from her eyes when Marianne had finished telling the story. Marianne didn't mention it. Instead, she showed her more pictures.

Sickness

When Leena woke, her muscles moved like they were made of bricks. She forced herself up, feeling as if she were walking through water. The sounds of her children were muffled, and her vision was skewed. She felt disoriented and drained. Her children needed her, so she pushed her body to move, but then collapsed on her bed. Her lungs burned, and she started coughing. It was futile to fight—a virus had caught hold of her. It took all her energy to lift the phone and call for help. She called Ron because she knew her mother was sick too.

"I'm sorry to bother you," Leena said, clearing her throat.

"You're never a bother. What can I do for ya?" Ron asked.

"I'm sick. I can't even get out of bed. I would have called my mom, but she's sick too."

"Okay. Well, I have something of a plumbing catastrophe going on at Bart's, but I know just who to send. I'll be by later to check on ya. Take care."

***

Anna wanted to help, but Leena's children frightened her. They were good kids, but reminders of her faults nonetheless, and they were a handful. Despite her reluctance, however, she owed Leena that much, and more. So, minutes after Ron called her with the news, Anna drove to Leena's house.

Leena looked like a caricature of herself, her face elongated around her red nose and her eyes unnaturally small as she squinted at Anna.

"Go to bed. It's your day off," Anna told her.

"Thanks, but I'll manage," she squeaked in a phlegm-filled voice.

Anna insisted, "Get to bed before I cart you there. Neither of us wants that. You need some help, so take it and don't give me a hard time." Anna enjoyed giving Leena some of her own hard medicine.

"Okay. Promise me that if you need help with Hank or anything, you'll come and get me. Molly and Jeff won't be home from school until 3:30, but I'm sure I'll be up before that."

"Get some rest. I won't need help, but I promise to ask if I do."

Leena ambled up the stairs to rest.

Although Anna had spent a lot of time with Hank, she didn't feel comfortable being alone with him. With his dark hair he reminded her of what Andrew might be like in years to come. She nudged the thought out of her mind and turned her energy toward Hank.

She looked down at the boy, whose face was clean for a change. "What do you want to do, little buddy?"

"Doctr, Mama."

"Oh, Hank, your mom needs sleep. We can't bug her."

"No! Doctr Mama," he insisted. Anna knew from watching Leena that if she argued with Hank, he would explode and become an intense mix of anger and tears. The situation called for distraction. Her mind had not yet reached its two-cup-of-coffee state of wakefulness, but she thought fast. She looked around and saw that dress-up clothes were strewn about the kitchen.

"How about we dress up? You can dress me however you want."

A smile curled across Hank's face. "*howbeber* I nant?"

"Yes."

"Otay."

Hank decorated Anna with princess clothing. He pushed small pieces of clothing on Anna's arms, legs, and feet. The rest he draped over any uncovered spots, covering Anna in mismatched pieces of cloth. She sat covered in a ridiculous mess of pinks, purples, and frilly yellows.

"One mint," he said as he walked away.

He returned with Molly's play makeup. "Now make more purdy."

Anna sighed. It was a small price to pay so that Leena could rest. He covered her with sloppy stripes of pink makeup. *Why does this stuff smell like plastic?*

"You purdy pincess," he said. He opened his arms wide and

gave her a hug. "I wuv you." He looked up at her with his beautiful brown eyes and long eyelashes, seeming to wait for a response.

"I love you, too," Anna said, and she meant it. In that moment, something fluttered out of her. Maybe fear? Whatever it was, it left like an exorcised ghost. Tears stung her eyes. She forced them back, just as she pushed back the memory of Andrew. Something shifted inside her, but what it was, she did not know.

Anna and Hank played more dress up. They ate fish crackers until they were stuffed. The dog, Sprinkles, greedily ate the ones that fell to the floor. They crashed cars together and played with Play-Doh until Anna's hands hurt. Their play spun forward like a home movie on fast forward. Running a half marathon made Anna less exhausted than her hours with Hank.

Finally Hank tired. He sat on the couch, watching television, and his eyelids became heavy. Sprinkles lay curled into a ball beside him. Anna warmed up some soup and put it on a tray with crackers and juice. She walked upstairs to offer it to Leena, who refused to eat, but took the juice.

Hank and Sprinkles were asleep when Anna returned. Quietly, she stretched out in the recliner. She fell into a deep, quiet sleep.

Small, hot puffs of air blew on her face, interrupting her dream. When she opened her eyes, Sprinkles and Hank were looking at her expectantly.

***

At 3:30, Molly and Jeff came home from school. Anna made them sandwiches and cut up two apples. She had no more ideas on how to keep them entertained, especially Hank. Ron had called earlier and said that he wouldn't be able to come until evening, but that he'd stay the whole next day. She was stuck for the long haul.

She asked Jeff, "What do you kids usually do when you get home?"

Jeff brightened with the task of taking charge. He guided her through homework help with Molly. The children played a few board games, and Anna brought them more snacks. The time whizzed by. Thankfully, Hank was less work with his siblings around him. They kept him busy.

Jeff cleaned Hank up and helped Anna through their bedtime ritual. She read them story after story until, their eyelids started to get heavy and she walked them to bed and tucked them in.

When they were all finally in bed, Anna wondered how Leena did all of this every day and still had time and energy for anything else, and how she so often managed to beam with energy. It occurred to Anna that she had survived a whole day with three children. It gave her hope.

***

When Ron arrived later that night, Anna wasted no time in making her exit.

"Hey, I see you have the 'in sickness' part down," she teased.

"Ha, ha. How's she doing?"

"She slept most of the day and she's sleeping now. I think you'll have a quiet night," Anna said as she walked out the door.

Ron would have been happy to do anything for Leena. To be around her when she was sick was better than not to be around her at all. He refused to give up hope completely, but began to suspect that his only role in her life might be as a friend. He couldn't decide if he should take a chance and try for more. What if it ruined their friendship? He needed Leena in his life.

Ron had grown to love Leena's kids. He had been a consistent presence in their lives over the last two years. Sometimes he dropped by to say hello and try to wear Hank out or play games with Molly and Jeff. He watched the kids for Leena whenever she asked, which wasn't very often.

The night settled into silence. He stretched out on the futon and slept until he heard the sound of small feet moving around the house. *This is what it would feel like to wake with them every morning.* Before he was fully awake, he packed lunches and ushered Jeff and Molly to the bus stop.

Ron knew what it took to wear little Hank out. He made a full pot of coffee and went to work. They played seven games of hide and seek, then stuffed themselves with bananas and crackers. Ron bundled Hank up for an expedition to sled a nearby hill. Hank took deep breaths as he trekked up the hill. His snow gear slowed his movement. Ron could hear him giggle each time he rushed down the hill.

"I tired," Hank finally complained when he reached the top of the hill once again.

"Let's go in. How about some lunch?"

"Otay."

They shuffled back inside. Hank watched as Ron heated up the soup he had brought.

"You know, there won't be much more sledding this year. Even though it doesn't feel like it, it's spring now."

"Where's the flowers?" Hank asked.

"They'll be here soon."

Hank ate the soup that Ron put before him. They both dropped crackers in their soup and fished them out with their spoons.

"Where bugs go in wintoe?"

"Some of them go deep in the ground where they don't freeze, some fly south like birds, and some have something in their body that lets them kind of freeze and then when it warms up they unfreeze. Some bees even huddle up together to stay warm."

Hank stared at him with his head cocked to the side. Then he said, "Is Sesme Steet on now? I love Elmo."

"Did you get enough soup?"

"All done."

"Okay, let's get you comfy. He tucked Hank under a blanket. Sprinkles curled up next to him.

Ron took a bowl of soup upstairs to Leena while Hank laughed at something on *Sesame Street*. He knocked softly on her door and then opened it.

"How's the patient?"

"Shitty."

"Here, sit up. I brought soup." He plumped her pillows so she could sit up and carefully placed the tray on her lap.

The Nature of Denial

"I'm sure this is good soup, but food sounds repulsive to me."

"Give it a try."

"I don't know, I—"

"Take two bites. Then if you don't want more, I'll take it away."

She reluctantly spooned some soup into her mouth. "Not bad," she said as she ate five more bites. "Thanks." She leaned her head back. "I'm so tired."

"Get some more rest," he said and walked downstairs.

***

When Leena finally woke again, it looked dark outside her window. She forced her achy body into the shower. Clean and cold, she walked downstairs to thank Ron.

The kids were already in bed, and the room was quiet. She saw Ron stretched out in her recliner, reading. The couch puffed out air when she sat. Words couldn't express her gratitude, but she said them anyway.

"Thanks for everything."

"No problem."

Leena's emotions bubbled involuntarily to the surface. "I mean thank you for *everything*. You're an incredible friend."

Ron closed his book and pushed the footrest of the recliner down. He moved to the couch and sat next to Leena.

What is he doing? Is he getting sick too? Leena wondered. His smile looked odd, like he knew some kind of secret.

"I'm glad we're friends, but I'd like to be *more* than that."

Leena looked away. She had no idea what to say. Her sister and Anna had teased her relentlessly about this, but she had never thought that Ron would ever pursue a relationship with her. Maybe it had been denial, but the words shocked her. She looked at Ron's face, which was crinkled with worry.

"I don't know what to say. I'm not well enough to talk about this right now. I'm sorry. Another time."

Leena hugged Ron, because she didn't know what to say and she didn't want to lose him. For a brief moment, Leena didn't want to let go.

Three days after her sickness began, Leena had improved enough to watch her kids, but not enough for work. Anna took over the rest of her shifts for the week. Leena gratefully accepted the reprise from work. She didn't feel equipped to see Ron yet. His words sat like a bear in the room—they couldn't be ignored. *Why'd he have to ruin everything? You shouldn't mess with what works.*

Visitors

Ron's voice sounded urgent, over the static of a weak cell-phone connection, "Leen, where are you girls?"

"We're in nature, enjoying the sounds of spring," Leena teased. "Is there some kind of emergency?" she chided. Ron had called her often to chat lately, but Leena preferred in-person talking, so she kept their conversations short. Thankfully, he hadn't mentioned anything about his late-night confession, so Leena just pretended that it hadn't happened.

"Tell Anna not to come to Bart's today. In fact, she should stay with you and not even go to her apartment."

"What's going on?"

"There's some guy asking questions. He wants to know if anyone new has come to town lately. Showed us pictures of Anna. We lied, but I get the sense he's hanging around for a while."

"How did he … ?"

"I don't know, but I heard that he talked to Nelly. You know how big her mouth is. I took a picture of the guy. I'll send it. See if she knows him."

Leena told Anna and showed her the picture of the man.

"I've never seen him before. Who is it?"

"Your husband must have sent him."

"Maybe it's time I left. I should hide somewhere else."

"We'll make sure he doesn't find you. Just stay with me for now."

The women wordlessly walked back to Leena's truck, with only the sound of melting, crunchy snow beneath them. They stopped at a bar outside of Mikamaw on their way home from their hike. They needed time to digest the news and create a plan before they headed back to Leena's.

"Is there anything you need from your apartment? Ron can get whatever you need," Leena suggested.

"I need some clothes and underwear, but honestly, I don't want Ron finding underwear for me. It's a little weird."

"Okay. I'll stop over there and sneak up and get some stuff for you."

"Thanks."

"I wonder how he found you." Leena said. She remembered that the police had been in town weeks ago, but she didn't tell Anna. She worried that Anna might not be able to handle another move. She wasn't strong enough yet.

"I used my phone a few weeks ago. I've gotten rid of it for good, but they must have found my location from it."

"We'll just have to let them believe that you've moved on."

"I'm just ... not ready to deal with this. I need this guy to go away. I need talk to David on *my* terms, when I'm ready. Not like this."

"Will you forgive him?" Leena asked.

Anna looked at her for a long moment. Leena couldn't read the look on her face. "I don't know."

They developed a plan over dinner. Anna would stay at Leena's and hide for a few days in hopes that the man would go away none the wiser.

***

Later that day, Ron stopped over at Nelly's house. He knew Nelly's ways. She probably spilled the beans to that detective faster than snow melts at the equator. Anger threatened to pour out, but he pulled it back. He needed to control himself.

Nelly opened the door, and a warm smile came across her face. "Hello. To what do I owe *this* pleasure?"

"May I come in and talk to you for a minute?" he asked as he flashed her a false smile.

"Sure," she said as she led him in.

As they sat in her living room, he wasted no time mincing words. "Why have you been talking to strangers about Anna?"

"What are you talking about?" Nelly cleared her throat and looked around nervously.

"I know you like to talk, Nelly, but you've gone too far. You know nothing about her. What right do you have gettin' into other people's business?"

"Someone asked a question and I answered it. Is that a

crime?" Nelly sat up straighter, more sure of herself.

"It could turn into one. Did you know she's hiding from a husband who beat her? What if she gets hurt now because of you?" He let that sink in for a few minutes.

Nelly looked down in thought. She slowly looked up. "I had no idea. I wouldn't have done that if I had. Sorry."

"Well, if you want to make it right, you've got to tell me everything you told that guy."

"I told him that Anna worked at Bart's and lived above it."

"What else did you tell him?"

"Nothing, really. I don't know nothing else about her."

"Okay. There's only one way to make up for it. You have to tell everyone in town that you've heard that she's moved on."

"Has she? Moved on?" asked Nelly.

"It doesn't matter. What matters is that we convince that man to move on. Maybe say that you heard she wanted to go to a big city or she wanted to live somewhere warm. Whatever you say, keep it consistent, and tell everyone you know. You don't want her blood on your hands, do you?"

"No, I don't."

***

Anna had spent three days at Leena's house and now she wanted to move back to her apartment. She felt caged. She cared for Leena, but required some space. Anyway, the investigator must have believed the rumors that Nelly spread. No one had seen him in two days.

Leena begged Anna to stay one more day to meet her sister, Meg, who would be visiting that day. Anna found it impossible to say no Leena's request.

The women cooked in the kitchen for hours. Their only breaks were to entertain Hank. They made homemade spaghetti sauce from tomatoes frozen the previous summer, chopped a variety of greens and vegetables for salads, and Anna made homemade bread and apple pie. She couldn't quite retire the baker inside herself. The sensations and smells brought both comfort and remorse. Anna missed her friends from Savory Scents. They were like family to her, her bread friends as she called them. She wondered how Savory Scents and her friends were doing.

As they prepared the food, Leena told Anna about her sister. Meg had known early in life that she would leave Mikamaw. She had traversed the country, looking for the place that suited her taste. Chicago seemed to fit the bill, and she remained semi-settled there, where she liked the pace of life and the seasons.

When Leena opened the door for her sister, Anna was stupefied. She expected some resemblance of Leena in her sister, but saw none. A petite, fashion-forward woman with blonde hair stood before them. There was no clinging to past decades for this sister.

As the afternoon progressed, Anna saw that Meg cut through small talk with a verbal knife and immediately marched to the point of conversation. She said whatever came to mind at the moment it arrived. Anna wished Leena had informed her of this fact ahead of time. It took some mental adjustment to get used to it.

After Leena's mother arrived, they sat for supper. Steaming piles of pasta adorned the table, which was surrounded by three generations of Leena's family. The smell of fresh bread and pasta sauce permeated the air. The conversation briefly paused as plates were piled with food.

"So, Anna, what's your story? How'd you end up in this shithole?" Meg asked before she scooped some pasta into her mouth.

"Meg!" her sister objected sternly, caught off guard with her mouth full of food. Molly and Jeff stifled a giggle.

"It's a long story," Anna said. She stared intently at her pasta twirling around her fork and hoped that would end the conversation.

"Okay, I'll take that as code for we'll talk about it later," Meg said. She flashed a brilliant, white smile and winked. Her next questions focused on Molly and Jeff. Then she doted on little Hank—sauce-covered face and all. As she talked with each child, she gave them her full attention, as if they were the most important person in the world. They looked at their aunt with admiration as they excitedly answered her questions. Anna admired Meg's matter-of-fact style with the kids, and they seemed to like it as well.

***

Later that night, after the kids were in bed and Jewel had left, Anna sat with the sisters at the kitchen table. They drank a concoction of Meg's making that combined a variety of liquor with some fruit juice. They drank the powerful blend and played rummy.

Leena caught Meg up on the town gossip and told her about Nelly and Alice's incessant gossiping about Anna since her arrival.

Incredulous, Meg said, "That Nelly's never learned how to mind her own business. I can't believe that after all these years she hasn't changed one bit!" She looked at Anna, "You know, she's been talking about people behind their backs since she was in diapers."

"She's caused trouble with all her gossip," Leena explained to Anna. She turned to Meg, "Remember when she told everyone Samantha Thompson was pregnant?"

"Yeah, and she wasn't! That poor girl wouldn't show her face for a week. Her mom had to drag her to school, humiliated and pissed." Meg shook her head, indignant at the memory.

"At least she put that anger to good use." They both laughed.

"You see," Meg informed Anna, "Samantha found Nelly after school and beat her to a pulp until she told the crowd that she had lied. Turned out that Nelly was upset because Samantha had caught the eye of Nelly's schoolgirl crush, Mark Jessip."

Leena loved Meg's visits and missed them. The only thing she didn't like was that over the past year, Meg constantly teased her about Ron. This day was no different.

"Speaking of crushes, have you given in to Ron's *charms* yet?" Meg asked, stretching out the word.

"I don't know what you're talking about Meg." Leena hoped her sister would drop the subject in Anna's company.

"Oh, come on." Meg waved her hand. "You can't be completely oblivious. I'd be on him like butter on toast, if you catch my drift."

"How could I miss it?" They all laughed.

"Really, how long are you going to make that man suffer? He's been in love with you since high school. Aren't you even curious about what it would be like?"

"He has not been in love with me, and I'm not even going to answer the 'it' question. Geez Meg, simmer down."

"Can't you see it, Anna?"

"I don't want to get involved in this one," Anna said, hands up.

"You worry too much," Meg said to Anna.

"Can we drop this for now?" Leena insisted.

"Okay, okay."

Leena had done her best to avoid the subject of Ron, and even Ron himself, lately. Since his confession, she had avoided him like a snow squall.

The conversation turned to updates on Leena's children. Leena beamed with pride when she discussed Jeff's gift for math and Molly's incredible stories. Then talk turned to Hank.

"And how are you handling things with Hank these days? Is all that better?" Meg asked.

"Meg, it's fine. You know it's fine," Leena said, annoyed. She discretely looked toward Anna to remind Meg that they were not alone.

Meg's cheeks shone red. She slurred a bit, "Oh, don't be so hush-hush. I just want to know you're all better. We're clearly among friends. Even if they are tight-lipped." She looked at Anna with raised eyebrows.

"That's okay, Meg. Let's change the topic," Anna said.

Meg took a long drink, and then blurted out, "This girl was crazy as a bat a few years back when I last saw her. That's what she doesn't want to talk about. But the way I see it, if we can't talk about the tough times, what's the point?"

"Real nice, Meg. What the fuck?" Leena turned away from her sister.

"I just want to know that you're okay." Meg looked at Anna, "Leena was a slip of herself. She lost so much weight so fast that she couldn't even breastfeed. I had to pick her up off the floor most mornings and she would either cry in my arms or scream at me. I make light of it now, but it was dark stuff."

Anna stood up. "I think I should go. Looks like you two need to talk." She started gathering up her things amidst pleas from both women not to leave. As she bent to grab her purse, which was on the floor by her shoes, she stumbled.

"No offense, Anna, but you're too shit-faced to drive. I'll cool down. I just genuinely want to know how things are with my sis. Clearly ... they are peachy."

Anna agreed to stay. They ditched the rummy game and moved to the living room, the air full of tension and regret.

Leena set Meg straight. "Just because you're an open book, doesn't mean we all are. I'm pretty open, but come on. You don't need to air all my business. That's rude." She turned to Anna. "I had severe postpartum depression soon after Hank was born. Not to mention," she turned to her sister, scolding, "I had just lost my husband not even a year before that. I couldn't force myself out of bed anymore and my mom called Meg to help. I don't remember everything about that time except that I worried I'd never learn to love my son and it was nearly more than I could bear. It was the postpartum depression though and it did finally pass. Took some time though, but it helped to put a name to it. I guess it's not uncommon, there are even different kinds. I had no idea. Anyway..."

Leena drank from her glass, mired in the past. "Meg was nice enough to come and take care of me for a while. Looking back, maybe that was a mistake," she said scornfully, looking at Meg.

"I'm sorry. I didn't mean to upset you. Really. I got carried away. It brought it all back when I saw you. I didn't mean any harm." She looked to Anna, "We don't see each other as much as we should. I haven't been here in a long time, but you've got to admit, it's a hell of a drive." Leena smiled and rolled her eyes at Meg's lame apology attempt.

The conversation turned to lighter matters, but Anna became quiet.

"You alright?" Leena asked her.

"Yeah, I'm just tired. I think I'll go to bed now."

***

Uncertainty crippled Anna. Like one of those perpetual motion toys, her mind swayed from one thought to the other, with no end, or decision, in sight. She'd never considered that her loss of sanity might be temporary. It shattered her ideas and plans like thin ice smashed by a freighter. It sat like a rock, boulder sized, in her stomach. Now she didn't know what to think or do. Her internal compass was broken. Had she left behind her husband, her baby, and her life for something that would have passed? *It couldn't be. It would be too simple, too coincidental, too naive.*

Anna laid on the futon for hours, a lump of indecision, with her thoughts competing with one another for attention. She knew about postpartum depression, but she didn't feel depressed — she felt crazy, or at least that she had been crazy — especially in the month before she left Andrew. *I can't give up now. Andrew needs me to be strong.* Her mind wavered between these alternate realities for an hour while she lay in bed, compulsively tapping her hand on her leg. It occurred to her to ask David what he thought, then reality struck the idea into submission. Guilt and confusion hijacked her brain. Cohesive thoughts became more impossible with each moment and the stress of it all threatened the progress she'd made.

When she thought of her family, David's smell eluded her, his touch a distant memory. Andrew's face was blurry — like an illusion. The essences of her loved ones were fading. *I want to be with them but I can't just saunter in and say, "Hey, I was wrong" and expect forgiveness. And I don't know if I'm wrong at all. My mom thought a lot of crazy truths herself. How do I know if I'm sane or only fooling myself?* She felt disconnected from within, the right mode of action absolutely unclear.

Anna made a conscious effort to change the topic in her mind. *I wish my sister and I could get along like Meg and Leena do.* A memory of Joanne washed over her, the day they bounced happily in the waves at the beach. Darkness clouded the memory, overtaken by the memory of Joanne ripping into Anna with words when she asked what was wrong with their mother. Joanne had exuded warmth and understanding when it came to their mother, but it was as if she had used up her quota of compassion when it came to Anna. Joanne turned cold many years ago and hadn't warmed since.

Found

The tight-lipped nature of the people Grendal Moore had encountered in Mikamaw surprised him. Usually, someone would trade information for a little cash. He had used an app on Anna's phone, which she obviously didn't know existed, to track her general location. The last time her phone was used, weeks ago, it showed her in this location, but nothing since. She could be miles away by now, but Grendal doubted it.

Finally, he got a break when he met a nervous woman named Nelly. She told him that Anna worked at Bart's Bar and lived above it. Grendal had a feeling this woman would rat her own mother out—too bad he hadn't found her sooner. So far, he found no evidence of Anna at Bart's.

Grendal decided to enact a new plan. It was time to disappear, because either someone was watching him or Anna had moved on. That nervous woman told him that Anna left town a week ago, but he didn't know if he believed her. He needed to create the illusion that he'd left town himself. He checked out of Walt's Hotel, the worst accommodations of his life, even by his low standards, and gladly moved into his van.

He left town for a few days and contacted David with what little news he had. David didn't take it too well. He wanted answers, but Grendal didn't have any for him. Grendal asked him to wait until he could learn more.

After two days out of town, Grendal slowly drove through Mikamaw in his rented Malibu. (He ditched his van for a while, lest he be discovered spying on Bart's.) Under cover of darkness, he planted a small camera across the street from the bar at the hardware store, hidden in some storefront decorations. Then he slept and watched the door to Bart's from a distance through the morning and afternoon.

His brief stakeout didn't give him much, but the camera he retrieved two days later did. Without a doubt, he saw Anna walking into Bart's. A man tried to hide her entry, but it didn't work. The windows weren't clear enough to see what she did or who she met there, but she didn't leave for seven hours. The next day he called David to see if he should confront her. David told him to leave—he would take over from there.

***

The news about Anna shocked David. *What the hell is Anna doing in the Upper Peninsula? I couldn't have paid her to go there.* He had begged her many times to backpack with him and enjoy what he'd spent the little free time he had in college doing. She always refused. Questions ran through his mind. *Is she being forced to stay there, or is she trying to stupefy me with an unlikely location? What's wrong with her? Is she mentally stable? Does she hate me?*

David couldn't focus on Andrew, because his thoughts were consumed by his wife. *Anna must be in trouble. I need to help her before she hides somewhere else.* He knew whatever was wrong must have been terrible for her to leave. Not knowing why his wife left made him spin in circles of conjecture and speculation. He needed to develop a plan and he needed help.

Kate answered on the first ring. He updated her with the new information. "What do you think I should do?" he asked. "I don't want to scare her away. Whatever she's going through, it's me and Andrew she ran from, but damn it, I've got to get her home."

"Who knows why she ran, but we need to be cautious. Do you want me to go check it out so you can stay with Andrew?"

"I can't stay here. I think it might take both of us. Let's drive up together."

"What about Andrew?" Kate asked.

"I could take him up, but it would be stressful for him. I can barely hold it together as it is, and I don't want to put him through that. I know it sounds silly, he can't even talk, but—"

"Not at all. I know what you mean. Where can he stay for a few days?"

"I'm not asking Bryan and his wife. They would have him wearing designer clothes and thinking he's better than everyone else by the end of one day. Not to mention that would piss Anna off."

"Okay. What about Amy?"

"I don't think so. For days it works, but she has night classes. I'm not sure if she's ready for nights *and* days anyway."

The conversation paused as they both thought. *This is part of the trouble when you don't have family you trust living close by,* David thought. When he thought of family, Joanne's image appeared to him.

"I wish my mom or normal brother didn't live across the country." He paused, worried Kate would balk at his idea, then asked, "How about Joanne?"

"Anna wouldn't like it, but it might be your only choice. She doesn't have a lot kid experience, though, does she?"

"She was good with Andrew when we stayed with her. Even with everything that was going on, I could tell she adored him. She might be my only option."

"Ask her then. It's worth a shot."

When he hung up, he dialed Joanne's number. His hands were damp with nervousness. He needed her help. He could ask his brother, Todd, to fly over, but by then Anna might be in another state.

Joanne answered the phone. David didn't bother with pleasantries, but immediately begged her for help.

She listened to his request. "I don't know. I've never been alone with Andrew for more than a few hours. Anyway, won't it make Anna mad?"

"You are a natural with Andrew. He adores you. And Anna's not here to make the decision, I am. Joanne, my family is too far away to ask and I need to get up there quickly."

"It will take me five hours to get there."

"I know. Amy can stay until you get here. I can't put Andrew through the stress of all that traveling ... and I'm so tense. I'm two seconds from snapping. He needs to stay here."

Joanne sighed. She started to say something, but stopped. "I don't want to do this." David felt a stab of anxiety. "But I guess I will ... for Andrew and you. Not for Anna. I still think it's despicable, what she's done and—"

"Thank you, Joanne. Thank you, thank you. When can you get here?"

The Nature of Denial

***

The haphazardly packed bags were piled in the backseat of the car, shifting at each turn and stop. The sun shone bright in the afternoon sky. David and Kate remained quiet, even though they'd been driving for hours. Thoughts boiled in David's mind, but he wasn't ready to share them. Too many emotions ran through him, and he didn't know which one to give in to. They drove silently for many miles.

When they reached the Mackinac Bridge, the situation became more real to David. They were on their way to find Anna, hopefully. The setting sun highlighted the beauty of the bridge that would lead them to upper Michigan. It always filled David with awe. Its crafted suspension stood like a piece of art, strong, yet flexible, enduring the winds and hard weather of the Straits of Mackinac. He noticed chunks of ice, like small islands, pushed up against the shore below. The thumping sound of the tires on the bridge seemed to coordinate with the sudden rushing of his blood.

The bridge turned a page in their adventure. They were still far away, but getting closer.

"I wonder what she was thinking," Kate said. "She's always told me what's going on. I still can't believe she didn't say anything. Not a word."

"I don't know. The whole thing is surreal. Somehow I failed her."

"It's not your fault," Kate assured him.

"We have to make sure she doesn't bolt again, once we find her. Obviously she's not in the right state of mind."

They talked for hours as they created a plan they hoped would be least likely to drive Anna away—a tricky task, since they knew so little about why she had left in the first place, except to protect Andrew, according to what she wrote in David's letter. By the time they reached Munising, they had agreed on a strategy and still had hours left to drive.

"It's so ironic that she's here, of all places. I know you asked her to hike here when you were first together."

"She tells you everything, doesn't she?"

"She did."

The headlights shone on another sign for Munising. The last time David drove to this part of the state was when he and Todd backpacked all over the U.P. They had painful welts from bug bites, farmer's tans, and the stench of the unshowered to prove the distance they'd covered.

"There's an incredible waterfall here," David mused. After a few minutes, he expelled something that had been nagging at him. "I get that it wasn't what she wanted, hiking and stuff, but she never even tried."

"She can be stubborn. She knows what she likes and sometimes doesn't bend." They both smiled. "I tried to get her to try golf with me. You know, I'm on the women's league. She's always insisted that golf is not her thing. She wouldn't even go to the driving range with me. So, you're not the only one, I guess."

"You have to admire, in a way, that she knows who she is and won't pretend for others." David tried to see the best in his wife.

"Or you could just call it stubborn," Kate said.

***

Anna walked into Bart's on a sunny, cold day for her afternoon shift. No one had seen the detective for almost a week, long enough for her to feel safe returning to work. The detective must have believed Nelly's story. Anna walked straight to the back of the bar to the kitchen without noticing the particular identities of the customers. There were always regulars sprinkled in with a few tourists. Anna washed her hands, wrapped herself with her half-apron, and filled her pockets with an order pad, change purse, and pen.

As Anna walked toward the tables to see what she needed to do, she noticed Marianne waiting with her camera to share some pictures with her. Harold looked down at his food until he heard Anna say hello, and then his demeanor changed and he contorted his face into a smile. Nelly sat at the table right in front of Anna, her attention taken by someone across the bar. Anna couldn't see the face of the poor sap who'd piqued Nelly's attention. George walked in, ready for a late lunch, while Anna made her assessment of Bart's. She walked toward him to ask for his drink order, although she already knew what it would be. She glanced at the table Nelly was staring at on the way over, and her legs turned to jelly — there sat Kate.

Anna walked back to the kitchen and asked Lloyd to take over because she had an emergency to address. She walked back to Kate and quietly demanded her to follow. Kate walked wordlessly out the door of Bart's and up the stairs to Anna's apartment.

Before the door fully closed behind them, Anna wheeled around angrily and demanded, "What the hell are you doing here?"

"Nice welcome, Anna. And how are you?" Kate smiled.

"This isn't a joke. How did you find me? You need to leave." Anna felt the sting of remorse, but her old life couldn't come crashing in on the one she'd created; it threatened her foundation. She wasn't ready for it.

"I know. I'm sorry. You haven't returned my texts or calls. I need you to sign some paperwork for your insurance or they're going to look for you. I did all I could about your car, but if you don't sign this stuff, they're going to think it's fraud. Then they, and the police, will start looking for you."

Anna paced the small living room. She tried to make sense of the shock of seeing Kate and comprehend the words she spoke. "So that private eye was for you?"

"Yes, sorry. I needed to know where you were. I won't bother you again. I didn't want you to be in trouble. Isn't that what a friend should do?"

Anna continued to pace for a few minutes longer, then suddenly stopped, a decision made. "Yes, it is. Sorry. It's a shock to see you. It's almost too much."

"I'm just trying to help."

Anna emitted a deep sigh as she lowered herself into the chair across from Kate. Her eyes darted at everything but Kate, and her hands nervously fidgeted.

"I don't mean to be any trouble, but do you have any coffee around here? I've been on the road for a while. I feel like I could fall asleep standing. I won't stay long, but I need to get these papers signed," she said, motioning to some papers she held in her hand, "and rest for a minute."

"Sure," Anna said pensively. She fumbled around the kitchenette, making coffee in her one-cup coffee maker. Confounded, she frantically contemplated the best course of action. Part of her was happy to see her friend—a familiar face whom she'd spent much of her life with—yet, more than that, the intrusion made her nervous. Before Kate had arrived, Anna had questioned her decision to leave David, but she wasn't yet ready or equipped to change course. She needed Kate to leave so she could think. *What words can explain this that won't hurt her? Maybe she'll just leave and I won't have to go there.*

Anna handed Kate her coffee mug and sat with her own.

"Your car is totaled. I'm glad you didn't get hurt," said Kate.

"They don't make cars like they used to," Anna said, faking a casual tone. "It didn't seem that bad."

"Well, your insurance company will send you a check. Do you want them to send it here?"

"Just have it sent to David. He can have the money. I don't want my address to be on any documents. Okay?"

"Yes. Of course."

"Don't tell David or anyone where I am. I know it will be hard, but please, for all we've been through. Don't tell anyone."

"I won't. I promise. So ... you work downstairs?"

Anna couldn't do it anymore. "I'm sorry, Kate. I can't talk like this, like nothing's happened—"

"Good. I'm so glad to hear you say that. I—"

"Let me sign the papers." She reached for the papers. "Finish your coffee—you have to go."

"Okay. But before I go, I have a few things to say, since I won't be seeing you again." She paused, "You have to come home."

"No offense, but don't tell me what to do. You don't understand!"

"You're right, I don't. But you didn't give me a chance to, did you? You didn't give any of us a chance. David is broken over this. Is that what you want? And Andrew needs you."

Anna stood and yelled, "Don't bring up Andrew!" She slowly

slumped back into her chair, briefly thankful that they weren't downstairs, and painted her face with composure. "I'm sure it will hurt him. But I've saved him from much worse. Please, don't bring up Andrew." Her eyes narrowed with fierceness.

"Anna. It's me. What the hell is going on? Why did you leave? I can help. I'm your friend. Remember?"

Kate was more than a friend to Anna, she was the sister that Joanne should have been. Anna had tried not to think of Kate over these months and what she must be going through.

"I'm sorry, Kate. You deserve better. I just don't have anything to give. I wish I could explain, but it's just too hard."

"Just tell me, are you okay?"

"I am ok. I am better than I was."

"Well, that's a start," Kate said. "Whatever's happened, you can go back. David loves you. He wants you back. Andrew needs you. The girls from Savory Scents miss you. Don't be afraid to come back because you walked away. People love you and want you back."

Anna started to tear up. "I appreciate that, but I'm not sure I can. I need more time." Anna began to weave a story. She needed Kate to leave. "I will call you soon and let you know. But I need you to go after you finish your coffee. I've got to get back to work. It gets really busy this time of day," she lied. After she signed the paperwork, she said, "If you're my friend, then keep my secret. My head is starting to clear, but I need more time."

Could I come back? she wondered. *I am feeling a little better.* Then she saw Andrew's bruised arm and heard his unanswered cry. She remembered the screaming, the foul words, and the brief moment when she imagined him dead. *I can't. What if it comes back? What if it's not postpartum anxiety? What if I'm like my mom? What if I'm worse?*

***

Back at the hotel, Kate updated David on Anna's fragile state.

"It was so hard to follow through with that farce. It took everything I had to leave her there. I wanted to shake her back to her senses and throw her in the car and take her home," Kate said while pacing the small room.

"Well, thanks for keeping your cool," David said, looking down.

"I still don't get why she won't just come back. In a way, I felt bad lying to her. We've always been honest with each other."

"It was necessary. Thanks for talking with her. Now we have a better sense of what we're dealing with," he said, leaning back in the chair and taking a lungful of musty air.

"I don't know about that. I'm more confused now than before I saw her. What happened to her?"

"I wish I knew. At least we found her. It's a start. We can't give her time to take off again." David tapped his fingers on his knee. He didn't know what to do with all the tension building inside him. "We should go over there now and just tell her that she has to come home."

"I don't think that's a good idea. Anna was shaken by seeing me. She seemed a little ... almost unstable. I think we should give her a day to calm down."

"What makes you think she'll calm down and not take off?"

"We'll have to take turns watching her to make sure, but I think if we just march in there now she's going to run away the first chance she gets. Let's give her time to simmer down and think about our next move. "

"I don't know. I don't think I can wait. This is killing me," said David.

"Anyways, we need to think about how to convince her to talk to us and come home. Marching in and saying "come home" is not going to work. Just give it one day, David. Will you trust me?"

Being so near to Anna made David's blood pulse forcefully with a rush of unanswered emotion. These months without her had been torture on him. He wanted nothing more than to see his wife and bring her home. After that, he wanted answers to heal his anger and pain. Maybe Kate was right, though. Maybe everyone's emotions were running too high for reasonable conversation. Maybe a day or two would make a difference. He would try, for Kate's sake, to wait a day, but it would be hard.

***

Anna owed Leena a face-to-face goodbye. Kate and David never received this courtesy, she thought, but she pushed that realization away, another sin to bury.

Leena opened the door on Anna's second knock. "What's going on? Are you okay?" She moved aside and Anna rushed in, a ball of walking stress and anxiety.

"Kate's found me."

"Who is Kate?"

"A friend," Anna said, full of regret.

"Ok. Maybe I haven't had enough coffee, but why's it bad to see an old friend?"

"She'll tell David."

"So, she's not a good friend?"

"She's the closest friend I've ever had."

Leena pulled out a chair for Anna. "Let's sit and talk. I have to admit, I'm confused."

Anna's lies had finally caught up with her. The truth refused to be contained any longer. She could feel it threatening to burst from inside her. It was as if the world were determined to withdraw the falsehood, like sucking out poison.

One more thing could topple Anna, like a row of standing dominoes, ending not with an amazing finale, but with her total destruction. She'd reached the limit of her ability to process life. Her past, present, and future hovered in front of her, coalescing, and threatened to knock her over with the truth of all that she'd given up.

"I haven't been honest with you," Anna admitted. "I'm sorry for that. I don't have a lot of time to explain because I have to go. But Kate was, I mean is, a good friend. That's why she'll tell David."

"Doesn't she know that he hurt you?"

"That's what I lied about. He never hurt me. I'm the one who hurt him."

Leena prodded her on: "What happened?"

"I don't know how else to say it but to spit it all out." Anna paused and thought about how to explain the months of turmoil to her friend. "David is a good man. We have a baby, Andrew. I ..." She cradled her head in her hands, making keening noises. She looked up, and time ticked with the pulsing of her blood. She needed to leave soon, before Kate returned. "I left them. I didn't want to hurt Andrew. I was scared ..." Anna's voice cracked. She looked down at the floor, but no answers were there. She took a deep breath, locating the last of her inner strength, and continued, "I thought I was losing my mind. I was scared I would hurt him. Certain that I would. So I left."

Leena moved next to Anna and put a warm hand on her shoulder. "I'm so sorry about your pain. I know I haven't known you long, but I know that you would never hurt anyone, especially a child. How come you didn't tell anyone what you were going through?"

"I couldn't. I thought I was bipolar like my mom. I didn't want to put Andrew through that, with violent urges on top of it. My mom was a lot of things, but she never hurt me physically."

"Anna, this can be fixed. You can be with your family. You don't have to leave. You just need help."

"I'm not ready to face them. What if it all comes back?"

"Don't let fear keep you from your family. You need to go to them."

"I will, but not yet. I'm not ready. Thank you ... for everything. You have been a great friend and you don't even know me that well. Obviously," she said in reference to all she'd just told her. "I have to go, but I'll be back. We'll talk more then."

"Stay, Anna. You don't need to do this alone. Your family loves you, and you have friends here."

Anna wished it were that easy. She needed time to think. *I'm not certain what happened to me. I need to think about it. I'm not ready to face David. I don't know if I can go back. What if I do hurt Andrew? What if David doesn't forgive me?*

"I will be okay. I'm not leaving you all for good," said Anna. *I hope.* "I just need more time."

"I wish you'd stay, but I can't stop you," Leena finally conceded. "I'll be here when you get back."

They said their goodbyes and Anna left. She needed to pack before Kate came back or Leena tried to make her stay.

The Nature of Denial

***

The lights were still on at Bart's when Anna returned to her apartment, which was unusual because they closed early on Sundays. *Probably the plumbing again. It doesn't matter because I'm out of here. Bart's will only be a memory.* Before Anna could put a foot on the stairs to her apartment, Ron ran up to her, his clothes disheveled, his face tomato-red and sweaty. "Anna, I've got him. You've gotta tell me what to do with him. Lloyd's with him."

"With who? Is Lloyd okay? What are you—"

"It's your husband," Ron said, avoiding Anna's eyes. "I roughed him up and he fell. He wants to—"

Anna ran into Bart's.

"—take you home," Ron yelled after her.

Inside Bart's, Anna knelt next to her rumpled, bloodied husband, who was lying on the floor unconscious. Silent tears streamed from her eyes. "He won't admit what he's done. He wouldn't apologize." Lloyd, the cook, usually so relaxed, was angry. "We found him sneaking around. We—"

"Stop!" Anna yelled.

Lloyd said, "You're safe. He's not gonna hurt you."

"He didn't hurt me!" Anna snapped. "I'm the one who hurt him." She put her arms protectively around David. Then she pulled back to assess him. His eyes were closed, his lip swollen and bloody, his left eye bulging and black. Under his nose, dried blood covered his upper lip and was splattered on his shirt.

"God forgive me. David forgive me," Anna begged as she held David close.

David's body moved. Anna leaned back and looked at him. He opened his good eye and looked at her. His eye squinted. Slowly, a look of recognition formed on his face, his bloody lips smiled, and then his head slumped over.

"Oh God, he's dead," she yelled at Ron. "You've fuckin' killed him! Get him off the floor! What the fuck? HURRY!" she screamed.

Ron gently shook him awake and helped him to a booth. David lay across the faux leather seat. Before anyone could react, he slumped under the table. His body moved like rubber and landed with a slight thud.

"Ron, you've got to get him upstairs. He needs rest, or maybe the hospital. What should we do? I don't want him to die! Don't let him die."

"He's gonna be fine. Don't worry," Ron said, though he sounded uncertain. "I don't want a man's death on my hands. I was just trying to help. I can ..." he lifted David over his shoulder and moved slowly, "... carry him."

***

David woke confused. Everything looked hazy and unfamiliar. His head ached with compression, like it was stuck in a vise. He tried to move and solve the mystery before him, but quickly stopped. A groan of agony escaped from him.

A figure moved toward him. A blurry person morphed in the dim light into a very lifelike version of Anna. He squinted, trying to determine the sense of this dream. Why did she look so real? Then he remembered— he had found her and then some asshole beat the daylights out of him.

"What the ... ?"

"It's okay," Anna said soothingly as she stroked his arm. "How's your head?"

"Why are you talking so loud?" Her voice rang like cymbals clashing next to his ears, and his head burned with pain. "Oh, my God. My head!" He cradled his head and groaned with pain.

"I'll be right back."

Anna ran downstairs, where Ron and Lloyd sat waiting for her return. They looked up expectantly. "He's got to go to the hospital!" she yelled. "Here," she threw keys at Lloyd, "get my car!" She knew that Ron had only his motorcycle that day, and Lloyd usually walked to work.

Lloyd ran outside and got her car, and Ron followed her up the stairs to her apartment. They each draped one of David's arms over their shoulders and helped him down the stairs. Then Lloyd took over and they helped David into the backseat. Anna followed and sat beside him.

Lloyd sat in the driver's seat and looked back at Anna, concern plastered across his face. Ron opened the passenger door.

"Ron, you stay here. I don't want him to signal you out as the one who did this until I have a chance to talk to him."

"Are you sure? I want to help."

"It's best this way. We've got to go, though. Shut the door." Ron closed the door and stood beside the car.

"Drive fast, but safe Lloyd. I believe you know the way." Anna referred to the time when Lloyd had held her in the backseat while Leena drove her to the Marquette Hospital.

He nodded and drove. They exchanged few words during the rest of the drive. Anna prayed silently for David's safety.

When they arrived, Anna told the intake nurse that David had been mugged and beaten up but they never saw who did it. The lie slipped off her lips so smoothly that even Lloyd looked convinced.

They took David into a room to evaluate him. Anna began to follow, and so did Lloyd.

"You can go now. Thanks for driving, Lloyd."

"I can't leave you here."

"It's going to be a while. I'd like to be alone with my husband. You can take my car."

"I'll get a ride so you have your car. But I don't feel right about leaving you here. Are you sure?"

"I'm sure. Thanks for getting us here."

"No problem."

After many hours, an orderly pushed David's bed from the emergency room to a hospital room, while Anna followed. It looked and smelled the same as the room she had occupied nearly two months before, and for all she knew, it could be the same one. The uncanny coincidence raised goose bumps on her skin. Now she stood over David's bedside—he suffered from the same condition, although caused by different means. He saw a different doctor, but the results were the same—he was going to be okay, with time. He needed rest to heal and painkillers for a killer headache.

***

David woke up wondering why his alarm sounded different. It took him a moment to absorb and recognize the beeps, antiseptic smells, and pressure on his abdomen. He looked down. Anna lay across him, sleeping, holding his arm like a lifeline. Relief filled him and pulsed through his body, like blood. *She's here. Alive.*

The anger inside him melted away. Feeling the warmth of her body over his gave him peace, like going home. Whatever happened, they could work through it. They were together. He gently stroked her hair. *I can't believe she chopped off her hair.* He knew how she prized her long, black locks. She was still beautiful. She didn't stir at his touch, but he did. He couldn't believe that even with a roaring headache and after months of heartache, his wife could still easily arouse him.

***

Lloyd called Leena with the news about Anna and her husband. "It's quite a coincidence. It probably means something, but I don't know what. I'm just glad I wasn't stoned at the time. That woulda been too much."

"Thanks for helping them, Lloyd. You're a good person. But I wonder why Ron didn't call me about it."

"I think he's embarrassed. He didn't mean for the man to get hurt like that, but he fell and that made him hit his head."

"I should have told him."

"Told him what?" Lloyd asked.

"I should have told him that Anna's story about her husband wasn't the truth. I suspected it for some time, but I didn't say anything. Then today Anna told me herself."

"Why would she lie about that?"

"It's a long story. I'll fill you in another time."

"Well, tell Ron thanks again for picking me up at the hospital. I didn't want to leave her alone, but she insisted."

"Ok, I'll thank Ron when I talk to him. Thanks, Lloyd."

The news astounded her. *I'm glad her lies are behind her. Maybe now she can move on. Too bad David got hurt. At least he found her before she left. I hope Ron's not too hard on himself.*

***

The next evening, Leena was shocked to see Anna at the restaurant. She immediately pulled her to the back room to talk. "What are you *doing* here?"

"Where else would I be?" Anna asked sarcastically.

"I thought we were friends, but if you're going to stand there and bullshit me, we're done. You haven't called me back and you could have gotten a lot of people in trouble, including Ron, but you stand there and act like nothing's happened?"

A sigh emitted from Anna, shrinking her. "I don't know what to say. I don't know what to do. I—"

"Let's go talk. It's dead in here anyway. Come on." Leena asked Amber, the other waitress on duty, to fill in for them, and they headed out.

Anna insisted that she check on David first. He slept in her bed. The two hadn't spoken many words since he slept for most of the last twenty-four hours. In the living room, Kate fumbled with her computer, trying to get some work done. Kate glared at Anna. They'd argued over the phone when Anna called Kate to tell her that David was in the hospital. Kate slung words, full of contempt, so fast that Anna could barely keep up.

Words between them had been sparse since David got back from the hospital. The tension between them grew thick so Anna insisted on going to work. She just couldn't face them both, sitting in her tiny apartment, waiting for answers. She needed a break.

Anna walked back downstairs and drove with Leena to Ned's. The smell at Ned's Grill never changed. Instead of a fried-potato smell, like at Bart's, it had a beer smell with a musty quality. The last time Anna and Leena went there, they argued. So much had changed since. Anna tried to make sense of what her life had become, but it was like trying to arrange a room full of furniture floating in water. She kept inhaling big breaths of air, trying to ward off the building pressure. She needed to tell her story, grit through it, and voice things in order to create some resemblance of stability in her mind.

Anna described to Leena the trip to the hospital with a broken and beaten David—a trip full of dark irony. Then Anna relayed her story in its entirety, from her intense love for Andrew to the nightmare of anxiety, depression, fear, and anger she experienced in the weeks following his birth.

"It's hard to say, but I thought I could hurt or kill my own son. What mother feels that? Then my anger and tension became uncontrollable. I didn't know what was going to happen, but I felt like a rubber band stretched out and ready to snap."

"I don't know what to say. That must have been awful. In all that time, why didn't ya tell anyone what was goin' on?" Leena asked.

"I guess I was scared of what would happen if I admitted it. I didn't want to go through what my mom went through or put Andrew through that. I thought I was a monster and I didn't want anyone to know. I realized through all this that I could never live up to my mom's devotion. She never gave up, and I walked away."

"I don't know if comparing yourself to her is a good idea. It's two different things."

"Maybe, maybe not. But the fact is, she would never have given up," Anna said.

Then she changed the subject. She told Leena how Fry wanted to do awful things to her and she contemplated killing him. "Should I care what happened to him?"

"No, I don't think you should. He deserved whatever came his way."

"Harold drove me here from that truck stop. I hitched a ride with him and he hasn't mentioned it since. I can't believe he's never mentioned it."

"Now it makes sense. I didn't think mere beauty could melt that man's heart. He must have felt some connection to you."

Anna's voice was hoarse. The release of her secrets lightened the weight on her shoulders. The women sipped on their sodas in silence.

Leena said, "I have one thing to ask you. Something you

haven't talked about. How the hell did you end up in Mikamaw, the middle of nowhere, as a place to hide?"

At that they both laughed so hard they had to use the table for support. When they calmed down, Leena said, "I'm sorry you had to go through that alone."

"I wasn't alone. Not completely, anyway." Anna looked toward Leena. She'd bared too much already to say the words out loud, but Leena had stood by her side. "I just don't know where to start from here. I believe I can get better. I think so anyway. I know David loves me, but how can he forgive me? How do I go back to being a mom? How will I face my friends? Part of me wants to run again."

Leena's face contorted with anger. "Don't say that. Don't even think it." Anna sank back into her chair. In a calmer tone, Leena continued, "As much as all this sucks, you have another chance. Your husband is here, your baby is alive. It's going to be hard, but you'll get through it. If your husband's worked this hard to find you, he's willing to forgive. The question is, can you forgive yourself?"

***

Leena's question lingered in Anna's mind. Forgiveness had become a theme in her life. Her failure to forgive her mother in time haunted her. In Anna's dream, her mother forgave *her* and this, whether real or imagined, gave Anna some peace. She and Joanne had spent years adding up their grudges and forgiveness didn't enter the equation. Look where it had led them. Her father often spoke of forgiveness. He urged Anna to forge forward in her relationship with her mom and sister—to no avail. Now, she struggled to forgive even herself. It sounded like a small word, for all that it required.

When Anna returned to her apartment, Kate plucked away at her computer, barely acknowledging her. Anna sat by her and waited for her to look up. Kate finally stopped typing and lifted her head. Her eyes gleamed with disappointment.

"Kate, I'm sorry. I—"

"I'm sure you are sorry. I just don't know if that's enough. I don't know what happened to you, but you could have gotten him killed with your lies. I'm not sure if sorry is going to cut it," said Kate.

"Can we talk? I think—"

"Some other time. I'm going to go downstairs and get something to eat."

"Why don't I go with you?" Anna asked.

"I think you need to focus on him right now," Kate said and looked toward Anna's room, where David rested. She packed her laptop in her bag and left with no other words.

***

He's sleeping. I don't know what to say anyway. Anna quietly opened her dresser and put away the clothes piled upon it. David stirred.

"What are you doing?" he asked. "Are you *leaving*?"

"No, of course not. I'm putting away some clothes. Sorry I disturbed you."

David sat up in the bed and rubbed his head. "Are you sure?"

Anna sat on the edge of the bed and looked at her weary husband. "I'm not going anywhere."

"How can I believe that? How do I know that you won't just take off again?" He squinted his eyes with confusion.

"I promise. I won't leave. Okay?"

He leaned back against the wall. "I can't believe you did this to us. Why didn't you tell me what was going on?"

Anna's words rushed out. "I didn't know how. I thought I would hurt Andrew. I kept thinking that I must be like my mom, but much worse. I couldn't put you both through all that pain."

"You don't get to decide that," he said forcefully. "Sorry. I didn't mean to say it like that. My head still hurts, I—"

"You don't owe me any apologies. I'm the one who owes you. I'm sorry, David. I'm sorry I hurt you. I thought I was protecting you."

"After all these years, I deserved to know. You kept me in the dark. Do you know what that's like? Not knowing?"

"I thought—"

"These have been the worst months of my life. I had no idea what happened to you. You deserted our family. We could have figured it out. Together."

"I wish I knew the words to make you understand why I did it."

"Try me. I deserve that much."

Anna sat still for some time, trying to arrange the events in her mind so that she could communicate to him. "After Andrew was born, I felt fine. Tired, but fine. As the weeks went by, though, something changed. I loved him, but part of me almost, this is hard to say, but hated him." Anna leaned her head in her hands. Then she sat up and continued, "Simple things started to make me angry, and I felt tight with stress all the time. I worried that I would snap. Then I did. More than once." She stared at the wall, remembering.

"What do you mean *snapped*?"

"I yelled at Andrew—screamed at him—more than once. I couldn't believe the words that came from my mouth. The day before I left, I gripped his arm and shook him. I bruised him, our sweet baby. What kind of mother does that? I knew then that I had to leave, David. I love Andrew and I didn't want to hurt my baby. I didn't know where this evil person had come from. It reminded me so much of what I went through with my mom, even though she was never evil, like me. At least she never gave up, even though I treated her horribly."

"Why didn't you tell me what was going on?" David's voice softened. "We could have found you help."

"I was too ashamed for you to see what I'd become. I couldn't face you. I was terrified that I would hurt Andrew." Anna's eyes filled with tears. "If I could go back in time, I would do it differently. I did what I thought was right."

"God, Anna." David ran his hands through his hair, like he always did when he was stressed. "Don't ever keep anything from me again. We'll figure out what happened. It will be ok, but don't ever leave me like that again. I can't live without you."

Live. Should I tell him what I did when I got here? Should I spare him that knowledge?

"There's one more thing I should tell you."

He stared at her, his emotions hidden.

Anna continued, "I don't want to tell you, but you should know. I don't want to keep anything else from you."

"Go on," he said.

"One night, not long after I arrived here, I tried to end it."

"What do you mean ... end it?"

"I tried to kill myself."

"Oh." He put his head down in his hands. He looked up, his lips trembling, his eyes wet. "Thank God you are okay." He reached out and put his hands over hers. "Please, tell me what happened."

"I don't feel that way anymore, David. I don't want to die, but I did that night. I drank myself into oblivion and I raced down the pier toward some of the biggest waves I've ever seen. The pier was slick with ice and I slipped and fell before I made it to the end. Leena found me and took me to the hospital. I had a concussion. Like you."

David moved closer to Anna and wrapped her in his arms. Their collective sobs released some of the Anna's sorrow. She didn't know what would happen from here, but at least she had done the right thing—for the first time in a while.

Later they sat at Anna's small kitchen table and continued their talk.

"I'm sorry I wasn't there for you," David said.

"How could you have been? It's not your fault."

"I'm still sorry for it." He was quiet for some time. "We're going to get help and work through this."

"Do you mean a shrink?"

"Yes. We can't go on living life as usual, Anna. How do we know this won't happen again?"

"I'm not sure I want to go through all this again with a shrink." Each retelling exhausted her.

"You will go and so will I," David said with certainty.

"Okay. I'll go. It's just so hard," Anna said.

"It will get easier. You can get some answers, and we'll start there. Anyway, we need it for us. I don't want to let this whole thing come between us. I can't lose you a second time."

"Ok, we'll talk to someone." A second time? She couldn't face losing David twice either. It occurred to her at that moment that it would be hard for him to trust her again. Hopefully with time, it could be fixed.

"One more thing," David said.

"Yes?"

"Why did that asshole do this to my face?"

"That was Ron. Actually, he's not an asshole. He's a good guy. I told everyone that my husband beat me and was looking for me. He was trying to protect me. I'm so sorry about that."

"That makes me feel a little better. Not that you lied, but that he thought he had a valid reason."

"I'm really sorry, David, about all of this. I can't say it enough."

"Then stop saying it. It's not going to be easy for either of us, but we'll get through this. I love you, Anna."

"I love you too."

***

When you have to think hard to figure out how many years you've been friends with someone, it's been a long time, Anna thought. She and Kate had been friends that long. They experienced hormone-infused adolescence, teenage rebellion, college turbulence, and the growing pains of adulthood together. They were friends who boarded the ship of life and set sail, devoted to their friendship, mending sails and altering course as needed.

Anna knew that when she abandoned Kate, she severed the code of their friendship. Kate didn't deserve it and her anger over it couldn't be missed.

As David slept that evening, Anna told Kate that they needed to talk.

"I don't know if now is a good time," Kate said.

"There isn't going to be a good time," Anna said.

"I don't think I can sit and listen right now. I'm too fuckin' upset," Kate said, looking at her. Anna could see the pain in Kate's eyes.

"Let's just try. All you have to do is listen. I want to tell you what happened. I want you to understand."

"I don't know—"

"Please. I know you're angry. Please, just listen."

"Fine." Kate leaned back and folded her arms over her chest, and Anna began.

It took hours for Anna to convey the events of the past months to Kate. The kitchen chair made her back sore, but she dared not move. Instead, she continued to talk. Kate listened, yet interjected with many thoughts and questions. Many times, she asked, "Why didn't you call?" or reiterated, "I would have been there for you, no questions asked."

When Anna finished the story in its entirety, the mental echo of her last words dissipated into the painfully silent air. "I'm sorry," she finally said.

Kate looked thoughtfully past Anna for many minutes. Anna waited and listened to David's soft snoring from his roost in her bed. The seconds seemed to tick louder on the kitchen clock as she waited for Kate to respond. The continued silence made her anxious. She knew the story was intense—she lived it—but the silence was deafening. Kate stood up and started to pace the room—not a good sign. Minute after minute passed in this way. Kate made her way around the small living room another time, then stopped and sat across from Anna.

"I can't pretend I'm not pissed. I want to, for your sake, but I can't." Kate looked around the room, her jaw clenched. "I can't sugarcoat it, it's not my way. I have to tell you how I see it. You shouldn't have shut me or David out like that. It's selfish. You should have told us. It might have avoided all this bullshit."

She's right. I was selfish. Anna looked down, and a sigh escaped from deep within.

Kate continued, "I know I should be saying I'm glad you're okay or sorry, and I am, but—"

"I'm so sorry."

"I know. But I'm mad. I'll get over it. If you promise not to do anything like that again. Next time, I won't be so nice." Kate gave her a half smile and then walked into the living room.

The Nature of Denial

***

Kate had spent most of her time the last few days thinking about Anna. She worried that Anna might run again. She suspected that Anna still feared motherhood by her lack of questions about Andrew. Shouldn't she be curious about her own son? Yet, she never brought him up in conversation. It was one thing for her and David to tell Anna that she would be a good mother, but she needed to see for herself that it would be okay. She needed to see Andrew. Kate believed that if they were to all drive back, Anna might flee somewhere along the way. She didn't trust her friend again yet. Anna still had a hard time even talking about Andrew. When David talked about him, Kate noticed a faraway look in Anna's eyes. What did it mean?

Kate woke one morning with an inspiration—a way to keep Anna from running and a way to get Anna and her sister to talk. Until lately, Kate had never considered that Joanne might not be a bad person. Her dedication to Andrew earned her new respect in Kate's eyes. Why shouldn't Anna and Joanne reconcile? After all, Joanne was the only family Anna had now. They should at least try to patch up their differences.

She told David about her plan: Joanne should bring Andrew north.

"I think this is too much to put on Anna right now. She's too fragile," said David.

"I agree, she is fragile. But Anna has a track record of running from things when they get hard. What makes you so sure she won't do it again?"

David looked hard at her. "I'm not," he admitted.

"If she sees Andrew and spends some time with him here, she won't run. Then she'll know that she can do it and be ready to go home."

"Why don't we ask *her* about it?" asked David.

"Come on. The stress of that could push her away. She'll say no. She shouldn't have time to think or worry about it."

David looked away, apparently lost in thought. "Maybe you're right about Andrew. Why do we have to throw Joanne into the mix, though? That is overload."

"If Anna's going through the wringer anyway, why not have her come out even cleaner in the end? Get it all over with?"

"I don't know. I think it's too much."

"Anna's dealing with a lot right now, and it might help her to see Joanne. They've lost their mother, for goodness sake. They should see each other."

"We could wait on the Joanne part. Let's do that when Anna's home and settled."

Kate loved Anna and would always support her, but she knew Anna had trouble with forgiveness and confronting issues. She felt certain that this needed to happen now. David wasn't going to agree. She needed to tweak her plan.

"Okay," Kate agreed, "we could wait on Joanne. But how will Andrew get here? You agree that she needs to see him, don't you?"

"Is it really going to matter if she sees him at home or here?"

"Think about it, David. What does Anna do when it comes to confrontation?"

"Well, she confronted Natalie pretty well."

"That's different. Natalie was never close to her heart. But think about the troubles she had with her mom and Joanne. Think about fights you've had with her. She has a tendency to walk away from things that hurt. She just spent the last few months running away from her troubles. She spent her entire life avoiding her own mother."

"You're right. She should see Andrew. I don't feel right about keeping it from her, though."

"Trust me, if you tell her, all bets are off."

"Ok, but if it backfires, I'm blaming it on you."

"So, how will we get him here?" asked Kate.

"I hoped that you would get him for me. Can you?"

"I wish I could, but my boss is giving me a lot of flak about taking this time off. They are cutting back on employees lately, and I don't want to be one of them. I would do it, but I could lose my job." Kate hoped the lies were convincing. "Who else can you ask?"

"I don't know."

"You could ask Joanne."

Spring

David stretched his body in the morning sunlight that shone through the window of Anna's apartment. She noticed the length of his body compared to hers.

"How are you feeling this morning?" she asked, resting her hand on her elbow as she turned her body toward his.

"I feel pretty good. My head feels fine, but my body is achy."

Anna knew that feeling from before when she laid on Leena's futon recovering. David had seemed tense since Kate left, and maybe an adventure would help him. "Would you like to go for a hike today? Do you think you're up for it?"

David looked at her, his mouth open with shock. "Anna, I never thought I'd hear those words come from your sexy mouth. I would love that."

After breakfast, they headed out to the trail on the edge of town that Leena had first taken Anna to see. She wanted to share the beauty with David. When they arrived at the trailhead, she noticed the chatter of birds, making arrangements for their spring rendezvous. Tiny plants pushed up from the snow-covered earth with small yellow flowers atop them. A year ago, she would never have noticed such things.

Anna never paid much attention to the seasons in the past; they were simply a part of the setting in which she lived. From her perspective, autumn consisted of two parts: when the leaves turned color and then later when they fell off. Winter was cold and spring was the time before the weather turned hot.

This spring Anna realized how much she had missed through the years. There were dramatic stages in between as tiny buds turned to leaves and leaves grew to cover trees and shrubs in their summer dress. She had first noticed the growing greenery on an early spring hike with Leena. In the weeks to come, she observed the subtle changes in her surroundings. It felt like her first spring, and with it she felt a renewal of her spirit, like a woman reborn.

People, too, she realized, changed in spring, at least in this part of the country. Cloudy days far outnumbered sunny ones in Michigan in the fall and winter. The final days of winter, when people wore their grumpiness like a shirt, changed with the start of spring. Was it her imagination, or did people's moods lift in direct relation to the extension of sunlight? *Why haven't I ever noticed how weather affects people? It seems I feel a bit depressed at the end of every winter, but I never thought it could be related to the weather.*

They walked for some time, David following Anna. The only sound was their feet hitting the trail.

"This is surreal. I feel like I'm in a dream," said David.

"Well, I can assure you, you're not," Anna said, laughing.

"I've dreamed of doing this with you for a long time."

"I know. I'm sorry that it didn't happen sooner. It's amazing. I mean, look around, these trees are enormous and so beautiful."

"What trees?"

Anna stopped and turned around to look at him. The trees groaned in the slight wind. "What do you mean what trees? Are you okay? Is your head okay? Maybe we shouldn't have—"

"Honestly, how can I notice the trees when you're walking in front of me? All I can see is your fine behind."

"Oh, come on," Anna said and continued walking.

"Really. I want to make love to you on this muddy ground. Are you up for it?"

"David," she said, turning to look at him, "give it a rest." Right at that moment, he stepped right into a muddy, melting pool. The mud held fast, angry at the disturbance. "Serves you right," Anna said in a playfully scolding voice.

She looked around at the tiny rivers of meltwater everywhere, feeding the pools of mud a seemingly endless supply of water. The sun shone at a beautiful angle through the woods, creating welcoming shadows along the trail. The familiar change in smell informed Anna that they were close to the big lake.

At the Lake Superior shore, piles of old, dirty ice slowly melted. The unusually calm water glistened a blue-green color. They walked toward the water, ingesting the beauty.

They stood before the greatness of the enormous lake and held hands. It was a rare moment of peace where all seemed right, even though it wasn't. David moved closer to Anna and wrapped his arms around her. In his arms, Anna returned home. His familiar smell and comfortable grip reminded her of how much she had missed him. She wondered how she could have left him, her rock, in the first place. For months, she worked to push David out of her mind, and now all that she had tried to forget came back with urgency—her loving husband, her son, her life. David looked down at her and wiped her face; she hadn't even noticed the tears.

"I love you," he said, kissing her forehead. "Are you okay?"

"No. But I will be." She squeezed him harder. "I've missed you."

He looked deeply into her eyes. She thought he could glimpse her soul with those eyes. She felt the stir of passion. They kissed soft and sweet and deep. Yet it didn't satisfy. They wanted more—to be as close as two people could get. They stumbled across the beach, intertwined, toward an isolated spot to satisfy the intense, urgent need. Although the cold bit at their skin, they didn't care. David laid his coat on the sand and they wrestled to unclothe one another. They laughed at the absurdity of making love on a beach near stacks of ice while the sun shone brightly in an unsuccessful attempt at warmth. For a while, they didn't feel the cold, only an intense satisfaction at being reunited.

No snuggle time was had that afternoon. Frigid air began to pinch their skin, so they clothed themselves immediately after. They stood again, where they had stood before they started, utterly transformed. David looked down at Anna. "I have missed you so much. Don't ever leave me again."

So many words came to her mind, a jumbled force, but all that exited her mouth was, "I won't."

A look flashed across his face. Was it disbelief? she wondered. Then he smiled. "I love you."

"I love you, too."

They hiked further through the woods. The birds sang their secrets to them in their ancient language of tweets and chirps. David held Anna's hand. "I can't believe we're here. This is amazing. What changed your mind about hiking? You told me you'd never be that kind of girl," he chided her.

"A good friend taught me I was wrong. I get it now."

"So, you're saying you'll hike with me again?"

"Yeah, I guess I am saying that."

"Woo-hoo," he yelled. He picked Anna up around the waist

and announced to the birds, "I love this woman!"

Anna couldn't help but laugh. It was good to be loved.

***

That night Ron and Leena went out alone, which was not something they often did. Leena said that she needed to talk about Anna and all that had happened.

Ron's good fortune made him dizzy with excitement. He would have sat next to Leena through a chick-flick just to smell her hair, which looked even better these days since Anna convinced her to retire her curling iron and go more natural. She looked beautiful before, but now he found her irresistible with her soft blonde, wavy hair. Living with the pretense of only friendship might no longer be an option, thought Ron.

They went to Ned's Grill, the only other local choice, besides Bart's, for drinks. They thoroughly fleshed out the happenings of the past few months, rehashing the hills, valleys, and murky waters of it all. They exchanged their thoughts until they could see it all through each other's eyes. There hadn't been so much excitement in Mikamaw in many years, and people would be talking about these events for some time.

The conversation flowed for hours, as did the frothy, cold beer.

Leena didn't have to worry about the time, because her mother agreed to stay the night and sleep in the guest room so not stay up past her bedtime to watch her grandchildren.

"Well, I guess Anna will be gone soon. I wonder if she'll come back to visit," Ron mused.

"Do you ever wish *you* could leave? I mean, do you miss teaching?" asked Leena.

"I do. But I'm happy where I'm at." He looked at Leena, trying to send a message, but Leena looked down.

"Well, good. I can't stand to lose two friends at once."

Ron started laughing into his beer. "Yep. Friends."

"What's so funny?"

"Oh, come on, Leena!"

"What?" she laughed, uncertainty in her voice.

"Leena Barberg. Don't bullshit me. Don't make me say it. It's bad enough …" he couldn't finish the thought.

"Hey, sorry. I'm not trying to upset you. Let's move on." Leena stood up and covered herself with her thick coat. "Let's walk over and see if Lloyd will give us a ride. We're too smashed to drive anywhere." She walked out quickly.

Ron chased after her. The moonlight and fresh, promising air of spring galvanized him. "Leena!" he called after her as she jogged down the sidewalk.

He decided on an impulse that he had to lay all his cards on the table. *If she won't give me a chance, it's time to move on.* Living so close to the person he loved and not being able to put his arms around her or kiss her had become too cruel to endure.

The few streetlights above them shone like tiny beacons on the deserted, sleeping town. Main Street stood dark and empty. Ron sped up and grabbed Leena's arm, gently turning her toward him. "You need to know why I laughed, Leena."

"Are you still on that? It's okay. Let's move on."

"You need to hear me." He gently put his finger to her lips when she tried to interrupt. Touching her lips warmed his body insanely, threatening to distract his thoughts. He took the plunge: "You have to know how I feel."

"I can't do this. Please stop." She tried again to walk away. He grabbed her again, this time in a hug-like grasp to keep her from leaving.

"I love you, damn it." Immediately he regretted his lack of romance, but he plunged ahead. "I've been in love with you nearly my whole life."

They looked into each other's eyes. Leena's look confused Ron. He couldn't tell if she wanted to kiss him or run away. She felt warm in his arms.

"Ron, you've been such a good friend through the years. My best friend. I couldn't have gotten through these years without you. You've been there for my kids, fixed what's broke, listened."

"And I was happy to do it all. But, I need to know how you feel. I can't stand by being your 'friend' anymore, unless I can be more than that too. It's killing me."

"I'm just not ready."

"You are too!" he said more forcefully than he intended. This was not going smoothly. More calmly, he said, "You *are* ready. The question is, are you ready with me?"

Before she could answer, he leaned in and kissed her. At first he kissed her softly, and then she pulled him closer and they stood there, under the spring moon, cold, drunk, and in love.

***

The next morning Leena awoke in Ron's bed. How was she supposed to act now? It stupefied her how quickly things could change. Should she feel embarrassed, relieved, or what, she wondered? Last night her beloved best friend changed instantly into much more and her love changed into something powerful. Had it already been there under the surface? She already knew everything about his personality, and now she knew they were physically compatible as well. More than that—they fit like jigsaw pieces. He lit a fire beneath her, igniting a part of her that she had forgotten even existed.

Ron woke as she stirred. He turned over to face her and put his tattooed, muscled arm over her. "You have made me the happiest man on the planet," he said with a groggy voice and a full smile. He kissed her cheek with warm, soft lips. "Would you like some breakfast?"

"Sure," Leena said, worried that if she moved too fast it would all disappear.

He smoothed her hair away from her face and looked her in the eyes. "I love you."

Before her brain could think, her heart responded, "I love you too."

Forgiveness

It took Kate one audiobook, four bathroom stops, and nearly all the songs on her playlists to drive home. While she drove, she thought about Anna and Joanne's relationship. Siblings often didn't get along, she realized, although she knew little about it firsthand, having none of her own. Kate had taken Anna's word that growing up with Joanne was hell and hadn't considered how their relationship became so ugly. Now, she wondered what would happen if they talked about it? Could a truce be made? They both loved their parents; they could start there.

The next morning, after a good night's sleep at home, Kate woke early and drove to Anna's house, where Joanne babysat Andrew. Kate tried to quiet her nerves as she drove. She and Joanne had never really fought, but she knew Joanne didn't like her. Joanne intimidated her — which made Kate a little unsure of herself. Kate was usually the one making others think twice. She reminded herself, as she parked in the driveway, that she was doing this, in part, for Andrew. Having kids wasn't part of her plan, but she intended to spoil Andrew like the nephew she'd never have. He deserved all the family and love he could get.

Joanne looked surprised when she opened the door and saw Kate. "Is everything okay?" she asked.

"Yes. Anna and David are fine. I'm just here to talk. I would have called, but I worried that you wouldn't agree to talk to me."

Joanne's eyes squinted with a thought she didn't express. She opened the door. Kate walked in and saw Andrew sitting in the middle of the living room floor, wildly swinging a soft rattle, laughing at the sound and pleased with himself. Kate squatted down and gave him a hug.

"Hi, Andrew, my little sweet. How are you?" she said in a sing-song voice.

Andrew stared at her with deep interest, and then looked to Joanne, seeming to gauge his reaction against hers. Joanne gave him a big smile and he grunted some sounds and began to swing around another toy. "I can't believe how much he's changed since the last time I saw him. Unbelievable."

"He's growing fast," Joanne said with obvious affection. She sat on the floor next to Andrew, and Kate sat on the soft carpet across from her. "So, what are you here for?"

Kate had rehearsed and planned her words, but now her plans seeped from her mind. Nothing but honesty would do, so she decided to let it all out. "I came to talk about you and Anna and Andrew—"

"I don't want—" Joanne interrupted.

"Can you just hear me out? I've driven a long way and slept very little, just to come here and talk to you. David wants me to talk to you. I know you respect him and love Andrew... so, for them, will you at least listen?"

Joanne sighed. "Okay, for them, but honestly, I don't see the point."

"I know you and Anna have a difficult history."

"That's putting it—"

"You said you'd listen," Kate interrupted.

"Go ahead."

"But just because that's how it's been, doesn't mean it has to be that way forever. I think you two need to talk. I know you're upset that she wasn't with you to bury your mom—you have every right to be. But, something happened with Anna." Kate shifted on the carpet at the thought of her broken friend. "She thought she was losing her mind. She wanted to protect Andrew by leaving. She was all alone during a rough time. You two might not be able to work it out, but don't you think you owe it to Clare and Trent to give it a try?"

Joanne sat quietly for some time. She watched Andrew play. "I'm sorry Anna had a difficult time, but what about before that? She wasn't there for our mom. She kept her distance, and I know it hurt my mom. I don't know if I can ever forget that. I don't know if I'll ever stop hating her for it."

"I'm not saying that Anna's perfect and didn't make mistakes. But are you ready to let Andrew go? You will be without any family if you don't make some peace with her."

"I know. I don't want to lose Andrew. He's the only good thing that came out of this mess." Joanne looked down at Andrew. Kate could see that she loved him. "I just don't know if I can forgive her. I'm not sure if I want to."

"Will you take some time to think about it?" Kate asked.

Joanne looked hard at her. She was quiet for so long, it made for an awkward silence. "I'll think about it."

Kate had thought she would be screamed at and thrown out by now, but this was much better. "Good. That's a start."

"I'm not promising anything," said Joanne.

"I understand. Either way, David wants Andrew to come up in a few days. He thinks Anna needs to see him before she comes home. He's worried she might not come home otherwise. I would do it, but I've got to get back to work. Would you at least think about taking Andrew up there, even if you decide not to talk with Anna? You don't want Andrew to grow up without a mom, do you?"

"I've got to think about it. I'll call you later."

"Sure. Thanks for talking with me."

Kate picked Andrew up and hugged him while she swung him in a circle. He laughed. Kate said, "I love this guy just as much as you do. The more family he has in his life, the better."

***

Being back with David energized Anna, like a new battery in an old toy. The stress and loss that she had experienced while away from her family decreased daily in his presence. The only blackness in her newfound joy was Andrew. She missed him, ached for him in fact, but wondered if she could be a capable mother. She couldn't reconcile the monster she had been with the good mother that she wanted to be.

Anna needed to process all that had happened, and David was her sounding board. They spent hours rehashing everything that occurred during their separation. Her anxiety decreased as she unburdened herself of the pain of the past two months. She felt lighter as she exercised her new freedom to talk about it.

David surprised her by his listening. In the past, he always tried to solve her problems, even though she explained that most of the time, she simply needed him to listen. The day after Kate left, they spent hours in Anna's apartment drinking coffee and revisiting the day Anna decided to throw away her phone.

He looked her and said, "I want you to know how sorry I am you had to go through all of that alone." He looked down. When he looked up, his eyes filled with tears, he said, "I feel like I should've known. I should've seen—"

"Don't blame yourself. I can't have that over my head too. It's not your fault."

He started kneading the back of his neck, a sure sign of accumulated stress.

Anna broke the silence. "Let's do both ourselves a favor and stop doling out blame. It's not helping us." She moved closer and cupped his face in her hands, looking him in the eyes, "Okay?"

His smile, punctuated by tears, was too much. She had to wipe the sadness away. She embraced him and they mended their sadness with the touch of their skin.

They woke in bed hours later. Despite the darkness outside, they were alert and energized, and would be for hours because of their long nap. They decided to go out for a drink since sleep wouldn't come until much later because of their afternoon nap.

They didn't go far, only downstairs to a quiet corner in Bart's. The smell of the salty, greasy fries tempted David as it did so many patrons of Bart's, and he gave in, an unusual choice for his well-cared-for body. Words were sparse, as they had already said so much that day, so they ate their food in comfortable quiet and ordered another round of drinks.

A strange look crossed David's face—one eyebrow raised higher than the other as he tore apart his paper napkin. Anna recognized that face as indicating guilt.

"What's wrong, David?

"I have something to tell you. You see, I spoke with Kate today and I have some news."

"That seems odd, you and Kate talking directly."

"After all that's happened, it's not that weird. Kate and I have helped each other through a lot." Anna gave him a questioning look. "Not like that, of course."

"I'm teasing. So, what'd your *friend* Kate have to say today?"

"Well, she kind of went on a mission."

"Oh?"

"Yeah. She asked Joanne if she would bring Andrew up here,

and she said Joanne agreed."

"What?" Anna asked, taken aback and indignant.

"Hear me out, okay? Joanne has become really close to Andrew over the last month. We stayed with her for weeks after your mother's funeral."

"And is she close to you?" Anna accused.

"She's not a bad person. She's hurt. Like you."

"Do not compare me to *her*."

"It's not about her. It's about Andrew. I want you to see him before you go home. Kate couldn't bring him, so I asked the only other person I would trust to."

"What right ..." Anna stopped, trying to calm herself. David wouldn't purposely try to hurt her. "What right do you have to do such a thing? Just because I've had a hard time doesn't mean you get to cozy up with Joanne and take her side."

"I'm not taking sides. If I were, it would only be your side and Andrew's. He loves Joanne and he deserves some family in his life. He needs some semi-normal people to cancel out my brother and Natalie." He smiled at her.

She rolled her eyes and followed their lead, leaning her head back to look up at the ceiling. A strange sound emerged from her throat. Anna tried to hold in her fury, but it couldn't be stopped.

"I'm sorry ... I didn't mean to—" he said.

"Too late for sorry. This is absolute bullshit! What makes you think you can start dictating my life? What gives you the right? Why didn't you ask *me* if I was ready to see Andrew? Or ask me if it was okay that Joanne bring him?"

"I'm sorry. You're right. I was just trying to help. I thought you needed to see them both. Andrew needs to see you. You need to talk to Joanne. Your mother is gone."

"Don't you think I know that?"

"Don't you think you should sit and talk with Joanne? Isn't that what your mother would want?"

"Don't you dare try to pull some guilt-trip bullshit on me! You're the one who's wrong here, not me! Don't think you get to make decisions about my life because of what happened. You don't!"

Anna stormed out. She vowed with ironic, black humor that she would never go to Bart's or Ned's and drink again. It always seemed to lead to a fight.

***

As she drove away from the bar, Anna felt a bit of pleasure at the thought of David worrying. He would think that she ran away. Guilt quickly replaced her joy, however.

Anna showed up at Leena's unannounced. To Anna's surprise, Ron's truck sat parked in the driveway. It seemed late for him to be there, and she wanted to talk with her friend alone.

She walked in and immediately unloaded her anger despite his presence. The story of her conversation with David oozed out of her, complete with contempt and disappointment.

"I'm confused. Don't you want to see Andrew?" asked Ron.

Anna glared at Ron. "I do. I just didn't want it thrown on me like that. Doesn't David think I can make decisions anymore? And it burns me that Joanne has spent more time with him lately than I have, even if it's what I deserve."

"I get that. But is she a horrible person? Would she treat Andrew badly?" asked Leena.

"No. I can't imagine that. But her being nice to my son and such a bitch to me is just another way for her to slap me in the face."

Ron looked out the window at the headlights coming up the drive. "Looks like we've got a visitor."

David's car sat in the driveway. "I'll go talk to him," Ron said. "Give you ladies some time to talk."

They watched Ron go out the front door. Leena sat up straighter and asked, "Is what he did really that bad? He wants you to see your son and make up with your sister. Don't you want to see Andrew?"

"I do, but the nerve of Joanne driving him. It's too much!"

"Would it hurt just to talk to her?"

"I don't know. Probably. You have no idea what she's like."

"It seems to me that most of your demons come from trying to outrun the past. Maybe it's time you face things—like your sister—and see what happens. Sorry, I know it's not what you want to hear."

Betrayal on all sides. No one around her understood. They were all trying to trap her. *I can't even call Kate, because she's in line with David,* Anna ruminated in self-imposed sorrow.

"Ron and I have been sleeping together," Leena said, changing the subject.

Anna looked at Leena. She knew Leena's distraction trick from Hank, but this was too hard to ignore. A smile emerged across her lips, betraying the heaviness within. "What? Really?" she asked, not able to resist interest at the course of events.

"Yes. It is *incredible*. So much has happened in the last few days."

Anna couldn't help herself. She had to know. She put her own misery on hold and demanded, "Tell me everything."

***

A half hour later, Ron walked back inside. "Is everything alright in here? David's waiting outside. He seems really sorry and he said he forgives me for hurting his head. He can't be all that bad," he said. Leena couldn't stop smiling.

Anna stood up, a smile upon her face. "I'm going now. It seems like I may have interrupted something," she laughed.

Ron flashed her a knowing smile.

"I'd better get back to my husband and let you guys get back to …" she looked at Leena and they laughed.

"Alright, alright. We're all adults here, aren't we?" Leena teased, and Anna left.

The news about Leena and Ron calmed Anna's anger as she walked to David's car. It injected her with mirth. She knew these two were supposed to be together, and it seemed so right that finally they were.

David sat looking at the vast forest next to Leena's house. Anna leaned toward the open window of his car.

"I'm going back to the apartment now," she said.

"Can I come too? Or do you want to cast me out to Walt's?"

"No, I wouldn't do that to my worst enemy. Can you do me a

favor though? Let's not talk about this anymore today."

"You've got it."

They both drove back to Anna's apartment in their separate vehicles, the talk about Joanne postponed.

***

Joanne knew the drive to Mikamaw would be difficult, but she hadn't anticipated hell. At first things went well, and Andrew took his morning nap in the car, but when he woke up, no action could subdue his desire to be free of the car seat. Joanne tried to sing and talk to him with no effect. Finally, she reached her hand back to hold his small hand, but nothing consoled him. His dismay turned into cries that threatened to injure Joanne's eardrums. She stopped to take him out and play for an hour until she felt confident in strapping him back in. Then she drove for a pleasant ninety non-screaming minutes. He began to fuss, so she entertained him by handing him toy after toy, which he would look at briefly and then throw into the pit of toys accumulating like unwanted memories on the back floor of her car. She stopped to feed him, collected the discarded toys, played with him, and called David.

"Sorry, but there is no way I'll make it there today," she said.

"Is everything okay?" David asked.

"It's just that I have to stop a lot. I think I'll take my time so it's better for both Andrew and I and get a hotel tonight."

David hadn't put much thought, until now, into what he was asking of Joanne. The farthest he ever drove alone with Andrew was five hours from Indiana.

"Thank you so much for doing this. It must be hard," said David.

"I'd say no problem, but I'd be lying."

"Well, you're a top-notch aunt, and I owe you a big favor. Is Andrew doing okay?"

"Yes, he's fine. I don't think he likes the car a whole lot, but he's fine. We should be there sometime tomorrow in the early afternoon. I'm not sure when. I'll call you."

"Just be safe and do what works for you. I really appreciate this. Thank—"

"If you thank me anymore, I'm turning around," Joanne teased him. "Have you told Anna I'm coming?"

"Yes. She's really excited to see you."

"You're not a good liar, you know. Anyway, I've got to go. I'll call you tomorrow."

"Alright. Talk to you later."

***

Anna and David sat at the small table in her apartment. The remnants of lunch sat on their near-empty plates. The afternoon passed in a bubble of quiet, with only necessary words exchanged. Anna didn't like the tension which grew between them.

Questions swirled in Anna's mind. What if Andrew knew on some primal level that she had already failed him, before he could even walk? What if he remembered what a beast she was before she left? How could she jump back into the role of motherhood, from which she had gone to such pains to escape? What if the anger came back to her when he frustrated her? What would he be like now?

The night before, vivid and intense dreams plagued Anna. They were so real that she could still grasp the colors, smells, and emotions of them. Her mother and father were above her, sitting on a glass floor, looking down. They sat in her childhood living room, all of it the same except for the glass floor where carpet should have been. They talked intensely to each other, but she couldn't hear what they were saying. She could tell by their content faces that they were happy. They stared at Anna and the look on their faces changed to disappointment. Andrew sat on her lap, drooling and playing with a toy. Her anxiety came back, she looked up, and her parents were gone. Only a little pile of black specks remained on the glass ceiling, as though they had evaporated and left behind any darkness they had left within. When she looked down from the ceiling, Andrew disappeared from her lap. She ran around the house looking for him. The house kept changing, like a carnival tent where the surroundings shift with the movement of mirrors. In a green room with green walls and enormous trees, Kate sat on a stump sharpening an enormous blade. When she saw Anna, she gave chase, wielding her sword like a warrior. Anna ran into her dad's living room and found Joanne and David on the couch kissing with their legs wrapped around one another. Anna ran toward them, ready to kill, and smashed into a glass wall. The force pushed her backward toward the ground, but the floor dropped and she fell down, down, and then she awoke with a start. She had no idea what any of this meant, if anything. The dream stuck with her in her daylight hours, just as vivid as it had been in the darkness.

David's phone rang. As he paced the room, Anna could hear him talking with Joanne. Traitor.

"Well, she's not going to be here until tomorrow," he said with a sheepish look.

"I'm relieved not to see Joanne today, but I was looking forward to seeing Andrew."

"Were you?"

"Of course I want to see him. I'm scared, but I miss him. I love him. What I did, I did out of love."

"I know that."

"I'm sorry I got so angry last night. It's a sensitive subject. I overreacted."

"I'd say so."

Anna glared at him.

"I understand, Anna. I sprung it on you. I'm only trying to do the right thing here," he said.

"Part of it is Joanne. It's hard to think of her as anything but the person who screwed me over. She's been judging me all her life, acting like she's better than I am. I get why she's upset, but she doesn't ever try to see my side. She's not as perfect as she thinks."

"None of us are. Maybe you two can start by tolerating each other. She's not perfect, but who is? And she loves Andrew. That means she can't be all bad, right?"

"I don't know. I'll try not to start yelling and kicking when I see her. That's the best I can offer." She looked up at David's face as he frowned with concern.

"What the—?"

"I'm joking, David! Geez!"

Anna pushed her thoughts of her sister deep below her river of consciousness. She didn't want to analyze all the ways Joanne had failed her, for the moment. She turned her energy toward Andrew. The thought of seeing Andrew made Anna buzz with nervous excitement.

***

With so many reminders of Anna around her, Joanne thought of little else on the ride north. Anna was the reason for the journey, her son cooed in the backseat, and memories of her cold detachment from their mother persisted in Joanne's mind. She tried to will it away, like the pain of a small scratch, but it ran deeper and couldn't be so easily dismissed. Too bad she couldn't let the past slip behind her like the driven miles. It took too much energy to be mad. She didn't want to stew anymore in the negative, but letting go of her deep-rooted hostility would be difficult. It had become such a part of her that, like a weed yanked from the dirt, it would leave scars and holes. But what did she gain from keeping hateful feelings? She might have been able to walk away and never talk to her sister again, if it weren't for Andrew. Her love for him took her heart the first time she held him. Walking away from him would be painful. Being in his life and reliving the anger she had for Anna over and over might be even harder. How do you move on from a lifetime of hate?

No matter what happened between her and Anna, Andrew needed his mother. Joanne knew firsthand how important a mother was, well or not.

She saw the sign for Baraga County and sighed, both relieved that the trip was nearly complete and worried at what would be at its end. She arrived in Mikamaw twenty minutes later. Kate's directions were accurate, and she drove right up to Bart's without getting lost or turned around. She appreciated clear and concise directions; so few people could do that anymore.

Joanne stepped out of the car and stretched her cramped

body. When she looked through the back window, she saw Andrew's heavy-lidded eyes near the moment of sleep. Quietly, she opened the back door and carefully withdrew Andrew from his car seat. He leaned heavily against her shoulder, drooling and contemplating sleep. Joanne walked past the doors that emitted a smell of greasy fries and opened a second, nondescript green door. She walked up the narrow steps, reached her hand out to knock, and the door quickly opened. Before she could properly view her surroundings, she and Andrew were tightly embraced in David's arms.

"Thank you so much! You are amazing!" He laughed with sheer delight over seeing his son. Joanne's eyes betrayed her and filled with tears at the happy father-son reunion. Andrew's sleepy body perked up at the sound of his father's voice. He made a chorus of sounds, as if he were catching his father up on the days he had missed. David gently pulled Andrew from Joanne's arms and squeezed his son with love.

Anna walked in from the bedroom, always lagging behind in action, Joanne thought. Her face shone blotchy-red, a nervous reaction that Joanne recognized from their youth. Anna looked toward Andrew, and tears rolled down her smiling face. Then she took a few fast steps toward Joanne and hugged her. Joanne received it stiffly, unsure how to react. They hadn't hugged since they were children. Anna cried and squeezed Joanne tightly.

Anna uttered strings of sounds, which took time to merge into recognizable words. "I'm so sorry about Mom. I wish I had been there. Forgive me. Thank you for bringing Andrew. I ..."

She let go of Joanne and lifted Andrew from David's arms. He started to cry. Her intensity seemed to frighten him in his tired state. David patted Andrew's back while Anna held him.

Joanne looked at her sister and saw her slightly anew. "Just sway with him. He's just tired, Anna. He was almost asleep when we got here."

Anna smiled, and her tears quieted, as did Andrew's.

***

The Nature of Denial

If another week or month had passed, Anna might not have recognized Andrew. His changed appearance startled her. His eyes shone a more vibrant blue, the same hue as Anna's. He controlled his body with much more skill. She watched, amazed, as he sat up on his own, observed the world around him with great interest, and commented upon it in his own language. Anna had expected him to be the same as when she left. It both delighted and disappointed her that he had changed.

A new world had opened to Andrew through the control of his hands—he particularly liked Anna's earrings and grabbed at them when she held him. Every time she wrapped her arms around him, her heart would jolt with electric joy. His baby smell lingered on her even when she put him down. She loved it.

Andrew looked at her as though he could see her for the first time. He examined her face with great interest. Anna suspected that, like his father, he had the ability to look right through her to her soul. *Would he always be able to do that?*

The proud parents sat on the living room floor of Anna's apartment and watched their son. He accomplished acrobatic feats on her resale flowered comforter, which she put on the floor so he could stretch out on something soft. "Look, he's doing his baby workout," Anna commented.

Andrew lay on his belly and kept swinging his weight, trying to get onto his side. "Look at our little guy, already trying to build his muscles," David said with obvious pride.

"Look, he flipped onto his back," Anna said.

"That's a relatively new one," said David.

"I can't believe how much he's changed. He looks so healthy and happy. Thank you."

"You don't have to thank me."

"I never thought this moment would happen. Seeing Andrew again is the best moment of my life."

"Wow, thanks."

"I mean—"

"I'm kidding, Anna. I know what you mean and I take *no* offense!"

She looked closely at David and kissed him with thanks. When they looked over at Andrew, he was perched on his hands and knees. The delighted parents cheered with praise.

In that moment, gratitude filled Anna. The things that she loved most in the world and thought she'd lost forever had somehow found her and were back in her life. After all that had happened, David could easily have chosen to hate her, but he didn't. He embraced her with open arms, with forgiveness and love. She didn't feel deserving of it, but she was definitely thankful.

***

Anna never would have guessed it could happen, but seeing Andrew changed Anna's attitude about her sister. She and Joanne would never agree on their perceptions of the past—they might never even get along—but she couldn't see any reason to keep her sister, who obviously loved Andrew, away from him. Not when he could have something she never had herself—a good relationship with Joanne.

Joanne agreed to meet with Anna before she went back downstate. She stayed the night at Leena's, who was gracious enough to save her from the experience of Walt's Hotel or Anna's small couch. The sisters decided to meet at a Lynn's Café in town. No more serious conversations would happen at Bart's or Ned's Grill. Anna had learned her lesson.

When Anna parked in Lynn's lot, wet with melting snow, Joanne's car was already there. Anna walked in and saw Joanne seated in the farthest corner, drinking from a large coffee mug. Anna's heart pounded anxiously. She walked over to the table, trying all the while to calm her nerves. Her gelatinous legs moved unsteadily and threatened to betray her at any moment, leaving her a crumbled mess on the floor. Joanne stood and stiffly received Anna's hug—their second in adulthood. They looked at the waitress walking over to take Anna's drink request.

The space between them filled with reluctant silence. Anna knew that once they started, it would all come out, and she feared the result.

"So, how was your night? Did you sleep well?" Anna asked.

"I did. Your friend Leena seems very nice," Joanne said.

"She is. I owe her a lot. She's an amazing woman," Anna agreed.

"She thinks highly of you, too."

Silence filled the air between them again.

"When are you leaving?" Anna asked.

"When we're done here, I'll be on my way. I may stop and say goodbye to Andrew first. I'm ready to get home."

"Thanks for watching him and bringing him here. It was very nice of you. Thank you."

"Andrew is a sweet baby. You're lucky," said Joanne.

"Thanks. He is amazing, despite his mother. Thanks again for bringing him."

"You're welcome."

Heavy silence filled the void as they exhausted small talk. Anna decided to take the plunge to the serious. She was reluctant, but ready.

She took a deep breath and held her hands tightly together in her lap for strength. "I'm sorry I wasn't there for ... Mom's burial. I hope you can forgive me for that."

Joanne looked somewhere beyond Anna. Her eyes reflected the start of tears. She breathed deeply, blinked several times, and sat up straighter. She finally looked Anna in the eye and said, "I don't know if I can ... I want to talk, but I don't know, I ..."

Anna forged forward. "I was sick for a little while ... in my head." She looked down at her hands, tightly embraced, trying to hold onto some invisible lifeline. "I thought I was losing my mind. That's why I left. When I found out about Mom, I wasn't in a state of mind where I could possibly have come to help you."

"Really. Too sick to come to your own mother's funeral? You were never there for her," Joanne's voice trembled, "not even at the end."

"I tried to kill myself, Joanne. Ironically, right at the moment I found out that mom was ... gone."

"You what?"

"I was in a very dark place. Otherwise, I would have never left David and Andrew. It was the hardest thing I've ever done. I tried to jump off the pier into the icy water, but I slipped and hit my head instead. I would have died anyway if it hadn't been for Leena."

A look of concern crossed Joanne's face. "Have you seen a doctor? Do you know what happened to you?" She lifted her eyebrows, intimating what she was too afraid to ask.

"I will when I get home. I'm feeling better now. I was worried it was ... like mom ... but I'm pretty sure it was postpartum anxiety."

"Just make sure to see a doctor. I'm sure you're right, but make sure."

"I will."

They were silent and took the opportunity to look at their menus. Anna's body ached with exhaustion. Until that moment, she hadn't realized how tense her muscles were, like fully stretched rubber bands. Each sentence of their conversation exhausted her like trekking uphill, requiring effort and endurance. These were the most civilized words they had shared at one time in twenty years.

They ate their sandwiches and drank their coffee, treading on light conversation — the perfect chewiness of the bread, the richness of the coffee, the beauty of the lake lit by the spring rays of sunshine. They had just run in the marathon of difficult conversations and needed a proverbial drink of water and catching of breath before they could move on.

"I'm sorry for what you went through," Joanne finally said. "I wish we could start fresh. I do. But it's just not that easy to pretend the past didn't happen. I wish there was a button I could push to forgive and move on, but I can't. I want to move on. But there's just so much ... anger. It's—"

"I know I've made mistakes, but don't pretend that you're faultless," Anna defended.

"What do you mean? I was *there*. I made sure Mom took her meds. I dedicated my life to her health. So, I'm not sure what I have to be sorry about. You're the one who cast her aside like an inconvenience," Joanne sneered.

"Wow, you really only see your side. You're right, I should have treated her better. I realize that now. I am sorry for that and I will have to find some way to live with that. But as far as our relationship goes, you're as much at fault as I am."

"Our *relationship* is what it is because of how you treated Mom. It made me hate you."

"Don't you remember," Anna's eyes narrowed, "when it all started? I was terrified when Mom changed. I couldn't ask Mom why she was acting strange, so I asked you. Do you remember what you did? You yelled at me, you pushed me around, you were evil about the whole thing. I was scared, and every time I turned to you, you were heartless. Don't forget that part of the story!"

"I don't remember that, Anna. All I remember is doing the best I could. It was scary, and I did my best to take care of our mom."

"I did my best too. It was confusing. One week she was energized, the next she barely moved. I made her eat when she camped in her bed for weeks. I tried, you know. But remember, I was eleven and you were fifteen. You kept saying there wasn't a problem."

"I don't remember that. I was always there for her. Anyway, if you cared so much, how come you kept her at such a distance?"

"Face it, Joanne, you two didn't need me. It was team Joanne and Mom, and I didn't feel particularly welcome, especially by you."

"That is a cop-out. Complete bullshit. You gave up on your own mother. Who does that?"

"How dare you? You have no idea what I thought or felt about Mom. I know I made mistakes, but honestly, I didn't know how to deal with it. After the accident, I was scared. I didn't know what she would do. You didn't make it any easier. You were a downright bitch, every step of the way."

They stared at each other. Anna could hear her heart pumping forcefully.

Joanne took a deep breath and leaned back in her chair. "That's not fair. I know that I'm not blameless. But despite all your excuses, I can't believe how you gave up. Mom was sick. She couldn't help it. She had good and bad moments, but in all of them, she never gave up hope in you. She spoke highly of you, when all you did was walk away."

"You took everything over, and there was no room for me. You drove over to Mom's all the time, but did you ever take me there unless Dad made you? Sisters are supposed to be there for each other, but all you did was berate me. You were old enough to know better." Anna knew this was not the type of conversation they should be having, that it could lead them down a path of no return, but she couldn't stop. "You wanted me to pretend everything was alright. It wasn't. I know I let mom down. It's a mistake that I can't make up for and I'm going to have to live with."

"When things get tough, you run. Just like this time."

"That's not fair! Can you really believe I wanted to leave David and Andrew? I did it because I thought I could hurt Andrew. I was terrified that I would."

Joanne leaned forward and put her hands on her forehead. She slowly moved her head back and forth. "You're right, that was low. I'm sorry. I don't want to do this. I guess I have a lot of pent-up anger. I wish it could be different, but I can't just wish it away."

"I know how you feel," Anna agreed. She sank lower in her chair, full of defeat. They sat for many moments of baffling silence.

Joanne looked up and gave Anna a half smile, which confused Anna.

Joanne said, "I don't know if our relationship's gone too far to repair or not. All I know is that I *would* like to be a part of Andrew's life. I don't want Natalie being the only aunt who spends time with him."

At that Anna couldn't help but laugh. "She is a bitch, isn't she? You should have seen how I told her off at Christmas."

"What?" Joanne laughed.

"She pushed me too many times. I had to give her a piece of my mind. I haven't talked to her since. So, you might not have any competition in the aunt department."

"That's great! She needed someone to put her in her place."

They drank their cold coffee, content that some words were said and they both survived.

Joanne said, "I'm just not sure how things are going to work with us. Maybe we can just take it moment by moment and see what happens. At least for Andrew."

It sounded like a start.

The Nature of Denial

***

Everything in Anna's life had changed since she came to Mikamaw. She thought that it was like water under the bridge. Then she realized, really, it wasn't, because the bridge would have been crushed by the vast, seething currents of her life's river. Yet, despite all that she had been through, she survived.

With so much uncertainty, she needed to collect her thoughts, like raindrops, to drink the truth of what had happened and what she would become. The day after she met with Joanne, she wrote the first page in a diary that she would fill in weeks.

I can't believe how much life can change in a year. This year I became a mom and lost my mom. I understand my mom better now than I ever did before. I wish I could tell her how sorry I am. Something tells me that she's already forgiven me, although I'm not sure that I deserve it.

It is ironic that my parents worked so hard to get Joanne and me to talk in life, but succeeded only in death. Andrew forced our first conversation, and he didn't even say a word. I know my parents would be proud. I wish they could have met Andrew.

I don't know if Joanne and I will ever be close, but I hope we can be civilized and learn to live in the present instead of the past. I think it would help heal us both. I would like to get to know my sister. (I never thought I would say that.) I know so little about her.

There is so much I'm uncertain of right now ... like what will happen with Joanne and I? Will Kate and my friends from Savory Scents forgive me? What kind of mother will I be?

Uncertainty makes it hard to move forward so maybe I should reflect on what I do know. I have to put my past in the past. I can't stay mired in it anymore or I will sink like a stone. I need to live in the present. I have to forgive myself to do this, which is easier said than done. I will need some help with this.

You can't choose your family or the people you love. You only get one shot at this life and it's too short to let go without a fight because really, love is all that matters. I know, it sounds cheesy, but it's absolutely true. I would do anything for Andrew. At first I thought that meant I had to leave him, but I was wrong. You have to work at love and keep it close. Whether it's the love of a child, a spouse, or a friend, we can't walk this life without it.

And finally, I will take a walk in the woods once in a while. It helped me gain a new perspective, and I don't want to lose it.

I'm sure there are other things I know, but I can't think of them at the moment. Wait, I take that back. I know that I'm ready to go home.

The Nature of Denial

ABOUT THE AUTHOR

Madelyn March's life is books. She can usually be found writing one, teaching someone how to read one, or enjoying one herself. When it's time for a book break, her favorite place to be is hiking in the forest with her family.

The Nature of Denial

Made in the USA
Charleston, SC
15 June 2016